2/17

The Guardians

The New Homefront, Volume 2

By Steven C. Bird

Lakeville Public Library
4 Precinct St.
Lakeville, MA 02347

The Guardians: The New Homefront, Volume 2

Copyright 2014 by Steven C. Bird

All rights reserved. No part of this book may be reproduced, copied, or shared without expressed consent and prior authorization from the author.

Written and published by Steven C. Bird at Homefront Books

Edited by Sara Jones at www.torchbeareredits.com

Illustrated by Keri Knutson at www.alchemybookcovers.com

Print Edition 3.16

ISBN-13: 978-1507808900
ISBN-10: 1507808909

www.stevencbird.com
www.homefrontbooks.com
www.facebook.com/homefrontbooks
scbird@homefrontbooks.com

Table of Contents

Disclaimer

The characters and events in this book are fictitious. Any similarities to real events or persons, past or present, living or dead, is purely coincidental and are not intended by the author. Although this book is based on real places and some real events and trends, it is a work of fiction for entertainment purposes only. None of the activities in this book are intended to replace legal activities and your own good judgment.

Some items in this series have been changed from their actual likenesses to avoid any accidental sharing of Sensitive Security Information (SSI). The replacement values serve the same narrative purpose without exposing any potential SSI.

Dedication

To my loving wife and children:

Monica, Seth, Olivia, and Sophia

As I continue with this series, you still inspire me and drive me to accomplish all I can. It is my constant desire to protect you and provide for you that drives my imagination in ways that allowed me to create this story, and to continue it into a series. Every day that I wake up, I hope that I can use that day to somehow improve myself so that I can be a better husband and father. Hopefully, this series will contribute to the things that will lead to a new and exciting life for us. I love you all.

Continued from - The Last Layover: The New Homefront, Volume 1

Introduction

Just over one year ago, a chain of events was set in motion that would forever change the United States of America. A series of strategic, non-military attacks was launched on our nation's key infrastructure components in an effort to bring our once thriving country to its knees. Oil refineries, electrical power plants, power distribution components, municipal water supplies, transportation infrastructure, food production and distribution, and financial institutions all came under attack.

Over the course of several weeks, as the attacks continued, enough of the nation's critical infrastructure components were destroyed or severely damaged, creating a state of emergency that left a majority of Americans to fend for themselves. They were left without the emergency response systems and government support they had come to expect. A society that had become completely dependent on complex, highly automated supply chains and financial systems, found themselves in a world devoid of all types of electronic transactions. This left them with no access to what had become nothing more than virtual money. Additionally, without the networked and automated logistical systems incorporated into nearly every modern supply chain, commerce came to a halt, leaving grocery store shelves empty with no readily available means of resupply.

As desperation set in, the dark side of humanity quickly overtook a once polite and peaceful society. Good people were forced to take desperate measures to provide for themselves and their families. The less than desirable elements of society quickly realized they could now come out of the shadows. These elements found a world where they could use violence and intimidation to take and do whatever they wanted, unencumbered by any sort of traditional civil authorities.

All levels of government also found themselves in disarray. With no specific group or organization clearly responsible for the attacks, as well as the existence of evidence that those involved were assisted by elements from within our own federal government, blame and accusations of guilt were pointed in all directions. Some of this blame was well supported by facts and circumstances while some was assigned simply to usurp power and to take political advantage in the vacuum of organized civil authority. As a former White House chief of staff once said, “Never let a crisis go to waste, and by that I mean we can now do what we could not get done before.”

Over the course of the year that followed, the country continued to decline to what some felt was an unofficial civil war. With resistance to a federal government that was now controlled solely by the president via the powers enacted due to the state of emergency, the country was severed into several regions of control.

The northeastern United States, starting from coastal Virginia, going all the way up the East Coast, and wrapping back around to Chicago, was strongly in the hands of the president’s regime. In addition, the federal government controlled most of the west coast, with the exception of the eastern areas of Washington and Oregon, which were heavily influenced by the Northwestern Defensive Coalition formed by Idaho, Montana, Wyoming, and Colorado. Most of the Midwestern states rejected the over-reaching authority of the federal government as well and remained autonomous, as did the states across the southern United States.

These political boundaries did not mean much in most places, as the state or the federal governments did not have the logistics and resources necessary to effectively govern very far outside of their capitols. For most people, criminal organizations or local citizen militias were the only sort of authority they were likely to encounter. The latter being primarily the case in the regions of the country where civilian gun ownership was high, such as the southern, midwestern, and northwestern states. The availability of guns and ammunition was a valuable asset for self-defense in these regions. The more politically oppressed parts of the country, such as New Jersey and New York, did not have a citizenry with prior access to arms and ammunition and easily fell in line with the ever-increasing encroachment of government in their region.

With food, fuel, and medical resources becoming increasingly scarce and electrical power still unavailable in most of the country, the barter system had returned as the primary means of person-to-person trade, as the U.S. dollar was now nearly worthless. It was backed by nothing but what had become a failed government and was abandoned as a reserve currency throughout the rest of the world.

Chapter 1: A Brother's Quest

It was a year ago to the day when Petty Officer Second Class Nathan Hoskins left his U.S. Navy duty station in San Diego, California. After the collapse and the struggle for power within every level of government, the military was purged of all senior leadership that did not show total allegiance to the current president and his administration. The power grabs and controls that the federal government attempted to impose on the American people, which often ended in violence against civilians, caused many to resist or refuse such orders. As patriotic servicemen and servicewomen resisted and were severely punished or imprisoned for doing so, mass desertions took place.

Some deserters left to try to link up with and find surviving family members. Others sought out and joined underground resistance movements and migrated to states with National Guard units that were still loyal to the Constitution. Petty Officer Hoskins, a Navy master-at-arms, fit into both camps. He was a naval security force patrol officer at Naval Base San Diego when it all went down. He saw enough government abuse of power after the collapse to realize he may be on the wrong side. With that realization, his first priority was to reunite with family and second was to find a place in this new world where he could once again serve and protect his fellow Americans, rather than oppress them.

His younger brother was a first-year medical student at Texas A&M's College of Medicine when the collapse began. He had not had any contact with his brother or his parents since then. His new mission was to reunite with his brother, and then he hoped they would travel together to Virginia to find their parents.

When he left his post at Naval Station San Diego, Nathan—or Nate as his friends and family called him—took with him his government-issued Benelli M4 shotgun and his Beretta M9 service pistol. These two items had saved his life countless times during his journey. With them, he was also able to barter his security services in exchange for food and shelter at various places along the way. Farmers had been having a serious problem trying to keep looters from devastating their crops and stealing their livestock. As a result, they were quick to hire on armed and experienced security personnel such as Nate.

His journey took him across the American southwest by way of the Interstate 10 corridor. He stayed clear of I-10 itself, as he knew it would be a line of drift for many people escaping the chaos of southern California. He used it as a general guide to follow, hand railing it by way of back roads and small towns along the way.

Being an outdoorsman, Nate used wildlife refuges and national parks as a refuge for himself during the journey. Although many people had taken to this way of thinking, there was still less chance of encountering trouble far off into the woods, than in places where people were expected to travel and congregate. He made stops in the Kofa National Wildlife Refuge near Yuma, Arizona; the Ironwood Forest in Marana, Arizona; the Coronado National Forest in Benson, Arizona; the Gila National Forest in Glenwood, New Mexico; and the Lincoln National Forest in Alamogordo, New Mexico. He came out of the Lincoln National Forest on its southernmost edge and continued southeast until he came upon Highway 285. He followed 285 south to Carlsbad, New Mexico, intentionally staying south of Artesia, New Mexico.

His goal was to remain south of Artesia to avoid the Federal Law Enforcement Training Center located there. He was not sure of the extent of the current federal presence in Artesia, but he knew, as a deserter, it was best not to risk getting too close. Once near Carlsbad, Nate knew he needed a break from his cross-country backwoods travels. On the southeast edge of town, on the southern bank of the Pecos River, Nate found employment as a security guard with a small family-owned farm owned by the Peterson family. He made a deal with the farmer to pay him only in room and board as well as credit towards earning a horse that he could use to continue his travels into Texas in search of his brother.

Over the course of several months, Nate became quite close with the family. They taught him the basics of farming and animal husbandry, and he used those skills to help in numerous ways on their farm in addition to his security duties.

As Nate began to get a little too comfortable with life on the Peterson farm, he felt that he needed to get back to his mission of finding his brother before he lost the fire in his heart. Comfort can turn into months and years that have gone by, and he wanted to keep his promise to himself to reunite his family. The Petersons, being a very tight-knit family, understood; they gave him a healthy, young mare and fitted him out with a saddle and packs to carry food and supplies.

After saying his goodbyes, Nate rode away from the Peterson farm and continued his journey by following the Pecos River down to Pecos, Texas. From there, he headed due east towards San Angelo. From San Angelo, he continued on to Brady and then across Interstate 35 near Temple and then on to College Station.

After a long and dangerous journey from southern California through Arizona, New Mexico, and Texas, Nate finally arrived on the outskirts of College Station. Having been hardened by a journey full of conflict and struggle, Nate approached the city with extreme caution.

Along the way, Nate gathered as much intelligence as he could regarding what to expect. Texas was one of the constitutionally loyal states that worked against the federal government and its attempt to use the state of emergency as an opportunity to impose its will on the states. Before the collapse, the Army and Air National Guards in Texas already had a healthy force strength due to the state's patriotic and proud population; however, with a flood of patriotic civilian volunteers and deserting federal servicemen and women, their numbers were nearly double what they were before the collapse. This made Texas a safe haven for those seeking to flee the near-totalitarian rule of the current federal government.

So far in his journey, he found Texas to be a much more stable place than the other states that he had traversed to get there. Some smaller towns even managed to get a partial electrical grid up and running for their hospitals and core infrastructure components, returning their citizens' lives to a certain level of pre-collapse normalcy. He was thankful his brother chose Texas A&M over the University of Massachusetts and Northwestern University in Chicago, as those regions of the country were devastated by both the terror attacks and the violence and lawlessness that followed. It was rumored that as much as fifty percent of the population died off in those areas and in others.

This exceptionally high mortality rate was due not only to the devastating attacks and the violence that followed, but also to the instability in the region; there was no supply chain from the other regions of the country that they normally depended on for food and supplies. Many people died of starvation and illnesses associated with malnutrition as well as other health problems that would have been treatable before the collapse. The areas of the country with populations that depended heavily on the rest of the nation for constant support and supplies simply could not defend or provide for themselves in the new reality.

Even with the hope that his brother was still safe and sound in Texas, Nate knew that finding him would take what seemed like an act of God. He avoided government authorities of all kinds during his journey, both because he was a deserter and because he did not want to get caught up in anyone else's struggles. He had reached the point, however, where he felt it was time to ask for help if he wanted any chance of finding his brother.

As he rode into the outskirts of town, he approached what appeared to be a Texas National Guard outpost. It had a sign posted, bearing the Texas flag that simply read "CS Post 19." His shotgun was in plain view in a homemade scabbard tied to his saddle, and his M9 was on his side, holstered, and in plain view as well. The guardsman standing watch at the entrance to the office stood up as he approached. Nate brought his horse to a stop and slowly climbed down from the saddle. As he got closer, he noticed the soldier wore the traditional National Guard uniform but appeared to be in his mid-fifties and had a short goatee beard. He had a Texas flag on his sleeve, but no U.S. government markings could be seen anywhere on his uniform. This gave Nate pause, as the man did not fit the profile of a traditional guardsman. He approached regardless, as he was desperate to begin the search for leads that may help him find his brother.

"What can I do for you, sir?" asked the obviously cautious soldier.

"What agency do you serve?" questioned Nate in reply.

"I only serve the people, sir. My name is Jeff Collins. I'm... well... we here, are with the Texas Citizens' Guard. We work in voluntary cooperation with the Texas State Guard."

"Do you mean Texas National Guard?" asked Nate.

"Formerly the Texas National Guard," he quickly replied. "When the state of Texas decided to take a stand against the regime's push for power, the governor dropped the word 'national' and severed all ties with the federally controlled U.S. Army and Air Force. There was already a Texas State Guard in place, which was a volunteer group that augmented the Texas military and civil authorities during a state of emergency.

"The governor merged the Texas Army National Guard and Texas Air National Guard with the Texas State Guard. As a result, the traditional Texas National Guard military forces and the Texas State Guard stand as one, organized like the traditional military side of the house, with a few special considerations here and there.

"The Texas Citizens' Guard is made up of civilian militia volunteers that work in concert with the State Guard in local areas. We are people who want to be the guardians of our own communities, on a strictly local level. Some of us can't just pack up and go wherever the governor needs us due to family constraints or disabilities, but we can help out in our own local areas. The affiliation with the Texas State Guard gives us more of a standing and trust with the people than if we were a bunch of different unaffiliated militia groups."

"That sounds like a damn good way to run things, at least in a patriot state like Texas," replied Nate.

"Yes, sir, it works for us. So, what can I do for you?" he again asked.

"My name is Nate Hoskins. My brother Luke is, or rather was, a medical student at the university when it all went down. I've traveled all the way here from San Diego to try and find him and I'm hoping you can maybe give me a place to start looking."

"Wait right here; I'll be right back," Mr. Collins said.

After a few moments, another gentleman followed Jack Collins back outside to where Nate waited with his horse and said, "Mark Tucker, it's a pleasure to meet you." He reached out to shake Nate's hand. "So you're looking for a medical student?"

"Yes, sir; my brother Luke Hoskins was a first-year med student here. I've not heard from him since the lines went dead."

"Well, I can't tell you about your brother personally, but the Texas State Guard set up a makeshift hospital/rehab center at the university to make up for some of the hospitals that were hit during the attacks. They offered the medical students food, shelter, and membership in the Citizens' Guard if they volunteered to stay on and help. There were a lot of initial casualties from the attacks as well as casualties brought on by the violence during the peacekeeping efforts that followed. Over the past six months or so, the cartels from Mexico have been rushing across the border, pillaging some towns and turning them into outposts for their smuggling operations. With the federal government only being concerned about themselves and their agenda, the border is effectively wide open. The university has a constant flow of border skirmish casualties from there as well. A lot of the students stayed on to help, so your brother may be there," Mr. Tucker explained.

"Great! How do I get there?" Nate asked enthusiastically.

"Well, you may not receive a warm welcome arriving unannounced with those guns, it being a base now and all. I'll go with you so I can introduce you to the right people," replied Mr. Tucker.

"When can we leave? I'm ready anytime," said Nate, excited about the possibility of finding his brother. The long, hard journey from California had taken a toll on him, both physically and emotionally. He was in desperate need of a positive turn in his life.

"Well, we can't both ride your horse and it's too far to walk. We have to ration our fuel around here as well, so we have scheduled runs in our van to get us around. The next one leaves at 1800 this evening. You can leave your horse here; she will be taken care of. Also, if you don't mind, you can leave your shotgun in our armory until we get back to get your horse. You can take your sidearm though, we encourage everyone to be armed, but we don't want to make anyone there question your intentions. A lot of the injured guys there have been shot up by their fellow citizens, so being low-key once we are inside is the respectful thing to do," Mr. Tucker explained.

"If that's what you need me to do, I'll do it," Nate apprehensively agreed. He had not been without both of his guns for even one moment over the past year. They had become an emotional and psychological crutch for him, having saved his life so many times.

"Jeff here will show you where you can water your horse, store your shotgun, grab a bite to eat, and wash up. Then meet me back here at 1800, and we will go see what we can find out," Mr. Tucker said as he shook Nate's hand while looking him dead in the eye with a warm and seemingly genuine smile.

Nate had not felt this welcome anywhere for quite some time. He felt like it was all too good to be true, but he just had to trust them—if for no other reason than the possibility of finding his brother. Now all he had to do was wait for 1800 to get here.

Chapter 2: Homesteading On the Homefront

After the harrowing journey to the Homefront in East Tennessee by Evan, Peggy, Zack, Judith, and the Jones family during the initial stages of the collapse, Evan and Molly Baird's little hundred-acre homestead had become a homesteading community. It was now home to not only the Bairds, but also Jason and Sarah Jones and their two young boys, Kevin and Michael. The group also included Peggy and her son Zack, Mike and Judy Vandergriff with their son Greg, and Judith. Fifteen people in all, spanning every age group, now called The Homefront home.

Immediately after last year's thwarted attack by a gang of looting marauders, the men went to work rebuilding and fortifying what was damaged during the attack. While they were doing the necessary exterior repairs, the women planned and arranged temporary living quarters for the new arrivals inside the home.

The men were pleased with the level of basic ballistic protection the home provided during the attack. Only basic repairs and modifications were needed, other than completely rebuilding the chicken coop. Jason destroyed the coop during the barrage of .300 Win Mag that he relentlessly pounded it with while ending the assault. They also felt that now, with their sheer numbers, they could defensively cover the property, especially after seeing what Griff and Greg accomplished alone when holding off the attackers.

Griff, whose specialty in the Marine Corps was physical security, was put in charge of making security assessments and recommendations to the rest of the group. His duties also included establishing a watch rotation, where someone would stand watch at night while the others slept. This person was relieved for a reasonable amount of time from any duties or chores for which they were responsible, allowing him time to prepare and then recover. The night watch stander was responsible for keeping an eye on security cameras as well as making rounds throughout the property near the house and the immediate perimeter.

Their staffing levels allowed for multiple night watch standers during periods of increased threat levels. On a regular basis, however, Griff recommended they use only one night watch throughout the night to help make life seem as normal as possible, especially for the children. In addition, their homesteading workload would become burdensome if they had multiple people standing watch each night and resting during the day. All of the adults, as well as Greg and Jake, were trained to Griff's standard and were rotated through the schedule. This meant each person only had to stand watch once every nine days. They were all trained to awaken Griff if any abnormalities were to occur—or either Evan or Jason when they were designated as an alternate watch leader for the night.

After much discussion and thought, the women came up with a way for everyone to live comfortably under one roof for the time being. Evan and Molly retained the master bedroom, Griff and Judy took a room of their own, as did Jason and Sarah. Peggy and Judith decided that they would be roommates by sharing a room. The older sons, Jake, and Greg, shared a room, as did the younger sons, putting Kevin, Michael, and Zack in a room. Lastly, the girls, Lilly, and Sammy, shared a room. This arrangement was cramped but equitable, putting all six bedrooms to good use and at full capacity. Eventually, if the situation ended up being long-term, they discussed building additional structures on the property, but for now, they had to focus on security and sustainable living.

It was fall once again, and they had just completed the last of harvesting from the garden. Processing the harvest, including dry storage and canning, was an all-hands-on-deck affair. Even the younger children were involved by breaking beans and recovering seeds. During the previous winter, the large number of people living in the home put a much larger dent in Evan and Molly's long-term food storage than was expected. This made production and storage of new food even more critical as another winter rapidly approached.

Their harvest was based on vegetables grown with non-hybrid heirloom seeds that Evan and Molly had obtained during their initial preps. Just as many other Americans that were beginning to get concerned about the state of things before the collapse, Evan and Molly had done a lot of research on how to maintain a sustainable garden. Non-hybrid heirloom seeds are critical in the self-sustainability of one's garden. Hybrid seeds, or GMOs (genetically mutated organisms), are genetically modified to obtain certain characteristics and traits that aid in large-scale industrial farming, such as disease and pest resistance, survivability of mechanical picking, long-range commercial shipments, color, etc.

Although to a commercial farm this may be of benefit, to the small-scale gardener or self-sufficient homesteader, there are many drawbacks. First of all, hybrid seeds do not grow true to the parent. In other words, if you harvested hybrid super tomatoes and then replanted their seeds the following season, they would not grow into another batch of super tomatoes. They may or may not follow characteristics of the parent plant, and therefore you cannot maintain a consistent crop yield from year to year using your own recovered seeds. This means when using hybrid seeds you must commercially purchase new seeds each year, and if the supply chain for seeds were to fail, so would your garden. In addition, as they are bred for commercial reasons, many hybrid plants and GMOs do not provide the same nutritional value as a non-hybrid plant. When you are surviving on the food that you produce and the yield of your crops are not guaranteed, the maximum available nutritional value must be taken into account. So in order to grow consistent crops year after year with the highest possible nutritional value, the Bairds like countless other like-minded Americans, properly planned for the use of and acquired non-hybrid seeds for their sustainable garden.

This first year's garden was productive. However, they learned a few lessons that they hoped not to repeat in the years to come. They viewed them as valuable lessons and teaching moments for the whole group, rather than failures and setbacks. Taking a positive attitude during a survival situation will go a long way towards ensuring success.

One of their lessons learned was not to assume too much. They planted several seeds, such as tomatoes, together in each hole assuming they would not get one hundred percent germination. They did this to ensure there was not any unused space in the garden that would yield weeds rather than vegetables. Fortunately, or rather unfortunately depending on how you look at it, they got what seemed to be one hundred percent germination from their tomatoes. This resulted in a crowded and tangled mess in the garden, rather than having things nicely spaced and easy to care for. This caused extra work when weeding and harvesting, as it was difficult to get to all of the tomatoes or even notice all of the ones that were ripe. This caused some of the tomatoes to go unnoticed and die on the vine.

Another lesson learned was that peppers do not germinate all that easily in the ground. Their pepper production was almost a complete failure. They had planted banana peppers, bell peppers, and cayenne peppers, and their overall germination rate was about thirty percent at best. This gave them just enough to recover the seeds for next year's crop; however, next year they would start the seeds in a greenhouse for later transplantation to the garden. Although the intent of the peppers was more for spice and variety than for nutrition, little things like that go a long way in terms of morale in a situation where you have limited food choices for extended periods of time.

One of the more substantial lessons learned was that it is best to grow melons vertically, or to at least give them a wide berth, as they will branch out and take over other parts of the garden as they grow. Of course, this was not a catastrophic mistake, but it did, just like in the case of the tomatoes, increase the workload required to maintain the garden as well as causing some production loss.

Although they had a few setbacks and learning moments, they felt that these lessons learned would help them better plan and coordinate their gardening/farming for future seasons at the Homefront.

In addition to their gardening, they focused hard on their livestock. Although they had lost several of their chickens during the raid, of which they all jokingly reminded Jason on a regular basis, Molly shifted her chicken focus from mostly egg production to a balanced mix of egg production and breeding. Luckily, their four roosters had survived the destruction of the chicken coop. One of the roosters had been acquired accidentally by purchasing a straight run bantam chick that later turned out to be a rooster. She originally purchased her three Bantams just for the hobby of it, as they are small and are not ideal for egg and meat production. Given the situation, however, she reluctantly decided to add them to the food supply. This gave her Bantam, Black star, Leghorn and Rhode Island Reds for her flock.

The rabbits were also doing well and producing a steady supply of protein for the group. Sarah volunteered to be their keeper since she and Jason had already been successful with their own rabbits back in Ohio. This not only helped take some of the workload off of Evan and Molly, it also gave her something to help her feel as if she was earning her keep.

Evan, Jason, and Griff had discussed hunting the deer and other game animals on the property, but they decided not to thin the herds too quickly. They knew that others in the area who had not been as prepared as they were would resort to hunting right away. With this in mind, they felt it would be prudent to keep the deer on the Homefront as a reserve food supply and to let their herd stay at abundantly healthy numbers. Keeping the property a low-stress area for the deer may also eventually lead to deer from pressured areas migrating towards them and onto their property. Their routine security patrols and watches would help ensure that others were not venturing onto the Homefront to poach any of their deer.

Another important addition to the Homefront was milk cows. After the attacks, Molly regretted not having already acquired a milk cow. What was once seen as good judgment in holding off on buying one until they felt they were ready, turned out to be a regrettable error. Molly joked that waiting to complete your preps until you felt you were ready was like waiting to have a baby until you are ready. "Sometimes you just need to jump in and do it before it's too late," she would say. Luckily, they had found a way to solve that problem.

After the dust had settled, Evan, Jason, and Griff ventured out into the surrounding county to reach out to their adjoining neighbors. Evan and Molly had not been able to get to know everyone prior to the collapse, as it was a very rural area with most homes being secluded onto tracts of land similar in size to the Homefront. At this point, however, they felt that all of the surrounding neighbors would mutually benefit from some sort of alliance, or at least a mutual understanding and cooperative existence.

During these outings, they got most of the surrounding neighbors on board with a plan to set up an informal barter system. They took a list of each of the goods or services that each of the neighbors felt they could offer as payment for the other goods and services that the other neighbors offered for barter or trade. There were twelve of the fourteen nearby properties that agreed to be a part of this voluntary cooperative.

The first deal Evan made with a neighbor was with Oliver Thomas. Oliver was an eighty-six year old Korean War veteran who lived on one hundred and fifty acres with his wife, Mildred. They had raised three children who had long since moved away and had not been heard from since the collapse began. Ollie, as he preferred to be called, raised cattle as a retirement hobby that turned into a life-sustaining endeavor for him and Mildred. He offered Evan the use of two milk cows to be rotated back into the herd and replaced with other milk-producing cows whenever necessary. This would ensure a constant supply of milk at the Homefront. In exchange, all he asked was that Evan, Jason, and Griff act as his security if he ran into trouble with outsiders or if they needed medical assistance since Molly was a registered nurse.

Chapter 3: Texas A&M

Six o'clock had finally arrived and Nate met Mark Tucker as was previously planned. The van that the Texas State Guard used for their around-town shuttle service was a Ford E450. It appeared to have previously been used as a hotel shuttle service van, as it still retained its hotel paint scheme yet had the addition of expanded metal screening over all of the windows and the radiator grill. The two men boarded the van, and Mark explained to the driver who Nate was and that he was his authorized escort. The van driver welcomed Nate aboard and left right on time for his scheduled route through town.

"What stop is the university today?" asked Mark.

"Fourth," responded the driver.

"We leave at a scheduled time every day," Mark said to Nate. "That helps simplify planning and logistics with limited comms, but our driver randomly mixes up the route each run, not telling anyone else until they are in the van. That makes it more difficult for anyone to ambush us along the way."

"You have a problem being ambushed here?" questioned Nate.

"From time to time," he answered. "The cartels are chipping away at us bit by bit, just as the insurgents used to do in Iraq and Afghanistan. They hit our personnel in order to discourage more people from joining us and helping us hold them off at the border. They see the southern U.S. as ripe for the taking without a federal government and U.S. Border Patrol," Mark explained.

"What happened to the Border Patrol?" asked Nate.

"I used to be Border Patrol," the van driver interrupted. "When it all started, the administration immediately dropped the U.S. border as a priority. They ordered us all to

Washington D.C. and other political locations of interest to keep them and their families safe. A few who either had nothing else going on or who were political loyalists, stayed with the Border Patrol and went; most of us, however, said to hell with that and bailed. I joined the CBP to protect my country, not to be a political bodyguard. Besides, we've got families to protect as well. So when the CBP basically dissolved overnight, the cartels instantly filled the power vacuum on the border. We'd be Mexico right now if not for the Texas State Guard and the Texas Citizens' Guard."

For the rest of the trip across town, Nate gazed out the window, looking through the expanded metal screen taking it all in. He saw and went through a lot over the past year, almost none of it being positive. Having groups like the Texas State Guard and the Texas Citizens' Guard was the first sign of hope he had seen. Hopefully, there were people out there in other parts of the country who were doing the same, serving as the guardians of their own homes and towns rather than depending on the rule of others to do so. If we were ever to have a hope of piecing the country back together it would need to start out like this, as the federal government, at least in its current form, was more of an enemy occupying force than a legitimate constitutional government.

As they approached the university, Mark said, "Well, Nate, here we are. Once we get inside, I'll take you over to the administration folks. Hopefully, if your brother decided to stay on, they will have a record of him. They run a pretty tight ship here personnel wise. They have to for security reasons."

Nate felt his stomach twist into knots as he realized that after his yearlong journey, he may be about to find out if it was all for nothing. If there were no records or sign of his brother, would he press on to the East Coast alone to try to find his parents? This possible reality was just now entering his head. *Hell, maybe I'll just stay on with these guys*, he thought for a moment. He had always envisioned making the rest of the journey with his brother, but deep down inside he knew things might not work out that way.

Mark and Nate stepped out of the van, thanked the driver, and then proceeded to the front gate where an armed checkpoint was in place. "They don't let the van pull onto the grounds, just in case the van was hijacked by the cartels along the way. We don't want them to get a Trojan horse inside," said Mark.

"Makes sense," replied Nate.

They walked over to the security checkpoint at the entrance of the facilities. Mark explained to the sentry standing guard who Nate was and gave them a discreet password in order to be allowed inside. He whispered it off to the side so that only he and the sentry could hear it. Nate, after all, was just a guest and did not warrant access on his own accord. The sentry waved the two men inside, and Mark said, "The administration folks are just a few buildings over. They are set up in one of the dorms where we house the folks assigned to the university. What's your plan if you can't find your brother?"

"I haven't thought things that far out," he replied. "All this time, the only thing that has kept me going has been finding my brother. I've played every scenario out in my head countless times, but never without him."

"Well, son, I hope things work out and you find him, but even if you don't, we could always use more patriotic prior service types like yourself around here. You would have a home and a purpose. You can help us put this country back together... starting with Texas, of course," Mark said as they walked towards the administration office.

"I appreciate that, sir, I really do, but once I find Luke, we'll be off to find our parents. I could never live with myself, and I'm sure he couldn't either if we at least didn't try to find them. I can't live with that dark cloud of uncertainty, not knowing where or how they are," Nate said, looking at his feet as they walked.

As they approached the administration office, Mark put his hand on Nate's shoulder and led him inside. They walked down the hall and passed several wounded personnel, some of whom were missing limbs and had other serious injuries from the attacks by the cartels. Mark said, "Most of the folks who work here who aren't medical personnel are casualties themselves. We need just about every able-bodied individual to staff sentry locations and checkpoints. That's in addition to our security patrols on the border and throughout all the areas where we have a presence. These folks are continuing to serve in any capacity they can, and we have a place for every one of them."

They entered the administration office and an attractive young female in her early twenties immediately caught Nate's eye. She was dressed in a Texas State Guard uniform and was sitting behind the desk. When she saw them enter, she looked up, smiled, and said, "Good evening, Colonel Tucker."

This caught Nate off guard, as he had been thinking of Mark Tucker as just an ordinary man. Nate was still not completely up to speed on the whole Texas State Guard versus the Texas Citizens' Guard thing. After all, he was not wearing any rank insignia and until now, everyone had been calling him Mr. Tucker or Mark.

"You're a colonel?" Nate asked with a confused look on his face.

"Yes," he replied. "Off-premises we stay pretty low-key. Our folks are all volunteers who could leave anytime, so there is no reason to push the hierarchy thing too hard. It's also a wise security strategy to keep our positions discrete outside the gates, given the cartel's penchant for kidnapping. I'd rather miss out on a few salutes and formalities than end up hanging from an overpass with a warning sign around my neck."

The young woman grinned at Colonel Tucker's explanation and said, "How may I help you gentlemen?"

"Nate is looking for his brother who was a medical student here at the university when it all went down. He has traveled a long way to find him, so we are hoping you may have some sort of record on him," said Colonel Tucker.

"What's his name?" she asked.

"Luke... well, officially Lucas Hoskins, but he always went by Luke, ma'am," Nate replied.

"Well, let me look," she said as she rolled away from the desk in a wheelchair. Nate was so taken back by her beautiful smile that he had not even noticed that the chair she was sitting in was a wheelchair. She was missing both of her legs from just above the knees. She noticed him staring, and he quickly looked away. She said, "It's okay. I get that a lot. The desk hides things. I was a TNG medic and was hit by an IED in an ambush while on our way to help an injured civilian. Unfortunately, that all happened to be a ruse used by the cartel to get us to the kill zone."

"Oh, no," he said in an embarrassed manner, "it's just been a long time since I've seen such a beautiful woman."

She blushed, smiled, and rolled over to her files. She went through several different cabinets until finally pulling out a file and said, "Lucas William Hoskins?"

"Yes, that's him!" exclaimed Nate. His heart raced at what felt like a thousand beats per minute in anticipation of the information she held in her hand. "Is he here? Is he okay?"

"He was here for a while, but he volunteered to be a field medic. It looks like he is currently with a unit that is on an extended patrol. That's all of the info I have here, as this is basic personnel info, but perhaps Colonel Tucker can help you find out more," she said as she returned to her desk and handed the file to Colonel Tucker.

"I'll see what I can come up with. The actual movements of individual units are kept quiet for obvious reasons. Let's head back to Post 19, where we met so I can reacquaint you with your horse and gear. You can spend the night there while I try to find out how to locate your brother. Hopefully, I'll have some more useful information for you by tomorrow," Colonel Tucker said as he took the file from the clerk.

"Yes, sir!" said Nate in an excited tone. This was the first time since it all happened that he heard anything at all about a family member. If Luke were with the TNG, he would surely be able to track him down.

"Thank you, ma'am, for the information. You've made my day," he said to the young woman as he turned to leave. "Oh, by the way, what's your name again?"

"Oh, it's Lisa Sanchez. Sergeant Lisa Sanchez," she said with a smile.

"Petty Officer Nathan Hoskins, if you want to put it that way," he said returning the smile.

"Okay kids, we've got to get back to catch the next van for the return trip. Thanks, Sergeant, for the information. I'll see you around," Colonel Tucker said as he led Nate out of the room.

As Nate and Colonel Tucker left the building and walked back to the guard shack to catch the van back across town, Colonel Tucker said to Nate, "We've got some makeshift sleeping quarters and shower facilities back at Post 19. You can check on your horse and we'll get you a shower and a rack for the night. I'll check around with our Ops folks to try and track down your brother, and we'll go from there if anything turns up."

"Thanks a lot, Colonel. I really appreciate what you're doing for me. This is more help than I ever expected or have received since it all began," Nate said with sincere gratitude.

"Call me Mark; no need for formalities between us. Besides, if your brother has been serving alongside us all this time, he deserves our help in getting you two back together," Mark said as he gave Nate a pat on the shoulder.

Just as Colonel Tucker had said, Nate was given a bed and had his gear, including his shotgun, returned to him. Before turning in for the night, he visited with his horse and gave her food and water which was provided by the TSG personnel. That night Nate tossed and turned in anticipation of what the next day would bring. A combination of excitement and uncertainty pumped through his veins as the culmination of his struggles during the past year's journey was about to come to fruition.

Chapter 4: The Confederacy

Early one beautiful morning, Evan and Jason were on their way to Ollie and Mildred Thomas' farm for what was now their weekly security visit. Being that the Thomas farm was only a few miles away, they rode Evan's and Jake's mountain bikes in order to conserve the fuel that remained in their supply cache. Mike Vandergriff stayed behind this trip to remain at the homestead for security. The three men always rotated this duty by sending two out on a run while one stayed behind with Greg and Jake to supervise the security of the Homefront.

Jake and Greg both grew up a lot in a short amount of time. With the stability that once allowed American youth to live without a care just a memory, maturity and work ethic were once again factors of survival. Everyone had to contribute to survive, and this included the possibility of being involved in an armed conflict. After the assault on the Homefront last fall, they both rose to meet the challenge, allowing the men to feel much more comfortable leaving the Homefront for supply and security runs. They planned to add Greg to these runs soon, with Jake soon to follow if it all went well.

"Well, if nothing else, at least we will never have to worry about getting out of shape having to travel like this all the time," Jason said as they pedaled their bikes up a fairly steep hill. The topography of East Tennessee made travel by bike or foot a workout, as it is extremely hilly and mountainous.

"Yeah, I'm saving a ton of money on gym memberships," Evan replied with a snicker.

As they approached the farm, they followed their normal security protocol and mixed up their arrival procedures, just in case the place were to ever be under surveillance by would-be looters. They did not want anyone with hostile intentions to be able to easily pattern them in order to undermine the security support that they provided for the Thomases. They stopped about a half mile away from the front gate and hid their bikes off to the side of the road, behind some bushes and foliage. "You swing wide to the left and come in through the hay field, and I'll handrail the road off to the right through the woods. If it all looks clear, I'll approach the house via the driveway so that Ollie and Mildred can see me coming. You stay just out of sight as usual until I get to the house, and I'll signal you to join us if all is well," Evan said.

"Roger Roger," Jason said as he ducked off into the woods, quickly disappearing from view as he blended into the natural environment. Both men now wore camouflage clothing year-round, as function took priority over fashion. Evan and Molly had stockpiled a decent amount of surplus camouflage, including several seasonal varieties of Swiss camo as well as German Flecktarn. Flecktarn was a good year-round pattern for the region and could be acquired cheap and in bulk prior to the collapse. Mike and Jason also both still had a stockpile of camouflage clothing from their military days, as well as from recreational hunting. They had both managed to bring some with them during their bug outs.

Both men were observant and stealth as they followed their respective routes. Nothing could be taken for granted; since the collapse, the decency of society outside of one's own associations could not be assumed. The members of their alliance constantly dealt with thieves and looters since most of the population of the major cities had become migrant groups of people in search of food and a new place in the world. At times, they seemed like plagues of locust, devouring resources as they moved from place to place. At first, many of them were simply looking for a handout, but the high mortality rate from exposure and starvation had hardened most of the survivors into bands of thieves and looters who would do whatever it took to survive. Without the basic food production and survival skill sets that rural Americans tended to be ingrained with, the lifelong urban dwellers had to take what they needed, and more often than not, it was by force. Evan often joked that the Hank Williams Jr. song "A Country Boy Can Survive" was proved right every day.

As Jason made his way around to the hay field, he set himself up in a position where he could remain inside the tree line, out of sight, and behind cover. From there, he would be able to engage any threats at or near the farmhouse with his Remington 700 in .300 Win Mag. He brought along his "Remy" on every outing to act as the designated over-watch while Evan or Griff took up the point position with a high capacity intermediate weapon such as an AR, AK, or VZ. Today, Evan brought along his beloved VZ58 side folder. For their runs outside of the Homefront, he loved its incredibly compact and easy-to-carry size when folded, especially when traveling via mountain bike. This combination of both a Remington 700 and a VZ58 gave the pair a high rate of fire and long-range capability, allowing them to address the myriad situations that may arise during a run.

Once in position, Jason clicked his handheld radio mic three times indicating to Evan that he was now on watch. This meant that Evan could approach the house with the confidence that he was in Jason's kill zone for fire support in the event things were to go south.

Evan heard the clicks through his earpiece and slowly emerged from the side of the road. He walked in plain view towards the house so that Ollie and Mildred could visually identify him. As he approached the house, the front door opened and Mildred came out and said, "You're just in time for coffee." This was their phrase to let them know they were not under duress, whereas she would use tea instead of coffee if someone were known to be listening or observing.

Evan clicked his mic four times to notify Jason that the home was secure and said to Mildred and over the radio, "Good, I could sure use a cup." With that, Jason emerged from his position, slung his rifle over his back, and proceeded to the house while Evan kept a watch over him. Once he reached the front porch, the two men joined Mildred inside.

"Good morning, boys," she said with a smile.

"Good morning, ma'am," they both responded.

"Ollie is out checking on the cattle in the back pasture. He should be back anytime. So how was the ride in this morning?" she asked.

"Nice and uneventful," Jason said as he reached out to accept the cup of coffee that she was handing him.

"Yep, other than having to wait up for Jason, it went smooth," Evan said with a devious smirk as he looked at Jason who was taking a sip of his coffee.

"Yeah, right," Jason said, returning the smirk. "I was just trying to set a slow pace for the old man here so he wouldn't overdo it."

"You two remind me so much of my boys, always picking at each other in fun," Mildred said with a smile, although Evan and Jason could both see the hurt in her eyes of not knowing what had become of her own children.

Just then, they heard the back door open with Ollie's familiar knock to let Mildred know it was only him entering the house. He had told her that if she ever hears someone enter the house without a sign that it is him, to run to the basement and lock herself inside. Their basement, being completely underground to act as a root cellar, had become their bug in or panic room if anything were to happen.

Ollie walked into the room and said, "Well, hello, gentlemen. How are things over on your little piece of the world?"

"We can't complain about a thing, sir. How are things going in the livestock business?" Evan replied.

"Mostly okay, I guess," he said as he poured himself a cup of coffee.

"Mostly?" inquired Mildred with a concerned look.

"Well, it may be nothing, but there are a few head of cattle I can't account for. They may have slipped through the fence somewhere, or maybe I missed 'em in the count. I'll count 'em again tomorrow," he said trying to dismiss his concerns as nothing to worry the others about.

"Why don't Evan and I patrol the full length of your fence with you while we are here to see if there is a place they could have gotten out?" Jason said. "We came all this way; we might as well help."

"I appreciate it, but that would take too long today. Some of it would have to be done on foot since there is a bit of a mud bog that the tractor can't get through right now. I'll count'em again tomorrow and we'll worry about it then if need be," Ollie answered with an insistent tone.

"Do you have a gun you take with you into the field?" Evan asked.

"I keep my shotgun on the tractor. That's all I've ever had a need for around here."

With that being said, Evan rotated the paddle holster holding his .45 caliber Springfield Armory 1911 that he had on his strong side, freed it from his belt, and placed it on the table with the muzzle pointed in a safe direction. He then did the same with his double mag pouch that was on his weak side and placed it on the table as well. "Keep this with you at all times. Have it on your side so that if you step off of and away from your tractor, you won't be away from your gun for even a second," he said.

"Oh nonsense, you keep that. You need that more than me," Ollie replied in protest.

"Trust me, I have more than this. It won't be missed. Just don't sell it on eBay or something," Evan said jokingly.

"E what?" Ollie asked.

"Oh, never mind. That was just a bad bygone technology joke," Evan replied. "So anyway, it's settled."

"Okay, fine," Ollie said. "So back to the other business at hand. How is the confederacy going?"

"Confederacy?" asked Jason in a confused manner.

"Oh, don't get wrapped around the axle on what you learned in school about the Civil War. A confederacy is a loosely formed alliance. We all share a common goal but stand as individuals. So we, as in our trade and barter group, are a confederacy of sorts."

"Oh, that," Jason replied. "Well, we have twelve of the fourteen surrounding properties onboard."

"Who are the two holdouts?" asked Ollie.

"The place just off of Big Ridge Road that has an old run-down farmhouse with a few doublewide trailers set up out back is one. The other is the Murphy place, a little on down the road from there. That is, I assume it's the Murphy place as that is what the mailbox says," added Evan.

"Well, that first one you mentioned is Frank Muncie's place. I believe he died a few years back. He was a rough ol' feller, but, overall, a decent man. His three boys, however, who should all be in their thirties or so by now, are a different story. Frank just didn't raise 'em right. He just let 'em do whatever the heck they wanted all their lives and, needless to say, they didn't turn out to be worth a damn. Frank Jr, the oldest, was in and out of jail by the time he was eighteen, mostly for theft and petty stuff. Once the other two boys got old enough, though, the three of them together went bad in a hurry. Word is they got into sellin' weed and from there got into pushin' prescription pain pills and such. Them ain't the kind of fellers you wanna be doin' business with anyway. Now the Murphys, on the other hand, that concerns me. What exactly happened there?" asked Ollie.

"We didn't even get to the front gate," Jason said.

"Yeah, we drove our ATVs toward the front gate and someone fired a warning shot over our heads, followed by someone yelling from the inside of the house to get the hell out of there. We didn't want to get into it with anyone, so we just complied and moved on," answered Evan.

"Hmmm... well, I don't know what to think about that," Ollie said as he looked down at the table with a concerned voice. His frustration and concern was evident from his demeanor. "Well, let's give it a day or two and then go pay them a visit. If I'm with you, maybe he won't go off half-cocked."

"What's the situation over there that's got you concerned?" asked Jason.

"Isaac Murphy and I go way back," Ollie answered. "He and I grew up together. We've lived here all of our lives, aside from our war years. He's a good man, but his wife passed on about five years ago and he didn't take it well. They had been married pretty much since the dinosaurs roamed these parts. He was just never the same without her. He went from being a friendly ol' coot like me, to being a cantankerous ol' hermit. Still, it doesn't seem like him to pop a shot off at someone, though, unless they earned it, of course. I guess I just haven't given much thought as to how he must be gettin' by out there by himself since the collapse. I feel like I owe it to him to go and check on him. For ol' time's sake."

"Well, we would be glad to escort you out there," Jason said.

"I don't need no damn escort! I'm not helpless! I just need someone to ride shotgun," snapped Ollie,

"Oliver! Mind your manners!" interrupted Mildred

"You're right, dear," he sheepishly replied. "I'm sorry, boys. There has just been a lot to digest lately and I let it get to me."

"Don't worry about it, sir," replied Jason. "We would be glad to ride shotgun for you."

"Okay, let's not get all mushy here; back to business. So other than those two, what are we looking at as far as this barter system goes? Who's got what?" Ollie said, changing the subject.

Evan dug a piece of paper out of his pocket and began to sift through what was written on it. "Well, you have cattle, of course. We have offered up security services as well as pick-up and delivery services for anyone who doesn't feel comfortable traveling right now to make their own trades. This, of course, requires payment in fuel to make the delivery, as well as some extra for our use back at the Homefront, or possibly a small share of the load. The terms of delivery will always be negotiable, of course. The Brooks Farm has general vegetables and such for trade. That could come in handy for lots of folks. The Deans still have their dairy up and running to feed themselves but say they can ramp things up to produce butter and some basic cheese products. They can also produce milk but aren't quite sure if the logistics of delivery would work out. Jimmy Lewis has been the local moonshiner around here for a while and has a stockpile of shine. He says he can fire it up and produce more if he can get the corn and sugar, but what he has will last a while. Even for the people who don't drink, it could be used as an antiseptic or cleaner."

"Or dragster fuel," added Jason jokingly.

"Yeah, you joke but you're not that far off base. That stuff can be used for all kinds of things," replied Evan. The Skidmores have chickens and pigs to trade. Lloyd Smith says his family will start breeding some of their egg laying chickens soon and will have plenty of extra eggs. He also has a good-sized garden and his wife is into canning, so he says they can also trade canned produce for winter use. Bill Duncan used to grow tobacco but switched to corn this season. He says he has a bunch ground up into cracked corn and corn meal."

"That's it for food, but it's a good start," Evan continued. "Other than food and our services, William Bailey has offered woodworking and carpentry services. He also has an old sawmill he can use to rip logs into boards. Charlie Blanchard owned the hardware store in Del Rio. He says he has a bunch of various nuts, bolts, nails, screws, tape, wire, and such that he could use for trade items. His brother Toby Blanchard has a junkyard of sorts with cars, equipment, appliances, and more. He said all of that could be used for parts and pieces for trade. Linda Cox previously had an alterations shop, so she has all of the fabrics and threads needed to make and or repair clothing. And last but not least is Daryl Moses. He's been into frontier days reenactment stuff with old muzzleloaders, long bows, animal traps, and stuff like that. He got so into it and wanted to be so correct to the period that he started making black powder from scratch, the old way, using a mixture of saltpeter, charcoal, and sulfur. He was into flintlock muskets so he makes it in FFG and FFFG grades."

"That could be some handy stuff," added Jason. "Heck, you could reload old hi-capacity case cartridges like .38 special, .45 Colt, .30-30, .45-70 and just about any other cartridge designed before the end of the 1800s with that stuff as long as you had a bullet mold and primers."

"Not to mention blowing out old tree stumps—or heck, even bombs if a fella' needed it," added Ollie. "Sounds to me like our little confederacy is off to a good start."

Chapter 5: Nightmares

There was a noise just outside the front door. They could not see what was there due to the power being out and the streets of their neighborhood being dark. Their flashlight batteries were all dead by now, so the young boy's grandmother lit a candle and handed it to his grandfather to go and see what was going on. He did not believe in having guns in the home, so all he had for protection was a cane that he occasionally used when his hip pain was flaring up. The hip replacement that he had received a couple years back had been giving him trouble over the past few months.

As the boy's grandfather crept into the living room to see what was going on, his grandmother led him to the utility closet and said, "Here, son, hide in here until your grandpa or me says it's okay to come out."

The boy nodded and did as his grandmother asked. The neighborhood had been getting more violent as each day passed. Not only were people running out of their basic supplies, it was also becoming clear that the police or any other sort of authority was not coming to fix things anytime soon. Several of the neighbors had been robbed over the course of the last few days, so they knew it was just a matter of time before they had to deal with the people migrating out of the inner city.

The boy sat quietly in the darkness of the utility closet. Sounds were all he had to paint a vision in his head of what may be going on in the house. He heard his grandmother whisper, "What is it?"

"I don't know," his grandpa replied. "I thought I heard whispering and some shuffling around the door, but it seems to be gone now."

He sat there in total silence for the next few minutes, trying his best to hear anything at all in the other room. Then he heard his grandpa say, “I think they are gone.” No sooner than he heard those words, he heard a violent crash and his grandmother scream aloud. Several loud male voices came running into the room yelling profanities and racist remarks as he heard thump after thump and his grandpa wailing and moaning. He heard his grandmother run by the closet towards their bedroom, slam the door, and lock it behind her.

“What were you gonna do with that cane ol’ man? Were you gonna try and hit me with it? I’m gonna beat you to death with your own cane you stupid ol’ fool,” shouted one of the strange men. He heard the sound of something swinging and thumping repeatedly as the man yelled, “Hit me with it now, fool! Hit me with it now!”

Several other men walked past the closet where the boy was hiding. He was now wedged behind the water heater, shaking in fear as he heard the horrific sounds coming from his grandparents’ home. He heard another crashing sound and screams from his grandmother as she was dragged past the closet towards the living room. When they got her to the living room, he heard her scream, “You killed him! You killed him, you bastards!” Her words fell from rage into a deep and sorrowful cry. He had never heard so much pain in a person’s voice.

He then heard a smacking sound as one of the men yelled, “Shut up, bitch!” He heard the sounds of tearing clothes as his grandmother sobbed painfully.

A few minutes of a muffled struggle went by and one of the men yelled, “Hurry up, it’s my turn.”

“I’ll be done when I’m done,” another voice said.

He could now hear footsteps coming to the closet. He tensed up as he heard the knob on the closet door begin to turn. The closet door opened and a bright flashlight shined in the boy's face followed by a large, dirty hand grabbing him by the arm. A voice from the figure in the darkness said, "I've got a young one!" And he pulled the young boy from the closet.

Peggy awoke to the sound of Zack screaming down the hall. She ran out into the hallway to find that Griff and Jason also heard the screams and had come running with their pistols at the ready, just in case it was an intruder causing the commotion. Griff was the first to arrive at the boy's room, as he was already up to stand watch that night. Jason followed closely behind having been awoken by the screams.

They ran into the young boy's bedroom to find Zack in his bed under the covers, kicking and screaming, "Get off her! Get off her!"

Zack, being the smallest of the three boys sharing the room, slept on one of the two bottom bunks. Peggy ran to him, pushing Griff out of the way and sat on the bed next to him. She put her hand on him to wake and comfort him. As soon as her hand touched his back, he flinched violently and then awoke to see that it was only his mother and not the intruder in his dream. He climbed into her arms sobbing, saying, "They wouldn't stop! They wouldn't stop!"

"Who wouldn't stop what, honey? It was just a dream," she said trying to comfort him.

"No! It was real! It was real!" he screamed repeatedly as the tears rolled down his face.

She hugged him and rocked back and forth trying to comfort him, saying, "It's okay, Mommy is here now, it's okay."

Jason said to his boys quietly, "Michael, you and Kevin come in here with me and your mom for the rest of the night. Let's give them some space." The Jones boys grabbed their pillows and blankets and followed Jason out the door. Pretty much everyone else in the house stood in the hallway at this point.

"What happened?" asked Evan.

"Boys, go on in there with your mom," Jason said as Sarah led them to her and Jason's room. After she had closed the door, Jason said, "Looks like he was having one serious nightmare. He kept screaming to get off her. It looked like a pretty intense dream."

"Well, from the way I found him in Newport, after witnessing what happened to his grandmother and grandfather, it's no surprise he's having issues. Frankly, I'm surprised it took this long for something like this to come up. That kid has gone through something worse than any of us have," Evan said.

Griff spoke up and said, "Well, now that everything is under control, let's leave him in Peggy's hands and go back to bed. We can talk to her about it in the morning. Right now, we are all just guessing. I'll make rounds through here occasionally to see if Peggy is up and in need of anything." With that being said, everyone nodded in agreement and they all shuffled off back to bed.

The rest of the night was uneventful. Most of the adults had a hard time sleeping after what had happened. They all had thoughts of the horrors that Zack must have had to live through before he was found by Evan, Peggy, and Judith at the home of Peggy's parents in Newport.

Six o'clock in the morning finally rolled around, and Judith walked into the kitchen to find Griff and his wife, Judy, sitting at the kitchen prep table. Griff was eating a bowl of scrambled eggs and potatoes while Judy looked around in the pantry. "Good morning," he said. "We made you all a pot of coffee. It's ready if you want some,"

"Oh, thank you so much. I really need it. I didn't sleep at all after what happened. I've been worried sick about poor little Zack. It was hard enough for me to get over what I saw in Newport, but that poor boy had to live through it. And with it being his beloved grandparents... just how does a little boy like

Zack deal with such a thing?" she said as she poured herself a cup of coffee.

"We can talk to the others later, but I think we need to rearrange the sleeping arrangements at a minimum for now so that he can be with his mother at night," Griff said, taking his last bite.

"I agree completely. Are you not joining us for breakfast?" she asked, noticing his empty bowl.

"No, ma'am. I'm whooped. That, and I have a lot to get done this evening, so I need to get to bed sooner, rather than later," he said.

Just then, Molly came into the kitchen and said, "Oh, good morning. I thought it was Peggy's turn to get up early to make breakfast, so I thought I would come down to help and just tell her to go back to bed and get some rest."

"That's exactly why I'm here," said Judith.

"Me too," said Judy. "I couldn't go back to sleep so I just came down to keep the hubby company and figured I'd cover for Peggy since I was already up."

Next, Sarah came through the door and paused, surprised to see the other women in the kitchen so early. Judy, Molly, and Judith just looked at each other and laughed. Sarah said, "What?"

"Oh, nothing," said Judith. "I guess we can all four just help each other with breakfast."

Realizing that she was there for the same reason as the other women, Sarah shared a laugh with them and said, "Okay, what are we making?"

With that, Griff said, "Well, ladies, I will leave you to your business at hand. I'll see you all this evening." Griff kissed Judy on his way out and the women got on with the business of breakfast.

A little while later, as everyone got up and gathered in the dining room for breakfast, they discussed the current sleeping situation. Sarah volunteered to move Kevin and Michael's bunk bed into her and Jason's room for the time being to allow Peggy the opportunity to be with Zack and to give them privacy. Everyone agreed and thanked her for volunteering a solution to the immediate problem while they tried to figure out how best to help Peggy with Zack in the long run. The ladies brought out scrambled eggs and potatoes with diced tomatoes with a pitcher of fresh cow's milk to wash it down. Evan led them all in a special prayer for grace before they ate, asking the Lord to look over and help poor little Zack and his mother, Peggy.

After their wonderful breakfast, they all went on with their day and life seemed, for the time being at least, to return to normal.

Chapter 6: On the Move

When Nate awoke the next morning, he was relieved to realize that he had finally fallen asleep. All he remembered was tossing and turning with thoughts of what may come the next day bouncing around in his head. The sun was now up and he could hear talking in the next room over, so he knew it was time to get up and see if there was any word from Colonel Tucker.

He got dressed and went into the main area of College Station Post 19, where he saw Mike Collins and another gentleman in a TSG uniform having a cup of coffee. He also noticed that another TSG member was at the sentry position out front. "Good morning, Nate," Mike Collins said as he noticed Nate enter the room. "Would you like some coffee?" he asked.

"Sure, I'd love some," he replied.

"Hello, Nate, I'm Sergeant Heath Wilson with the TSG," the other man said as he reached his hand out to Nate. Sergeant Wilson was in his early thirties and seemed to wear his uniform with pride. He was wearing the TSG's multi-cam field uniform with a matching multi-cam boonie style hat and desert tan suede boots. He had on a molle load-bearing vest that held six AR15/M4 magazines. He also wore a drop leg holster, which carried one of the Marine Corps' new Colt M45 1911 pistols. His sleeves were crisply rolled up, revealing a Marine Corps globe and anchor tattoo.

"Pleased to meet you," said Nate as he returned the handshake.

"So you're a squid, I hear," said Sergeant Wilson with a smirk on his face.

"I was an MA2 to be exact," referring to his rating as a Master at Arms Second Class, which is a Military Police E-5, equivalent to a Sergeant in rank.

"I was on the green side. Like you, I couldn't see myself serving in the capacity that the higher-ups these days wanted, so I bailed. I joined up with the TSG here and they've been my brothers ever since. Colonel Tucker sent me to see if you wanted to join my guys and me on a run. I was a 3531 in the Corps," Sergeant Wilson said. As he looked at Nate, he said, "I see you looking at me with a blank look, so I guess you don't know what that is. It's the motor vehicle operator MOS. I was a motor transport guy so I have lots of convoy experience. Anyway, they've put me to work in that capacity, delivering supplies to our forward deployed units and bringing back the wounded when necessary. We have a run going out tonight to take ammo, MREs, and mail down to a unit that's been mixing it up with the cartels pretty heavy. They are trying to hold them off from entering an area south of Beeville, which seems to be the cartel's next point of interest. There is a medic at a mobile medical unit there you may be interested in seeing."

"Luke?" Nate said with excitement.

"That's what I'm told," replied Sergeant Wilson. "Anyway, we are loading up a convoy of three Humvees, five guys total, six if you want to ride shotgun for me."

"Hell yes!" said Nate.

"Good. Get your stuff and come with me. We'll be leaving this evening at dusk to arrive by morning. I'll get you some TSG gear and get you suited up like us. We'll need to go over a few standard operating procedures so that you can work in sync with us if something goes down along the way."

"Sounds good," Nate said with enthusiasm. He went back to his rack and gathered his things. On his way out, he went out back to check on his horse. He kissed his horse on the head and said, "Don't you worry ol' girl, I'll be back. These guys will take good care of you until then." He then turned and walked towards the door, pausing to turn and look at her one more time with a strange feeling in his gut. He then turned and went back inside to meet up with Sergeant Wilson.

Sergeant Wilson was standing out front smoking a cigarette with two other TSG guardsmen. Both of the men were rough and weathered looking. One, a Caucasian man a little over six feet tall with a slim build, had a sleeve tattoo on his left arm and had severe scarring on his neck and the side of his face. The other was a Hispanic male with a stocky build that stood about five foot nine and weighed around two hundred pounds. He wore a Catholic rosary around his neck and a boonie style hat with a miniature Texas flag on a toothpick safety pinned in place.

"Hoskins," Sergeant Wilson said in a loud voice when he saw Nate come out of the building in order to get his attention. "Smoke?" He offered Nate a cigarette.

"No thanks, I don't smoke," Nate replied as he walked over to join them.

"Good. These things are worth their weight in gold these days," he said with a crooked smile.

"Hell, Sarge... you don't buy 'em. You get 'em off of dead Mexicans," the taller of the men said.

"What this insensitive jerk means is dead cartel gunmen, not Mexican civilians," responded Sergeant Wilson as he flicked his ashes at the man. "Besides, every situation I get in where I can pick up a pack of smokes is a situation where I can get smoked, so it's not like I'm rushing right out to get more. Anyway, this is Corporal Jeff Shockley. We just call him Shock because it shocks us that he manages to stay alive. He was an Army Ranger when the shit hit the fan. That probably explains a lot. This other fine specimen of male crudeness is Private Jose Garcia. We call him Chop for reasons you wouldn't tell your mother."

"He ran out of ammo during an ambushed supply run and ended up chopping his way out with an old rusty machete he found in a shed that he dove into for cover," Shock said. "He was such a demon-possessed freak, some of the cartel thugs that had ammo actually ran from him. Then again, seeing some of your compadres literally lose their heads will do that to a lesser man." Chop just took a draw off his cigarette as if the trash talk didn't faze him.

"So anyway, guys, this is the squid I was telling you about. He will be riding with me," Sergeant Wilson said to the guardsmen. He looked at Nate and said, "These two knuckleheads will take the other Humvee and the supply guys will take the third. We are supposed to meet up with them later at the depot. We are basically the point and rear guard for the run. I'd give you an M4 carbine to carry, but it's against SOP to arm up unverifieds. We've had way too many of our own weapons end up pointing back at us."

"I've got an M9 pistol and my 12 gauge that I plan to bring along unless you object," responded Nate.

"Oh hell, yeah! Bring 'em. I was afraid you'd be dead weight," Sergeant Wilson said enthusiastically. He tossed his cigarette butt on the ground and stomped it with his foot. "Okay, ladies, let's mount up."

Nate couldn't believe it. He was finally on his way to find his brother. Not just to find out more information or follow more leads, but to actually go and find him. He was motivated beyond belief. As he and Sergeant Wilson pulled away in their Humvee with Shock and Chop following close behind, he turned to Sergeant Wilson and asked, "So, where are we heading?"

"I can't tell you that just yet. It could compromise our OPSEC. If you got snagged by the cartels and they started sawing your head off with a rusty knife, you'd more than likely give up our destination, which would let them know where our boys are and it could blow everything," Sergeant Wilson said as he drove. "By the way, keep an eye out at all times. You're in a moving target now. The cartels make southern Texas feel like Texghanistan with all of the IEDs and ambushes. It doesn't help that these turd National Guard trucks aren't up-armored. Avoidance is our only defense. That's why we are heading out at sunset. With no electrical power in most places, it gets pretty damn dark at night, so we drive with NVGs and our lights out. It's the best cover we've got."

"I understand, but you can trust me not to give anything away if I'm interrogated," Nate said as he turned his attention outside of the window as Sergeant Wilson had directed him to do.

"Everybody says that until the knife is slicing into their throat. You'd be amazed how many people give it all up with their last breath," he replied.

After an uneventful drive through town, they came upon a fortified warehouse that was serving as a supply depot for the remotely deployed TSG units in the region. They pulled up along the street and parked in a row of other TSG vehicles. Sergeant Wilson shut the truck off and said, "You can leave your guns out here. I can't bring in an armed outsider. This street is heavily surveilled, so they'll be safe. We don't take vehicles inside unless necessary. Our third Humvee is already inside and it will come out loaded when we leave.

"Roger that," responded Nate, complying with his request.

They then met up with Shock and Chop, who had just parked behind them on the street, and proceeded to the entrance. The facility was heavily defended with two SAW machine guns set up behind makeshift bunkers at ground level and what appeared to be several marksmen on the roof with scoped M-14s. Sergeant Wilson exchanged some paperwork with the sentry who appeared to be in charge, and then Nate and the others were led inside.

"Shock, you two go and find our supply guys, and I'll get Nate here suited up in some of our gear," said Sergeant Wilson as they walked across the warehouse floor. To Nate, he said, "Follow me and we'll get you some proper threads."

Nate followed him through a door in the back of the facility, down a dark hallway, and then into a dingy room. The only light in the room was from skylights in the ceiling overhead. "What's your size, Hoskins?" asked Sergeant Wilson.

"Large/regular," replied Nate.

Sergeant Wilson dug around in a box for a minute and then tossed him a pair of BDU multi-cam pants and blouse. "They ain't new, but they'll work. Hat size?"

"Seven and a half."

Sergeant Wilson tossed him a multi-cam boonie hat and asked, "Boots?"

"Ten and a half."

Sergeant Wilson tossed him a pair of desert tan boots. "Eleven is the best we can do; wear extra socks. There is a trash bag full of socks over in the corner. Find yourself some with some life left in them and get dressed and meet us out in the staging area on the warehouse floor."

As Sergeant Wilson turned and walked out of the room, Nate said, "Roger that." He could not help but think of how crude and to the point these guys were compared to Colonel Tucker and Mike Collins back at Post 19. *I guess these guys, being out in the suck of it all, have been hardened a bit*, he thought to himself. Being former military police, Nate had never experienced combat directly; although he had several friends who had been in sustained combat operations and he had seen similar traits begin to show in them. In retrospect, he could see that he had changed a lot over the past year since the collapse. He had seen and done some dark things in order to survive. *We've all changed a lot, I guess.*

He snapped himself back to reality and got dressed. He folded his old clothes and put them back in the corner of the room out of the way, just in case he came back to the warehouse so he could retrieve them. He then backtracked his way down the dark hallway to meet back up with Sergeant Wilson and the guys.

"There's our squid!" said Shock from across the warehouse floor. Shock, Chop, Sergeant Wilson, and two other men stood around a loaded Humvee, going over a map. Sergeant Wilson folded the map up and put it into his pocket as Nate approached.

"Hoskins, this is Specialists Parker and Clarke. They'll be driving the supply truck positioned between us in the convoy during tonight's run," Sergeant Wilson said.

One of the men reached out his hand and said, "John Parker, pleased to meet you."

Nate returned the handshake with a nod and a smile as the other man said, "Howdy, I'm Will Clarke." He reached out to shake Nate's hand as well.

"Okay, ladies, now that we all know who we are workin' with, let's go over some ground rules." Sergeant Wilson went over the standard protocols and procedures for tonight's run. After he finished, he said, "Any questions, comments, additions, or concerns?"

"Can we stop for a beer along the way?" asked Shockley.

"Shut up, Shock," Sergeant Wilson said, dismissing the comment. "Anyone else? No? Good. Now, let's break up and meet back here at nineteen hundred hours. Get in a nap if you can, it'll be a long night."

Chapter 7: For Old Time's Sake

Two days after Evan and Jason's last visit with Ollie and Mildred, the two men were once again on their way to the Thomas farm, as they had agreed to accompany Ollie to visit Isaac Murphy. Griff volunteered once again to stay back at the Homefront to provide security while Evan and Jason were away. Although it was his turn to go into rotation for a run off of the property, he felt that since Evan and Jason were both already involved with the situation, it would be best for them to see it through.

As was now the routine, Evan and Jason rode their mountain bikes to the Thomas farm and approached with their standard operating procedure of Evan approaching the house from a random direction while Jason provided over-watch with his Remington 700. They found everything to be secure at the home and as usual, they were ushered into the home by Mildred, who was putting on a fresh pot of coffee.

As they sat down to enjoy their coffee, Mildred said, "Ollie will be in any minute. He's in the barn getting the tractor ready so you can all ride on it and leave your bikes behind." As she pulled up a chair and sat down to enjoy a cup of coffee herself, she looked both men in the eyes and said, "Please take care of my dear Ollie. He's not what he used to be, but in his head, he is still ten feet tall and bulletproof. He is my entire world. I can't live without him. Please bring him back to me."

Evan reached out and took her hand, looked her in the eye and said, "Ma'am, I promise you, we will use every precaution and will fight tooth and nail if it comes to it to make sure we bring him home safe to you. Just say a prayer or two for our safe return and we will do everything we can on our part. I'm sure everything will be fine."

"Well, I have faith in you boys," she said, welling up with a tear. "You're like family to us now. It was very scary and lonely around here over the past year until you two and Griff began coming around to check up on us. It sure has made a difference in our outlook on the world and our future."

"Ma'am, the pleasure, and the honor have been all ours," Jason said.

The back door opened and they heard Ollie's familiar knock. He walked into the room, hung his hat up on the hook on the wall, and said, "Well, boys, our ride is ready."

"So what's our ride?" asked Evan.

"We're gonna take that old Massey Ferguson tractor I've been tinkering on. I had an old six-foot Bush Hog mower deck that was junk. I pulled the blades, PTO shaft, and everything else that was no longer needed and tossed it. I tack-welded a foot high rail around it, added a sheet of half-inch plywood to make it not so rough to sit on, and basically made a flat pickup bed out of it. I'll hook the three-point hitch up to it, lift it up off the ground with the hydraulics, and you guys can ride back there in style. Heck, I can even throw a hay bail on it if you guys want something a little cushier. It being a diesel, it just sips fuel putting along like that, and being open cab and you guys being in the open, if we run into trouble we can just bail off of the thing and run. Most importantly though, I've had that ol' tractor for forty years and Isaac should recognize it from a distance and know it's me. Maybe that will calm that ill temper you fellers had the pleasure of experiencing," Ollie said as he sat down at the table and joined them.

Evan and Jason looked at each other and simultaneously said, "Sounds good."

"Well, drink your coffee and let's get a move on. It'll take a little while to get over there and I've got to find out what's goin' on with Isaac or it's gonna drive me nuts."

"Yes, sir," Jason said as he set his empty coffee cup on the table. "Thank you, ma'am, for the outstanding coffee, as usual."

"Well, boys, enjoy it while you can. We are getting down to our last bit we had stored up, and since I didn't hear coffee on your list of barter items, I imagine we will be running out soon," Mildred said.

"Well, stop wasting it on us then," replied Evan. "We don't want to eat into your stores like that."

"Oh nonsense," she said. "If you can't be a good host, then what's the point of this world, anyway?" she said.

"C'mon boys, she'll talk your ear off all day if you let her," Ollie said as he leaned over and gave her a kiss.

She grabbed him, gave him a big hug and kiss, and said, "Now you come back to me, you ol' coot. I can't work these cows alone!"

"Yes, ma'am," he said with a smile.

With that, Ollie, Evan, and Jason walked out of the house and went around to the barn to get the tractor. "I see you are wearing the pistol I gave you. Good!" said Evan pointing at the .45 on Ollie's hip.

"Yeah... well, I didn't want to get any lip from you, so it's just to shut you up," Ollie said in reply.

Evan just chuckled and said, "Whatever it takes."

"Well, boys, climb on," Ollie said as he climbed up on the old, red tractor and fired it up; the Massey responded by belching diesel smoke into the air. Evan and Jason hopped on the old Bush Hog and sat down with their rifles in hand. Ollie lifted the mower deck up off the ground with the three-point hitch and slipped the tractor into gear. With a jerk, they were on their way.

Most of the journey was uneventful. The tractor settled into a comfortable cruise down the old back roads. It was a bumpy ride for Evan and Jason, with the sloppy linkage of the three-point hitch letting the old mower deck shift side to side with every bump, but it was easier than pedaling their bikes.

The old road had many twists and turns and had trees and foliage beginning to overtake the pavement. The road had not been maintained in over a year and it was beginning to show; the lack of vehicle traffic and the kudzu vines that plagued the area were making the road seem narrower by the day. It was surrounded by tall hills that constantly kept it in the shadows, limiting visibility for those traveling on the road. *It's perfect for an ambush from virtually any position*, Jason thought to himself.

As they rounded a corner, Ollie slammed on the brakes, jarring Evan and Jason against the rear fenders. They turned around to see Ollie pointing ahead and to the left.

"What's up?" asked Jason.

"A horse just left the road and entered the woods right there," Ollie whispered as he pointed.

Evan and Jason's first thought was to split up and take cover on each side of the road, but they could not leave Ollie out there on that tractor exposed and alone. Evan hopped down and walked around alongside Ollie with his VZ at the ready. Jason took a kneeling position on the Bush Hog deck and scanned the area where Ollie saw the horse with his scope. A few moments passed and they neither saw nor heard anything more.

Evan said to Jason, "Cover me. I'm gonna sneak up there and see what I can see."

"Roger Roger!" replied Jason as he shouldered his Remington.

Evan crept up the side of the road near the ditch line. He had to step over and around the vegetation that was taking over the road, which was slowing his progress. The only clear path was in the center of the road and that would leave him too vulnerable and in the open. As he approached the area where

Ollie said he saw the horse, Evan heard a snort. He pulled his VZ up to a high ready position, scanning the woods and then heard, “Evan, is that you?”

“Who’s askin’?” he replied.

“It’s Daryl Moses. Put that thing away; I’m coming on out,” the man said as a large bearded fellow on a brown horse came into view while picking his way through the woods. “I came around the corner and saw that tractor and took off into the woods until I figured out who it was. I didn’t want to find myself stumbling across any looters or anything all alone.”

“You sure walk the walk and talk the talk. You look like you are straight out of Grizzly Adams or something,” Evan said to Daryl, commenting on his frontiersman attire.

“Well, there ain’t no better camo than the original camo. The frontiersman of the past didn’t need all of those fancy digital camo patterns and stuff, they simply wore what nature provided and it works to this day.”

In addition to his buckskin clothing and brown boots, Daryl was wearing an 1875 Remington on his side and had a Winchester Model 1886 lever action rifle attached to his saddle in a homemade leather scabbard.

“Are those things real?” Evan asked.

“The guns?” Daryl replied. “Well, the pistol is an Uberti reproduction of a ’75 chambered in .45 Colt. I wouldn’t be able to afford a real one; not to mention .45 Colt ammo is a lot easier to find than .44-40. The rifle is a true Winchester ’86 in .45-70. It’s old like me, but it still thumps hard and puts meat on the table. What are you fella’s up to? Are you on a supply run?”

“No, not today,” Evan replied. “We’re headin’ up to the Murphy place to try to make contact with him. The last time Jason and I went up there, we were shot at. This time, Ollie is going with us to see if we can get him to talk.”

"Oh hell, is that Oliver Thomas?" Daryl said as he squinted to see down the road. "Well, it is ain't it? I haven't seen ol' Ollie in quite some time."

Evan waved Jason and Ollie forward. Ollie fired the tractor up and they drove on up to where Daryl and Evan were stood on the side of the road.

"Good to see you, old man!" Daryl said to Ollie with a big smile on his face shining through his beard.

"Same to you, mountain man!" said Ollie, returning the smile. "We've all been so holed up since everything went to hell that we've damn near lost touch with everybody around these parts."

"About Isaac Murphy," Daryl said. "I don't know what's goin' on up there myself. I rode up there about a month ago to see if he needed anything and the place looked like a dump compared to how I remember it last. There was a bunch of crumpled up beer cans lying around the front porch and cigarette butts everywhere. From what I remember, Isaac didn't drink or smoke. Did he?"

"No, he sure as hell didn't," replied Ollie. "I don't like the sound of that."

"We never got close enough to see anything like that when we were up there last week," added Jason. "We didn't even get past the gate in the driveway before he... or someone, popped a shot off at us."

"Well, that doesn't sound like him at all. Something is up. I'll follow you fellas up there if you don't mind," Daryl replied with concern.

"The more, the merrier," Ollie said. "Let's get movin', the day's a wastin'," said Ollie as he fired up the tractor. "Hop on, boys," he said.

Evan and Jason hopped on the Bush Hog, and with a jerk, Ollie let out on the clutch and the tractor lunged forward from pulling out in fourth gear. Ollie was tired of talking about it and was determined to get up there and see what was going on for himself. Daryl Moses mounted his horse and followed along behind. After twenty minutes or so, they arrived just short of the Murphy place. Ollie shut down the tractor and let Daryl catch up. Once they joined up, Ollie said, “So how do you boys want to handle this?”

Jason spoke up and said, “I’ve got the high-powered scope so let me sneak around to the side of the property and glass the place. Once I’m in a position where I can see what’s going on, I’ll radio Evan on his handheld. Then as you proceed up the driveway, if we get to that point, I’ll be able to cover you if anything fishy is going on.”

“I can get up around back in a hurry with Ben here,” Daryl added, referring to his horse. “That way I can cover things from the back end, just in case. I’ve got a set of binoculars in my possibles bag. If all is well and you guys make contact and it’s all good, I’ll come on down. If not, I can either assist from there or create a diversion for your retreat.”

“Well, that about covers everything then,” Evan said. “Ollie can drive the tractor, which like he said, hopefully, will make him recognizable to Isaac, and I’ll ride shotgun for him. Daryl, you and Jason get moving. We will wait here until Jason gives us the signal.”

“Roger that!” said Jason as he slung his Remington over his shoulder and headed off into the woods.

“Stay safe,” replied Daryl as he disappeared into the woods on the back of his trusty horse, Ben.

As Jason made his way around the side of the home, he paused occasionally to glass the area with his powerful Nightforce scope. The home was in a terrible state of repair. It appeared to be completely neglected with litter and beer cans strewn around the entrances, just as Daryl said. At this point, however, he still had not seen any signs of possible occupants. He crept through the woods, taking up a vantage point directly off to the side, giving him the best overall view of both the front and back entrances to the house. Just as he began to glass the property, he saw someone come out of the back door. It was a young, white male with a mullet style haircut who Jason estimated to be in his late twenties. He took the last drag from a cigarette and tossed it into the back yard, followed by a beer can. He then turned and went back into the house. Jason pulled his handheld radio out of its pouch and whispered to Evan, “Ev... you there?”

“Yep,” Evan replied.

“We’ve got movement–white male in his late twenties. Looks pretty trashy. Also seems to be the source of at least some of the beer cans. Is there anyone that may be with Isaac that fits that description?”

Evan turned to Ollie and having heard the transmission from Jason, Ollie said, “Not that I am aware of. Distant family perhaps, but there wasn’t anyone living with him prior to the collapse.”

“Well, I guess we need to confront him or them somehow,” Evan suggested. “We need to get a dialog going to find out if Isaac is with them or not.”

“Just how do you propose we do that?” Ollie asked.

“I guess I just have to walk up there and ask. They may be here legitimately so we can’t just attack the place. And if they see me sneaking up on them, they will have every right to deal with me as an attacker, just as I would deal with them if they approached my house in such a way,” Evan said.

“Makes sense, I guess,” Ollie said. “Sounds stupid as all hell, but makes sense.”

“Jason, do you see Daryl anywhere?” asked Evan over the radio.

“Negative,” replied Jason.

“Well, I’m gonna make contact. I’ll keep my radio on with my earpiece in and try and hide it under my hat with the wire around the back of my neck. Keep me informed and do whatever you have to do," said Evan as he got his gear ready. He folded the stock on his VZ and slung it over his back to where it would not be readily visible from the front. He also arranged his radio and earpiece in such a way to hide its presence the best he could. "Well, here goes," he said.

Evan stood up, walked around the corner, and proceeded up the driveway in plain view. He got to the front gate and stopped just short of entering. He put his hands together and yelled, "Hello there! Is Isaac Murphy home?"

The front door to the house opened to the inside with the screen door still closed, masking the view to the inside of the house. A gruff voice yelled, "He's not here right now. Go away!"

"We are friends of his; we need to talk to him. We have some stuff to give him," Evan yelled back.

"Whatever you have to give him, leave it at the gate and we will come down to get it and give it to him later," the man from within the house yelled.

"Ev... someone is coming out the back door," said Jason over the radio. "It's a threat! He's got an AK!"

"On my command, Jason," Evan said.

"Roger," he replied.

"Tell your guy around back to drop his gun or he gets smoked!" Evan yelled. "The place is surrounded. We are here for Isaac; we are not leaving without him. You can cooperate, or..."

"Or what?" the man interrupted with an increasing tension in his voice.

"Or we will treat you like you are a threat to Isaac," Evan replied. "We don't tolerate people who are a threat to our friends."

"Get your sorry ass off of this property. It's mine now and that's just the way it's gonna be!" the man inside the house yelled in an agitated and threatening tone.

"You're leaving us no choice now," Evan replied. "We would rather not have to look for Isaac by force, but if you insist, that's how it will be."

Just then, a gunshot rang out of the house through the screen door, directed at Evan. He dove to the ground to take cover and yelled, "Waste 'em," to Jason over the radio.

As soon as the word rolled off Evan's tongue, Jason squeezed the trigger and let an open tip .300 Win Mag fly. It instantly smashed into the man carrying the AK. It hit the man directly in his chest, blowing out of his back. The man fell limp to the ground like a rag doll. Evan dropped to the ground while swinging his VZ into firing position. He lay just behind a fencepost, getting partial cover while he extended his stock.

"Any other movement?" Evan queried Jason.

Before Jason could answer, a barrage of gunfire came out of the front of the house from the door and from two of the windows. Two of the shooters seemed to be focused on Evan's location while the other made wild, random shots in Jason's direction. Bullets danced all around Evan. His cover was not adequate to repel this level of fire for long. Luckily, for him, it was not very focused or disciplined. He could not help but think about how this had not played out very well on his end. Jason attempted to lay down suppressing fire, shooting blindly towards the windows of the house. He could not get a view of any of the shooters, so he assumed they were farther back into the room, firing from a distance. This was smart he thought, as he would otherwise be able to pick them off easily.

The next thing Evan heard was the sound of the old Massey Ferguson's diesel engine as it came chugging up the hill. He looked to see Ollie backing up the driveway with the Bush Hog deck flipped up like a shield. *He must have taken the top link loose, stood the sucker up, and secured it standing on end somehow,* he thought. The steel deck and the plywood that he put over top of it seemed to provide enough ballistic protection from the small arms fire as the occupants of the house directed their fire at Ollie and the tractor.

Ollie backed the Bush Hog deck all the way up to the fence, and Evan scooted over behind it to take cover. "Brilliant!" Evan exclaimed.

"Do you start this much trouble everywhere you go?" asked Ollie.

"Lately, it seems," replied Evan.

"Ev... another threat just came out the back door. He went around the other side of the house, though. I can't see him. Be careful; he may be coming to flank you and Ollie," Jason said over the radio.

"Let's get a move on," Evan said to Ollie.

Ollie slipped the tractor into gear and began to creep forward as they looked over to see a man preparing to fire directly at Ollie. Evan swung his VZ around to fire on the assailant, but before Evan could get the gun into position, he heard a shot ring out and saw a flash of light. Everything went quiet, and his heart seemed to pause as he feared the worst. *Did the man just fire upon Ollie?* Evan thought in the slow motion of his mind. As Evan finally got his aim on the man and began to pull the trigger, the assailant fell forward and collapsed dead on the ground. He then saw Daryl off in the woods with a cloud of smoke still in the air from his black powder loaded .45-70. The gunshot he heard was Daryl's; Ollie was fine, and the tractor began to lunge forward. Evan hopped up on the running board of the tractor, alongside Ollie, and got back on the radio to Jason.

"Report!" he said.

"Accounting for the guy on the flank, I have only seen one location for muzzle flash from the house."

"Good, keep 'em occupied for a moment while I get Ollie out of here. I'll get back to you in a sec."

"Roger that," replied Jason as he began to maintain a steady fire on the front of the house, varying his point of aim from window to window and then back to the door.

Reaching the bottom of the hill and rounding the corner for cover, Evan said, "Great work, Ollie! Now stay here. I'll be right back." Evan then ran up the hill and through the woods towards where they had seen Daryl.

Daryl saw him coming and broke cover to get his attention. He then ducked back down behind some brush and Evan joined him. "Damn good shooting!" said Evan.

"Thank God I made it down the hill in time," Daryl replied. "I saw that guy come around back and around the side where Jason couldn't get a shot at him. I knew if he got to you, there would be trouble."

"Did you see anyone else from back there?" Evan asked.

"I was just counting gunshots, and based on that, we are down to one shooter that I know of," he replied.

"Good. Lead me back up the way you came down and let's get in position behind the house. You can cover me as I make my way to the back door. I'll have Jason unleash hell on the front to keep the shooter's attention while I try and make entry from the back."

"Will do," Daryl replied.

The two men worked their way back up the hill. They climbed through the woods to get uphill and above the back of the house. "I can cover you from here," Daryl said. "Are you sure you don't want me to come with you?"

"No sense in both of us taking the chance of getting killed. Besides, if he gets past me, you can stop him as he runs out the back door," Evan said as he patted Daryl on the back and then headed down into the backyard. The back door had been left open as the other man hastily vacated the house. He sliced the pie around the door with the muzzle of his VZ58 in line with his field of view. The kitchen looked clear so he slipped into the house. There was so much trash strewn around, it was hard to move without making noise. Once he made his way across the kitchen to get a view into the living room, he saw a grungy-looking fellow in his early thirties with a Ruger Mini 14. Evan raised his VZ and said, "Drop it! Now!"

"Don't shoot, man! Don't shoot! We were just defending ourselves! Don't shoot!" the man said as he cowered in the corner with his hands in the air.

"Where are the others?" demanded Evan.

"They all bailed. I'm the last one here. I swear."

"Where is Isaac?" Evan demanded again.

"He's out hunting. He's letting us stay here for a while," the man replied.

"Where is his wife? Did she go hunting with him like she normally does?" asked Evan.

"Yeah, man, they both went. They've been gone a couple days."

"Wrong answer!" Evan said as he cracked the steel side-folding stock against the man's head, knocking him unconscious. He then took some zip ties from his vest pocket and secured the man's hands behind his back.

"J... shooter is secured. Move in and help me secure the place," Evan said over the radio.

"Roger that! On my way," Jason responded.

Within a few minutes, Jason and Daryl both entered the house via the kitchen to find Evan standing over the unconscious man, with his VZ pointed at his head.

"Daryl, grab your horse and ride down and get Ollie. I don't want to leave him down there just in case there is another unaccounted for dirtbag around there somewhere. Jason, you clear the house while I keep watch over this guy."

Daryl ran out the back door to do as Evan had requested, and Jason immediately began clearing the house with his sidearm. He went through the laundry room and two of the three bedrooms, confirming clear as he went. He came upon the master bedroom and pushed the door open. There was blood on the wall by the bed and what appeared to be a shotgun blast, with the associated blood spatter, but there was no body. The blood was dry and looked as if it had been there for a while.

He crept over to the master bathroom and nudged the door open, taking a step back to see inside. To his horror, there was a young teenage girl bound and gagged. She was naked and shivering. There were bruises all over her face and body and she was chained to the back of the filthy toilet. She was terrified to see Jason but could not scream, as she had been gagged by her kidnappers.

"It's okay, it's okay now. It's all over," Jason said. "Those people can't hurt you anymore."

He looked at the chains and saw that there was a padlock on it. He had no clue where the key might be, so he kicked the toilet relentlessly until it broke free from the floor. As water began to flow out of the bottom of the toilet, he pulled the chain out from underneath, holstered his pistol, and picked up the shivering, scared, young girl. He wrapped her in what was the cleanest looking towel in the room. He carried her into one of the other bedrooms to get her away from the horror scene that she had been living in for who knows how long, laid her on the bed, and covered her up. "We are gonna get you help now. No one is ever gonna hurt you again," he said. "I'll be right back."

He walked back into the living room where Evan stood over the bound man. Jason walked over to him, pulled his pistol, put it to the back of his head, and fired, blasting his brains and bits of skull all over the floor. Evan stood there in shock of what Jason had just done. Jason turned and walked back into the bedroom to get back to the young girl.

Evan followed Jason into the next room, trying to figure out what was going on. As soon as he saw the young girl, he understood the extent of Jason's anger. She looked as if she was maybe thirteen years old or so. He was appalled at the terrible condition she was in. Jason looked through the drawers, trying to find some clothes for her to wear. He found a robe and an old nightgown. He assumed it used to belong to Mrs. Murphy, but now, none of that mattered. He needed to get her covered up and treated with respect like the young girl that she was, rather than the toy those men had brutally used her for.

Evan then began to look around in the other rooms. They still needed to try to find out what happened to Isaac. In the master bedroom, where the dried blood was spattered on the wall, everything that had previously been in the drawers was strewn about. It looked as if the place had been ransacked. He kicked some of the clothes around that were on the floor and found a wallet. The wallet contained Isaac Murphy's driver's license and some old photos of his dearly departed and beloved wife.

Evan looked at the blood spatter on the wall again and had chills go up his spine, realizing what had probably happened. In the middle of the night, while Isaac was asleep in bed, they broke into the home and worked their way to the bedroom. He could picture Isaac awakening to find the intruders present, and when reaching for his gun next to the bed, a blast from a shotgun tearing him to shreds. That would certainly explain the dried blood-spatter and its location in proximity to the bed.

Evan then heard Daryl and Ollie enter the home. He walked back into the living room to meet them and found them standing there, looking at the man Jason had just executed on the floor.

"What the hell happened while I was gone?" Daryl asked.

"Jason took care of something that needed to be taken care of," Evan responded. "It needed to be done."

"What, why?" asked Daryl.

"These scumbags were keeping a young girl chained to the toilet in the master bathroom. She was naked and clearly had been abused. Only she and God know what those evil monsters did to her. It also looks as if they took over the home by force and murdered Isaac," Evan said as he reached out to Ollie to hand him his old friend's wallet.

As Ollie began to thumb through the wallet, Evan continued, "It looks like they killed him as he was getting out of bed. They've pretty much torn this house apart. My guess is they were just going to squat here, having their way with that little girl while using up all of Isaac's resources. When the food and supplies were exhausted, I imagine they would have moved on and done the same thing to someone else. Who knows which one of us would have been next on their list? There is nothing else we could have done. We don't have the resources to keep violent criminals like this locked up forever, and there doesn't get much more of a threat to our loved ones than this. Jason did what needed to be done, without question."

"Some might argue that he deserved a trial, but I'd have shot him my damn self if Jason hadn't already done it," Ollie said as rage-filled tears welled up in his eyes.

Chapter 8: Wilson's Run

Nate had tried his best to get a nap in before the night's run. He and the other guys found a dark hallway in the back of the building. They each took a spot on the floor, propped their heads up on their packs, and racked out for a while. Judging from the snores, several of the guys clearly didn't have a problem sleeping. For Nate, however, this wasn't just a normal supply run. This was his moment of truth. It was the culmination of the efforts of the past year all coming to fruition. At a quarter before departure time, Sergeant Wilson came into the hall, banged on an old, out-of-service water fountain and said, "Rise and shine, ladies! Your chariots await. Don't be late for the ball."

With a few grunts and moans, the men gathered themselves, suited up, and headed on out to the front of the warehouse. Sergeant Wilson was leaning on the supply-laden Humvee with a dip of Copenhagen snuff in his lip, occasionally spitting into an old canteen. "Last chance to back out, Hoskins," he said.

"Hell no! I'm already there. I'm just waiting for you," Nate replied.

"Good then, here is the deal: Hoskins and I are gonna mount up in the lead Humvee and pull out into the street. Ponch and John here are gonna come out of the depot and form up behind us, then Shock and Chop will bring up the rear. We all know that's where they like it anyway," Sergeant Wilson said with a straight face, as everyone else except the named individuals chuckled.

"You mean Parker and Clarke in the middle, right?" Parker said.

"Nope, tonight you're Ponch and John. I always loved that show. All right, let's get moving. We'll see you guys out front," he said to Parker and Clarke as he and the others headed out of the building to the entrance of the depot. The men boarded their respective Humvees, fired them up, and Sergeant Wilson pulled out into the street. The front gate to the depot was opened by two of the sentries at the entrance. The supply Humvee entered the street and positioned itself behind Wilson and Hoskins, as planned. Shock and Chop formed up behind them in the rear. They gave the signal, and the convoy began its journey.

"There is no question that they have spotters who report movement in and out of the depot, so be on your toes for anything out of the ordinary. Not that there is an *ordinary* these days," Sergeant Wilson said to Nate.

"Roger that," replied Nate.

"We'll leave the lights on until we get clear of College Station. We don't want to run over a civilian in our own town because they couldn't see us in the dark. With no streetlights, it gets pitch black out here."

Nate sat with his shotgun lying across his lap, with the barrel pointed towards the passenger window. He mentally went over what it would be like to engage a target on his side of the vehicle. He would almost have to shoot left handed he thought.

As they left the city and entered Highway 21, Sergeant Wilson said over the radio, "Lights out, girls." He picked up his NVGs and put them in position, ready to flip them down. "Report," he ordered.

"Ponch and John ready," he heard over the radio.

"Shock and Chop ready," was said over the radio as well.

"Hit it," he said as he flipped down his NVGs and killed his headlights with the two Humvees in trail doing the same.

Nate said, "Damn it's dark without headlights or street lights."

"Oh sorry, I forgot to tell you. We're on a shoestring budget, so there's only one set of NVGs per truck. Without the headlights on, your eyes should adjust so that you can see a little," replied Sergeant Wilson.

They drove slowly and cautiously down the old rural roads. Nate still didn't know where they were going. All he knew was that his brother was supposed to be at or near their destination. He hoped Sergeant Wilson wouldn't hold out too long. It was a very uncomfortable feeling for Nate to be completely dependent on others after having lived life on his own terms for the past year.

After about an hour of driving, they approached a small town. Nate wasn't exactly sure where they were, and he didn't see any clear signs or markings at first, especially in their lights-out configuration. Sergeant Wilson said over the radio, "Okay, boys, lights on for now." He and the other two Humvees clicked their headlights on and illuminated the street.

Nate saw that they were in a run-down little town. There were windows broken out, and several doors looked as if they had been kicked off the hinges. Many of the homes appeared to be abandoned. "This town looks like they've had it rough," said Nate as he scanned the side roads for threats.

"Yes... yes it has," replied Sergeant Wilson. "The drug thugs tried to roll over it, but we fought them off. There are a few good folks left here that refuse to be run out of their own town. I can't say I would blame them if they left, though. Personally, I would rather die standing and fighting on my own two feet than running like a coward. But then again, I don't have a family to think of. Where else would they go, anyway? Unless you're a thief or a swindler, you pretty much have what you had, or less, from when it all started. The economy hasn't really been bristling with opportunity, ya know."

Sergeant Wilson took a left turn at a four-way intersection in the middle of town. The other two Humvees followed behind at a tactical bound. "Even though these supply runs are kept discrete, we stop off along the way at a few friendly points to act as a security patrol rather than just a supply convoy. Doing this accomplishes two things for us. First, it shows both our allies and our enemies that we are still around. We don't want either of the two to think we've moved on or lost interest in the area. Second, it helps to mask our true intentions of our movements. If we can get the cartel's informants to buy our ruse that we are a security patrol, they will transmit flawed reports. That's why I wanted you in TSG gear, so you look like another one of us. This may keep the cartels in the dark about the fact that we have a force in place that needs resupply. If they can draw conclusions as to where they are, they would stand a better chance of cutting them off from us and then taking them out."

"There is our man now," Sergeant Wilson said, pointing up ahead at three men on horseback. He pulled up alongside them and said, "¡Hola, gentlemen!"

"Buenas noches," one of the men said in return.

"Where is Carlos? I expected him to be here," Sergeant Wilson said as he shut the engine off to be able to hear the men better.

"They got him," said one of the men. "They got his whole family. They were on their way to church last Sunday and they mowed down Carlos, his wife, and their two little boys."

"Oh my God!" Sergeant Wilson exclaimed. "Who did it? Were there any town insiders that may have been involved?"

"It was the cartel, as far as we know. One of the gunmen had been seen around town before. He had been seen talking to Jose Gutiérrez a time or two. Gutiérrez has sort of always looked down on us Citizens' Guard types. He calls us militia and says the town needs a mayor and a police chief instead of the Texas Citizens' Guard. He and Carlos didn't see eye-to-eye on much. Most of us think he wants to take over the town then bow down to the cartels and get rich by selling out his own people, as has been the case in so many other towns."

Sergeant Wilson just sat there for a minute, visibly upset and holding back the rage. "Do you boys want to pay that chicken shit a visit tonight?" he asked the men.

"Hell yeah!" the men replied. "We were hoping you would say that."

"Sit tight, I'll be right back," Sergeant Wilson said as he opened the door and got out of the Humvee. He went back to the supply Humvee and motioned for Shock and Chop to join them. Nate tried to see what was going on; he could not get a good view from where he sat. Sergeant Wilson then returned to the Humvee, looked at Nate, and said, "These ain't your monkeys and this ain't your circus. Just sit tight when we get there. This won't take long." He then looked at the TCG locals on horseback and said, "Lead the way, my brothers."

The men on horseback led the convoy a few blocks over to a street that had a sign on it that said "Gutiérrez Way." *Well, that's new*, Sergeant Wilson thought to himself. They proceeded down the street until the men on horseback stopped and got off their horses. They all wore blue jeans, cowboy boots, and hats but had on TCG multi-cam tops and carried AR15s, each customized to the owner's liking. Their guns showed a lot of wear, with multiple layers of camo paint that looked as if it had been worn off and reapplied several times over. *These guys have clearly been in the mix for a while*, Nate thought to himself.

"Stay put," Sergeant Wilson said again to Nate as he exited the Humvee and joined up with the others.

Nate again tried to see what was going on from his vantage point. The five TSG members and the three TCG men seemed to be making a game plan of some sort. Shock left the group for a moment, and then returned with some rope that he had retrieved from one of the Humvees. The men then split up and disappeared into the darkness of the neighborhood.

After a few moments of silence, Nate heard a gunshot, followed by several others. Another minute of silence went by and then another shot was heard. This time he noticed a muzzle flashlight up a dark room inside of a large two-story house at the end of the street, located in a cul-de-sac. His eyes focused on this house now, as he desperately wanted to know what was going on. *What have I gotten myself into, teaming up with these guys*, he thought.

Just then, Nate saw a woman and a small child run out of the house in their nightclothes followed by Sergeant Wilson, who was dragging a man by a rope that was tied to his neck. The man was desperately struggling with the rope around his neck as he was being dragged across the yard. One of the other Humvees behind Nate started up and drove past him and into the front yard of the house. At this point, Nate could not believe what he was seeing. While Sergeant Wilson was holding the man down with his boot on his neck and his M45 pistol pointed at his head, Chop threw the rope over a branch of a large tree that was in the front yard. They tied the loose end of the rope to the front of the Humvee as it began to back up, pulling the man up into the air by his neck.

"Oh my God!" Nate said aloud to himself while he sat and watched from the Humvee. Do I get in the middle of this? Should I get in the middle of this? If I do, what will become of me? I am an outsider here and these guys are my only link to my brother. Unanswered questions swirled around inside of Nate's head. He was totally confused about the situation. He assumed this must be Jose Gutiérrez, the man believed to be behind the killing of Carlos and his family. Maybe it needed to be this way. Then again, maybe they are wrong. Maybe he had nothing to do with it and they are stringing up an innocent man. Nate's hand clinched the door handle of the Humvee, ready to exit the vehicle at any second, but he was paralyzed by his confusion.

The Humvee pulling the rope stopped just as the man was on the tip of his toes. He was being strangled by the rope but was still gasping for air and still alive. *Maybe they are just trying to scare him to get him to talk*, Nate thought to himself. That thought quickly passed, however, as the Humvee was again directed rearwards by Sergeant Wilson, and the man was pulled up into the air and hanged completely. He flailed around, desperately trying to get his fingers in between the rope and his neck to breathe, but his movements soon began to slow. After a few last twitches, the man went limp, hanging silently from the tree. Shock got out of the Humvee, and he and Chop untied the rope while they held it to keep the man in place. They then tied the end of the rope to the fence along the sidewalk to keep the man's lifeless body suspended in the air.

Nate was horrified. He had seen a lot of violence and suffering over the past year, but it was usually a cut-and-dry case of the innocent and guilty. He had not witnessed such a brutal act, one that caused him to doubt who the good were versus the bad. His hand went limp and fell to his side, off of the door handle. Shock and Chop got back into their Humvee and drove out of the yard, back onto the street. Parker and Clarke, who had been standing guard over the events taking place, returned to their Humvee as well. Sergeant Wilson walked back over to the TCG horsemen who had just come back out of the shadows. They apparently had been lying back in the darkness while the acts of violence were carried out. Sergeant Wilson shook their hands, and they mounted up and rode away. He walked back over to the Humvee where Nate waited, as ordered, and climbed back inside. He started the engine and they drove away, forming back up with the other two TSG Humvees.

The first mile or two out of town was eerily quiet. Nate stared off into the distance while Sergeant Wilson drove. The only thing to break the silence was Sergeant Wilson fumbling around for a can of Copenhagen as he packed a dip into his lower lip. "That had to be done," he said.

Nate just sat there silently, not knowing how to respond. Sergeant Wilson then said, "Look... I know that was a tough thing to watch, especially being new to things around here. You have to trust me, though. It had to be done. There isn't any real law around here. Carlos was as close to a lawman—who acted only in the best interest of the people—as they had, and he was taken out for it. The cartels are hot and heavy on towns like these. All they have to do is apply the same force and intimidation as they did in their own towns in Mexico, and soon the resolve of the people to fight back, without support from a stable authority, simply collapses.

"They put men like Gutiérrez in power as a puppet mayor who simply does their bidding. The town's people are held captive in their own homes, knowing that the streets are ruled by the cartels. Right now, this town is on the edge of caving to the cartels. Acts of violence against people like Carlos and his family, if gone unanswered, will simply intimidate the next man who may have stood up. We need to show the people in this town who are working as the eyes, ears, and networks of the cartels, that any act that is complicit in turning on your own people will result in the same extreme response that they aim to inflict. We've known about Gutiérrez for a while now. The people here tried to work against him in a civil and rational manner, but the slaughtering of Carlos and his family was the last straw. That sort of thing simply will not stand."

"What if you were wrong?" asked Nate. "What if Gutiérrez wasn't involved? Without a trial of some sort, will you ever really know?"

"Trial?" responded Sergeant Wilson. "A trial by whom? Any person who would step up to sit on a jury would have their own families murdered and their houses burned. Our federal government abandoned the people in the border towns long before it all fell apart. Now, except for us, they are completely alone. These are not people you can deal with on a rational level. You can't good-guy your way through a situation when your opponent is pure evil. Just look at the crap our guys in Iraq and Afghanistan had to deal with. Rules of engagement that were designed to make the media and political pollsters happy, rather than allowing our guys to be in a fair fight. We were cut to pieces in the name of decency. Letting my men die, so that the jihadist has a fair chance, isn't my idea of decency. It's sick and twisted. If the bastards writing the rules were standing in front of those bullets and driving by those IEDs, they wouldn't be so pussy-foot with the enemy. These cartel scumbags are no different. They will do the unspeakable to women and children to scare and intimidate, and you want me to wonder if Gutiérrez was really guilty and let other good people die while we try to sort it out the political way? I don't think so. Enough good people have died playing that game. Trust me, if you had been in the middle of this for as long as I have, you would would see things the same way."

"My bad. I shouldn't have said that," replied Nate. "I've pretty much been on my own for the past year. I've seen some bad things, but I haven't been deep enough into the weeds to get into a situation like this. I guess it's just a lot to take in all at once."

"It's all good," replied Sergeant Wilson as he spit his dip into an empty water bottle. "Just don't second guess anything if it all starts to fall apart while we are out here. If we are taking action, it's because it needs to be taken... Period."

"Roger that," Nate replied.

Chapter 9: Haley's Journey

After the events at Isaac Murphy's place, the people of the Homefront and the rest of their confederacy felt uneasy about how close to home such a horrible thing could happen. After the dust had settled, Evan and Jason made their rounds to the rest of their partner homesteads to let them know what happened. They wanted to make sure that the relative safety of the hills of East Tennessee did not lull anyone else into complacency in regards to their security. What happened to Isaac could have happened to any of them.

Ollie and Mildred volunteered to take in the young girl who was rescued from the Murphy home. They had plenty of room, and Mildred had all the time she needed to look after the girl and care for her during her physical and emotional recovery from the horrors she had endured. The girl's name was Haley Middleton. She was only thirteen years old and had been held captive for the past two months. Haley had not yet begun to talk much about what happened. She was very quiet and often seemed to be lost in her own thoughts. Mildred was a very patient woman though, and she was just what Haley needed to begin to trust again.

The only details that Mildred was able to get Haley to share with them was that she lived in a mobile home park in Cedartown, Georgia, which is located just northwest of Atlanta. Her parents did not have much before everything fell apart, so when it did, times were exceedingly hard on them. Her parents decided to try to make the trek to Chattanooga, Tennessee, where they had relatives who lived on a small rural farm just outside of town. They felt that it was their best chance of survival in a world now filled with starvation and need. This need was reaffirmed by the hordes of people vacating Atlanta in search of food and opportunity, spilling over into the outlying rural areas such as Cedartown.

After dinner, one evening, Mildred, Ollie, and Haley sat down to enjoy some fresh-baked apple pie. Luckily for the Thomas family, being homesteaders before the term was even a household word meant that they still had the means and the stores to eat and live well after the collapse. Life with Mildred and Ollie was the closest thing to the old normal Haley had seen in the past year.

As they sat there enjoying their pie, Haley spoke up and said, “Daddy got bit by a snake.”

Ollie and Mildred just looked at each other and Mildred said, “What was that, dear?”

“We were riding our bikes to Chattanooga. That’s when Daddy got bit,” Haley replied.

“So you were riding your bikes to get to Chattanooga from Georgia?” asked Ollie.

“Yes, sir. Daddy said we didn’t have any gas for the car and couldn’t get any. He said that even if we did have gas, somebody would try to take it. He said we would just ride our bikes with our backpacks and it would be like a camping trip,” replied young Haley.

“Your daddy was a smart man,” said Ollie as he swallowed the lump in his throat. “If you’re traveling by car these days, unless you are well-protected, people will want to take your fuel. And if they know you have food, they will want to take that too.”

“Mommy, Daddy, and I were riding our bikes down a little back road. Daddy didn’t want to take the big roads. He said there were too many people on them. We had been riding and camping for about three days. Mommy couldn’t ride very far each day because she had been sick for a long time. Daddy made us a camp off in the woods and was going to try to catch us a rabbit or squirrel for dinner. I thought that was gross at first, but after I tried them both I thought they were yummy," said Haley with a smile on her face for the first time in days.

"Yes, they are both quite delicious. Mildred here can cook up a delicious pot of rabbit or squirrel stew anytime you want it," Ollie said with a smile.

"Let her finish, Oliver," Mildred said, giving him a look that he understood very well after years of marriage.

Haley then continued, "When Daddy went off for food, he never came back. It got dark and Mom was afraid to leave camp in case he came back, so we just stayed there. The next morning, Daddy still wasn't back so we packed up our things, hid them, and went off in the woods looking for him." Haley's mood began to get noticeably more somber. "Later that day, we found Daddy by a creek. He was all swollen and pale. He wouldn't wake up. He just lay there shivering and sweating. Mommy saw a snake bite on Daddy's leg. It looked awful. Mommy started to cry and said she had to go get help. She told me to stay with Daddy until she got back. I just sat there with Daddy waiting for Mommy to come back, but she didn't. It got dark and I didn't have my sleeping bag or anything. I was really scared. There were all kinds of sounds in the woods. It sounded like animals were walking all around me in the bushes. I just prayed and prayed and finally the sun came up.

"I tried to wake Daddy again, but he was cold," she said as she began to tear up. "'Daddy, wake up, Daddy wake up, please don't leave me here, Daddy,' I said over and over again, but he never woke up. I sat there with Daddy for two more days waiting for Mommy, but she never came back. I finally walked out of the woods and found our bikes right where we left them. There were still some old biscuits that Mommy made with the last of the food from our house. I ate some of them and kept the rest. I got on my bike and rode for several hours looking for Mommy, but I never found her."

Ollie and Mildred looked at each other with broken hearts, listening to the young girl's story. She continued, saying, "That's when some men took me. They drove up in an old van. I was scared and didn't know what else to do, so I asked them if they had seen my mom. They said to get in and they would drive around and help me look, but they didn't."

She stared at the floor as she continued her story. "They kept me and made me do bad things. After a few weeks, those men traded me for some drugs and other stuff to the ones you found me with. They were even worse than the others were. They would just take over house after house, never staying anywhere for long. They chained me up like a dog, wouldn't let me wear clothes, and barely fed me. I prayed every day for God to rescue me. I started to give up hope. I just wanted to die. And then you and the other nice men found me." She looked at Ollie with gratitude.

Mildred kneeled down in front of Haley's chair, wrapped her arms around her, and the two cried together. "We will never let anything bad happen to you again. You will always have a home here," Mildred said through the tears.

"Amen to that," said Ollie as he looked up towards Heaven and thanked God silently that he led them to her.

Just then, they heard their dogs barking at something outside. Ollie jumped up, grabbed his shotgun, and headed over to the window. The tension in his gut immediately went away as he noticed Evan approaching by himself via the middle of the road as usual. Ollie opened the door and gave him a wave. Evan then motioned behind him and around the corner came Molly, driving the Baird's old Ford tractor, pulling a utility trailer with Judith and Griff on board. As they pulled alongside Evan, he hopped up onto the trailer and joined them for a ride on up to the house.

Mildred and Haley joined Ollie on the front porch to welcome them in. "To what honor do we owe this visit?" asked Mildred.

"Well, Judith and I heard you had a young lady over here that may want some pretty new clothes," Molly said. "Judith and I are gonna take some measurements, with her permission of course, and we are going to see what we can whip up. Linda Cox donated some very beautiful fabrics and some patterns for the project as well," Molly said with a smile.

"Oh, how nice of you all. Come on in for some pie. It's fresh out of the oven," Mildred said as she and Haley led the two women into the house.

On their way into the house, Haley turned to Evan and Ollie and said, "Where is the other man?"

"Which other man?" asked Evan.

"The one who unchained me and got me out of the bathroom," she replied.

"Oh, that's Jason. He's back at our place keeping an eye on things," said Evan.

"Well... tell him he is my hero. I'll never forget him for that," she said with a smile.

"Will do, ma'am," Evan said as he tipped his hat to her with a nod.

As the ladies entered the house and closed the door, leaving the men alone on the porch, Evan turned to Ollie and said, "Ollie, you know you can all come over to the Homefront with us if things get any more out of hand around here. If nothing else, do it for the sake of Mildred and Haley. You've got that old travel trailer out back that you could bring over and we would get you hooked up to our well water and everything."

"Yeah, there is safety in numbers, and we've got the numbers and the guns," added Griff.

"Well thanks, fellas, but we're fine here for now," Ollie replied.

"We figured you'd say that so we brought you something," Evan said as he pulled a rifle out of the trailer. "It's a Ruger American in good ol' .30-06. The scope is zeroed in and she's ready to go. It may be a basic hunting rifle, but on this large property you may need to hold someone off farther than that shotgun or .45 is good for."

"Here's a box of three hundred rounds of ammo, too," said Griff as he handed it to Ollie.

"Well, thank you, boys. I really appreciate it," Ollie said. "And don't worry; if it comes down to it, I'll bring Mildred and Haley over. We are happy here for now, though."

"Good enough," said Evan.

"So, how about that pie?" asked Griff.

Chapter 10: A Culmination of Events

With a bump, Nate was jarred awake. "Welcome back to the world, Sleeping Beauty," said Sergeant Wilson.

"Oh crap, sorry," said Nate as he gathered his presence of mind, realizing it was now almost two o'clock in the morning. "Ah man, how long was I out?"

"A little more than an hour," said Sergeant Wilson. "Don't worry. You didn't miss much, just dry Texas desert. Climb back in the back and get out that mid-sized OD green bag. It's got a thermos with some coffee in it. Dig it out and pour us both a cup."

"That sounds like exactly what I need," Nate said as he unbuckled his seat belt and climbed back to the rear of the truck. He dug around through several bags and could not find the coffee. "Where did you say the coffee was?" he asked.

"The OD green bag. No, wait, my mistake; it's in the desert camo duffel," Sergeant Wilson replied.

"Oh, here it is," Nate said as he pulled it from the bag and turned to show Sergeant Wilson. As he turned and looked forward, he heard a loud *POP!* followed by the windshield of the Humvee shattering. Sergeant Wilson's head flung back as his brain matter and bits of skull and blood splattered all over Nate's face. The truck swerved violently to the right and plummeted into a large irrigation ditch, rolling onto its top in about two feet of standing water.

Nate was pinned against the ceiling, nearly buried by the bags of gear and other supplies that were left loose in the rear cargo area. He struggled to hold his breath as his head was under water. The damage to the top of the vehicle, combined with the load bearing down on him made it difficult to move. After several moments of struggle, he finally managed to get into a position where he could breathe. He found himself in complete darkness. He struggled to get his senses about him with his head now above water. He could hear gunfire in the distance. It sounded as if it was coming from where they had previously been driving on the road. *The rest of the guys must be fighting them off*, he thought. It seemed like an eternity waiting for it to end. Surely, Shock and the guys would come down to check on him and Sergeant Wilson when they got things under control.

His left leg was throbbing with pain. In the position he was in, he could not move it at all. It seemed pinned down by something. Being as confined as he was and in total darkness, he could not tell by what. Eventually, the gunfire began to subside. *Any minute now and they will come down to get us*, he thought.

As the gunfire came to a halt, he could hear screaming off in the distance. It was a loud, agonizing, torturous scream. *What in the hell is going on?* He soon realized the screams were coming from Shock. It was as plain as day to him now. All of a sudden, he felt sick as he realized the TSG guys had not won the fight. Shock's agonizing screams slowly subsided and then stopped. Nate's imagination raced as he could not help but wonder what sort of inhumane form of death was dealt to him.

Terror set in as he realized if they came down to check on his Humvee, if they found him alive, he would almost certainly face the same sort of gruesome death. His mind raced, trying to figure out a defensive strategy, but in his state, he had very few options. His Beretta was on his side, but his shotgun, along with Sergeant Wilson's M4 carbine, was somewhere in the front of the vehicle just out of reach. He dug down under the water to find his pistol and struggled to unholster it in his tight confines. Once he got it freed, he held it above the water to try to drain the contaminants from it in order to make sure it was battle ready. In his panic-induced haste and due to the tight quarters and the total darkness of his surroundings, Nate accidentally hit the pistol against the aluminum of the truck. As he felt and heard the thud, his heart skipped a beat in terror. *Crap! Did they hear that? Holy crap. They had to have heard that.* His pulse raced as he tuned his ears to the outside world and tried to hear movement outside of the truck.

After a few moments that felt like an eternity, he heard boots sliding down the side of the hill as some men entered the irrigation ditch. He heard muffled voices; it sounded like they were speaking Spanish. Nate flashed back to his Navy days in California and how he had always intended to buy Rosetta Stone so he could learn Spanish. Being in Southern California, Spanish almost felt like the national language. He resented himself for having procrastinated back then. Being able to talk to these men, if necessary, would surely come in handy. If nothing else, just being able to understand what they were saying would help him understand his situation.

He snapped back into reality as the boots got closer and closer to his wrecked Humvee. A few of the men shouted some words in Spanish, which he could not understand. One of the men kicked the side of the Humvee. Nate flinched with the deafening sound of the thud of the boot against the side of the truck's aluminum body. *Did I just make a sound? Did I move the water when I flinched, making a noise they could hear*, he questioned to himself. He rested his pistol across his chest. *If they find me, do I take a few of them out in the process, or do I just use this on myself to save myself the horrors of the gruesome sort of death that Shock had to suffer through?*

As he silently rotated the safety of the Beretta M9 off to ready the pistol, several shots were fired into the Humvee. The sound of the rounds penetrating the aluminum from underneath was deafening. He resisted the urge to shoot in the direction of the shots. *This puny, little nine millimeter wouldn't have anything left after it impacted the truck body compared to the rifles those men have, plus it would only give away the fact that I am here as well as my position in the wreck*, he thought. With that in mind, he held his fire for the moment. Three more rounds ripped through the Humvee, this time closer than before. Two of the rounds impacted the duffel bags that were pinning him down under the weight of the truck. He could feel the shudder from the impact of the bullets.

The men conversed back and forth for a moment as one walked around to the driver's side of the truck. The man yelled something to the others and then a few more of walked over to the driver's door area. They began to lift and tug on something. *Are they trying to move the truck all by themselves?* He could then feel what he believed to be Sergeant Wilson's body being tugged in their direction. He could feel the movements of the water and the sound of what he perceived to be flesh and clothing being dragged against the structure of the truck.

One of the men yelled something in disgust and the forceful tugging came to a rapid halt. The men spoke for a few more minutes when Nate heard a commanding voice yell something from the road up above. The men answered back and then began to climb back up the hill, out of the irrigation ditch, and towards the road.

Is it over? He lay there in the water for at least another hour, not making a move or a sound. He listened intently for signs that they were still nearby.

Satisfied that they were gone, Nate had to figure a way out of this mess he had gotten into. His leg was still trapped and, now that his mind was back on his immediate situation, began to throb again in pain. He tried moving his leg to free it, but a sharp, searing pain shot up the nerves in his leg like an electrical shock. *Well, that's not going to work*, he thought. He felt around, trying to get a mental image of the gear he had within reach and found what he believed to be Sergeant Wilson's pack. While blindly rummaging through the pack, he found a cigarette lighter. *Great*, he thought, *now I can get some light*. Just as he began to flick the lighter, he realized there might be spilled fuel in the water or fumes trapped inside with him. He would rather remain blind than contribute to his own fiery death, so he put the lighter back. *I'll just remember where that is for later*. He continued to feel around and found Sergeant Wilson's helmet-mounted Surefire HL-1 light. He flicked it on, and for the first time since the accident, he could clearly see his situation.

What he saw only added to his horror. Most of his body was submerged in the stagnant looking water. There was a lot of blood in the water as well. He knew that Sergeant Wilson died a very physically destructive death. Was this Sergeant Wilson's blood or his own? Was it coming from the pain in his leg? If he had an open wound that would yield that amount of blood, this stagnant water would not be doing him any good right now. He continued to dig around in the bag for gear and found a Gerber folding shovel. *This might actually be of some use*, he thought.

He poked around with the shovel, hoping to find a way to use it to pry his leg loose. He knew he had to get out of the Humvee, even if it required painful and desperate measures. All he needed was rain upstream to raise the waters of the irrigation ditch to a level that would easily drown him. On the other hand, he could simply die of starvation or of his injuries, which at this point were still unknown to him due to his confined position.

He managed to lodge the shovel between something that he felt he could put leverage on and possibly free his leg. Unfortunately, he could not see his leg due to the water and debris. He tried to move the gear from his lower legs but realized the only room he had to move it to was the space immediately surrounding his head, so he again ran out of options.

Oh well, he thought. *I would rather die trying than die waiting*. With that, he blindly began to apply leverage with all the strength he could muster on whatever was on his leg. He felt something begin to give. He felt some pressure being released from his leg. His leg began to tingle, followed by a searing, burning pain like nothing he had ever felt. He screamed aloud in sheer agony. He broke down into tears. *I'm going to die here. I'm going to die in this God forsaken ditch, trapped like a rat. I made it this damn far to find my brother and this is where I am going to die!* He punched the aluminum of the Humvee over and over again as his world faded to black.

Chapter 11: Building a Community

As the confederacy of homesteads in East Tennessee began their trade and barter cooperative efforts, they felt a sense of community that none of them had felt since the initial stages of the collapse. At the Homefront, since Griff's primary responsibility was the physical security of their homestead, Evan and Jason were doing most of the coordination of their local trade network. They began making regular weekly runs to pick up and deliver the goods and materials promised to other members of the group. Most people were more than glad to have Evan and Jason do the pickup and delivery for a small cut of the load or for fuel or other items needed on the Homefront. The trade and barter system quickly created a much-needed boost to the quality of life of all of those concerned. The availability of new foods made mealtime, which had gotten quite monotonous over the past year, a treat once again. Additionally, the trading of goods, services, and dry goods replaced the stores that had run out for many of the homesteaders. A freshly made set of clothes or construction materials made the delivery day feel like Christmas morning, as they were the first new items most people had seen in all that time.

As Evan and Jason made their rounds, they gathered the thoughts and recommendations of each of the homesteaders to try to improve their system. At first, information and trade negotiations traveled slowly, as the lists of haves and wants were merely relayed during pick-up and delivery. However, it was soon realized that nearly everyone had a CB radio in one form or another. Most were twelve-volt automotive units while a few had in-home CB base station models. Evan and Jason coordinated an effort to get everyone's unit connected to a power and charging supply. The automotive units were as simple as using an old car battery, which was easily charged by solar panel charging systems, portable generators, or by mounting an automotive alternator to a small gas engine, such as an old lawn mower via a belt and pulley for a makeshift twelve-volt power supply. Minimal fuel was needed in a small engine to get a battery charged enough to power a mobile CB radio.

With the radios in place, they not only found that it was dramatically easier for the homesteading households to communicate between one another to make trade and barter deals; they also found that they were getting to know one another on a personal level, helping to build relationships within their community. This was especially important for the women, who tended not to venture out from their respective homesteads as often as the men, if at all. They also felt much more secure, due to the fact that if there were any strangers passing through, they could inform each other and then keep in contact, just in case the passersby became a threat. After what happened at the Murphy place, this was a real concern.

Judith became the unofficial CB radio operator for the Homefront. She enjoyed keeping all of the families up-to-date on the goings on and became a real treat to listen to for all of those in the area. One day, Linda Cox contacted Judith for their daily chat and recommended that Judith also become a regular HAM operator, as the Homefront was already equipped with a HAM system. She said, “Judith, you’re already our voice of the community; why don’t you be our ears and our voice for the outside world as well?”

The thought of taking on that potential responsibility excited Judith and gave her a way to feel more useful to everyone. Being without any family of her own, she felt like the odd woman out, even though the families at the Homefront treated her as one of their own. She replied, “Oh Linda, that’s such a wonderful idea. Thank you so much for recommending it. I'll talk to Evan and the men about it to make sure there aren't any security concerns."

"Well, I hope you do it. Maybe even for selfish reasons. Life sure would feel a little more normal around here with a daily update," Linda replied.

"I have to sign off for now," Judith said. "I'll talk to them tonight and see what they say. I'll let you know how it goes tomorrow. They've kept me alive all of this time so I will respect their judgment, whatever it may be."

With that, the two ladies said their goodbyes and went on about their respective days. Judith couldn't wait until dinner that night to get the men all in one place to ask them what they thought.

Later that evening after dinner, everyone at the Homefront sat around outside, surrounding the fire pit and relaxing on the outdoor furniture, enjoying the beautiful Tennessee mountain sunset. Although it wasn't cool enough to need a fire, the fire pit became their outdoor gathering place. Griff built a small fire and set it up to be a smoldering mosquito smoke. It kept the bugs away quite well, which could get pretty annoying that time of year in East Tennessee.

"I swear I think the bugs have gotten worse this year," Judy said.

"I was thinking the same thing," replied Griff.

"I'll betcha it's due to the fact that there hasn't been any commercial spraying going on," added Jason. "People have much larger pests to worry about these days."

Molly chimed in and said, "That's just what we need—more bugs. All we need is a West Nile outbreak, or something, with our country in shambles right now. With the medical system being in a state of ruin, people wouldn't even know what they had. The word wouldn't even get out, with electricity still being down."

"Speaking of word getting out," Judith said, seeing the opportunity to bring it up, "Linda Cox and I were chatting on the CB today and she came up with a great idea. She said since I'm already the unofficial radio person for the homesteads, I should start using the HAM radio you have set up here to keep up with the rest of the country. I could then relay how things are going out there, or as Molly said, even important things like health concerns could be shared with the group."

"That sounds like a great idea," said Molly and Judy together.

The men looked at each other, and Jason said, "That's probably not a bad idea."

"I was just thinking the other day how it seemed we had all but forgot about that old thing," replied Evan. "We've been focused on our own little world here all this time. What do you think, Griff?"

"I like it. I would caution the use of any transmitting, though. A HAM signal can be homed in on and tracked from quite a distance. After last year's attack, we know there are people out there that want to take our stuff, and if you have a HAM, you probably have stuff."

"Good point," said Evan. "Judith, go for it, but let's not do any talking for a while. Let's listen in on the HAM and then relay on the CB to keep everyone in the loop. We can reevaluate the situation after we've listened for a while, and then decide if we want to relay or chat over long distance."

"That sounds good to me," said Jason.

"Me too," added Griff,

"Great, I can't wait to get started," said Judith with excitement in her voice.

"Where is Peggy? She should be out here enjoying the evening, and Zack could be playing with the boys," Sarah said, pointing to Kevin and Michael as they played on the backyard play set the men built that summer out of random materials.

"Lemme check," replied Griff as he picked up the rechargeable handheld radio. "Greg is on watch; he may know." He then called for Greg on the radio. "Rover, you up?"

"Affirm," Greg replied.

"Where's P and Z? Have you seen them?"

"Affirm, passing one now. I'll stop by," Greg replied. Greg was on roving watch and passed the front gate near the house. One referred to the numbered position on the Homefront's security grid that corresponded with the front gate. As Greg came around the front of the house, he walked over to his Dad, Griff and said, "She's in the cellar. Zack was hiding in there crying again. The last I saw, she was in there snuggled up on the floor with him. I didn't say anything to her. I just left them alone."

"Where is Jake?" Griff asked.

"He told me he was going out to one of the treestands to chill and maybe draw some. He took a radio in case we need him," Greg responded.

"Poor little Zack. He hasn't been dealing with what happened very well," said Sarah.

"Oh, I know," replied Molly. "I wish there was something we could do to help."

"I'll talk to Peggy later and see how things are going," added Judith. "I'm gonna go clean up the kitchen while there is still daylight coming through the windows," she said.

"I'll help and then we can play with the HAM afterward," said Molly with a smile.

Sarah got up to go round up her boys from the play set while Judy followed Judith and Molly to the kitchen.

After the ladies were gone, Evan, Jason, and Griff just sat around the fire pit sipping their homemade dandelion tea when Griff spoke up and said, "So when are we building a home brewing setup? I could sure use a beer."

They each looked at each other with a straight face and then simultaneously busted out laughing. Jason said, “How did we go all this time without anyone thinking of that?”

Chapter 12: Awakening

A bright light shined in his eyes while his head pounded relentlessly. Everything was blurry. The bed he lay on bounced on occasion while forces tugged him from side to side. *Where the hell am I?* Nate thought to himself. His vision was blurry, his hearing seemed muffled, and he felt chills running through his body. He tried to speak, but his words failed him. He heard muffled voices and saw shadows moving through the light, but who were they? He closed his eyes to ease the dizziness that he was beginning to feel. As he rested his eyes, he drifted off into a wonderful dream about his family, as he once again faded into darkness.

Coming out of his haze, Nate began to awaken. This time everything felt different. His bed was silent and still. The room was completely quiet. He could even hear the ticking of an old analog clock. As he opened his eyes, the bright lights momentarily blinded him, but unlike before, his hazy vision began to clear. There stood his brother, Luke. *I must still be in my dream. Where are Mom and Dad? They were here before*, he thought to himself. Then he noticed an armed TSG soldier guarding the door; his brother also stood there in a TSG uniform.

He then felt a sensation on his arm as his brother touched him and said, "Nate. Are you in there, big brother?"

"Oh my God, it's real!" Nate exclaimed. The medical heart monitor he was hooked to surged with his excitement. "Oh my brother, is that really you?" Nate asked as he began to weep uncontrollably.

"Shhhhh, it's okay. Just relax," his brother said in a soft and reassuring voice. "You're safe now, but you're pretty banged up. Just rest for a while. I'll be right here when you wake up." Luke injected something into the IV taped to Nate's arm. "This will help you rest. Sleep tight, brother." Nate, once again, faded into black.

Nate opened his eyes to see an elderly Hispanic woman wiping a wet washcloth across his forehead. He flinched at first, still not having any idea what was going on. "It's okay, don't be afraid. Your brother is here somewhere. I'll go and find him for you," she said as she put the washcloth back into a pail of water and got up to leave the room. She stepped out into the hall for a moment and then returned with Luke.

"Lucas, oh my God, Lucas. You have no idea how happy I am to see you," Nate said as Luke sat down in the chair next to his bed.

"What in the world are you doing here? How did you get here?" Luke asked.

"Where is *here*? Sergeant Wilson said for security reasons I couldn't know exactly where your unit was."

"We are in the town of Victoria, Texas. We are in a makeshift medical facility set up by the townspeople for us. We guard it and they staff it with volunteers, with a few of us to augment them when needed. My unit has been operating to the southwest of here inside of cartel turf. We've been doing hit and run harassment operations. We want to keep the general population aware that there is a resistance so they don't give in to the cartels very easily. It also keeps the cartels focused on us, instead of moving into new towns. So that's why I'm here. What about you?" asked Luke.

"After it all started falling apart, most good guys I knew started to bail from the service. We didn't like the turn those in charge were taking. We didn't sign up to be an occupying force in our own country and turn our weapons on our own people. I reported for my shift one day, checked out a shotgun and nine millimeter, and flipped the place the bird as I drove out of the front gate, never looking back. I've been trekking my way across the country ever since to find you. After I arrived in

College Station, I hooked up with a TSG Colonel who set me up with Sergeant Wilson and his crew for a supply run out to your area," Nate said as he began to remember the events that landed him in a hospital bed.

"Yeah, that's where a good portion of our guys came from. Active duty, that is. Like the guys you were found with. I'm sorry, though. They didn't make it," Luke said.

"What the hell happened, anyway?" asked Nate. "It all happened so fast, I can barely remember any details."

"We had reports from spotters in La Grange about what you guys stopped and did to one of the cartel insiders," replied Luke.

"What they did," insisted Nate. "I had no part of that. I sat in the truck as instructed and just watched the entire horrific scene."

"Well, either way, it's not like Gutierrez didn't deserve it," Luke said. "Turncoats like him are responsible for thousands of horrific deaths at the hands of the cartels. We have to cut them from the herd like you guys... I mean, they did. The problem is, we aren't the only ones who have spotters there. That info was evidently relayed to the cartels. They have eyes and ears everywhere and were probably able to put together a probable route from a series of reports and set up an ambush for you. You're the lucky one, being pinned underneath that truck in the ditch. Looks like all but one of your group went down in the firefight; one unlucky SOB was cut up pretty bad. The cartels are full of sadistic scum that relish in every moment of human suffering."

"That was Shockley, I believe. I heard a lot of what went on. I've never heard screams like that. What did they do to him?" asked Nate.

"They basically gutted him like a deer and then packed his mouth and throat full of his own bowels. It appears he suffocated from that before the gaping stomach wounds got him. The other guys, except the guy in the truck with you who they apparently couldn't get out, were all beheaded and their heads were lined up in the road and shot up like tin cans. It was a revolting scene. It took us a while to clean it up. If they knew you had survived and were under there, they would have hacked you up as well. It's their way of trying to scare our guys off."

"No wonder Sergeant Wilson and the others seemed so crude. You'd about have to be a hardened SOB to make it out here," said Nate as a tear rolled down his cheek.

"Our guys barely found you in time. They hooked a winch to your Humvee and began to drag it up out of the ditch when they saw your boot and realized someone else must be in there. They stopped the winch to double check and found you," explained Luke.

"How did they see my boot if I was inside the truck?" asked Nate in a confused manner.

"Your lower leg was sticking out of the rear side window and was pinned between the bank of the ditch and the truck. We weren't able to save it, by the way. Your bones were riddled with fractures and the weight of the truck had cut the circulation off for too long. There was nothing they could do," Luke said to his brother with a sorrowful tone.

Nate raised the bed sheet and saw a bandaged stump, about six inches below his left knee. He lay back on his pillow to soak it all in for a minute. He started to well up with tears, but then shrugged it off. "At least I didn't end up like Shock. That had to be an unimaginable hell he suffered through. Losing my foot saved my life. If I wasn't pinned down, I'd have gotten up to fight. Then I would have been killed or worse, as well. You can't wish to undo a situation. What you think would have been a better turn of events, could have gone a whole different way than what you have in your head," Nate said.

“That’s a fine way to look at things,” said Luke. “So back to my first question, what the hell are you doing out here?”

“Looking for you, little brother. I’ve spent the better part of the last year doing and seeing the worst in humanity to get to you. I figured once I found you, we could team up and go get Mom and Dad,” Nate said.

“Mom and Dad? Have you heard from them?” asked Luke.

“No, but I hadn’t heard from you either, but here you are,” replied Nate.

Luke just sat there for a moment, then turned to Nate and said, “I can’t go with you. These guys are like a family to me now. I can’t just walk away from everything we’ve done here to chase an impossible dream. We don’t know where they are. They may have taken to the sea for all we know. Virginia is a long way from here.”

“Mom and Dad aren’t LIKE family; they ARE family. THE family,” Nate said in a stressed manner. “I had no idea if I would find you, where you were, or if you were even alive, yet here we are, in the same damn room! What’s wrong with you, little brother? If God brought me to you, it was for a reason. It was so that we could go and help Mom and Dad.”

“Well, if there is a God, why are we going through this? If this is the rapture, he sure forgot a lot of us,” Luke said, looking visibly distraught.

“These guys may have done a lot for you over the past year, but don’t forget what Mom and Dad did for you for your entire life. You wouldn’t even be here if they hadn’t cashed out some of their retirement savings to put you through medical school. Besides, it’s not as if these guys gave you a free ride. You’ve done a lot for them as well. You’ve earned your keep and then some saving lives. As soon as I can hobble on crutches, I’m heading east. I may or may not find them, and I may die trying, but at least I’ll die with self-respect, knowing I put my family above all else," Nate said as he slammed his head back in the pillow.

Luke sat there staring at the floor. After a few moments of silence, he said, "Okay, Brother, you need your rest. You've got a lot to soak in and there are a few other patients I need to help. Get some sleep and I'll be back in the morning."

As Luke got up and walked out of the room, Nate lay there clouded by both physical and emotional pain. He knew most everyone had changed over the course of the past year. They pretty much had to in order to be tough enough to make it. He just had no idea that his brother, his dear younger brother, could have changed so much that he now doubted his faith and was not equally motivated to help him find their parents. He ran through the events of the past year over and over again in his head. He could not help but wonder if his brother would do the same. He said a little prayer asking God to guide his brother, Luke, back to him and to move him to join his quest for their parents.

After he said his prayer to himself, he resolved that, no matter what his brother's decision turned out to be, he would continue his quest, with or without him.

Chapter 13: Trespassers

It had been a week since Molly and Judith accompanied Evan and Griff to the Thomas farm to meet and welcome young Haley into the group. The two women had been working hard, making her some clothes from the measurements they took. They felt it was important for her to be able to feel ladylike after her ordeal. They made her a few sets of pajamas, several blouses and skirts, two casual dresses, and three pairs of pants. In addition, they made her some underwear out of t-shirt material and elastic band material. Having come into their community wearing nothing but chains, she needed a little of everything.

The group was discussing their next trip to the Thomas farm to deliver her clothes. Judith said to Jason, "Jason, you definitely need to go this time. Haley was asking about you. I think you need to go and say hello."

"Yeah, it's my turn to go on a run anyway," replied Jason. "Peggy, you should go too. Sarah can watch Zack with the boys. You need to get out and stretch your legs a bit. You've been going through a lot lately, and you need a break. Having a lot of female interaction is probably what Haley needs right now, anyway."

"What about Sarah?" asked Peggy. "She may want to go herself."

"Oh, we wouldn't want to leave these two hellions with anyone." She was referring to her and Jason's boys. "Not anyone we liked, anyway. They can be a handful. They've got way too much of their daddy in them," she said, jokingly. "But Zack is easy, he would be a pleasure."

"I'm just afraid he would have one of his episodes while I'm away," Peggy replied.

"We've all been involved enough to be able to deal with it. You need the break. End of story," Sarah said with an insistent tone.

"Well... okay then, I'll go. I'd love to meet everyone over there and I could use a break," she said with a smile.

"That settles it then. Jason, Judith, Peggy, and I are on the next run. Griff will handle security with the boys, and Molly, Judy, and Sarah will handle the kids," Evan said.

"Hey Dad," said Jake, who was listening in on the planning.

"Yes, son?" Evan replied.

"Can I go too?" he asked. "Haley is about my age. It may help her if another kid is around to get to know and hang out with instead of always being in a world of adults."

Evan looked at Molly and she nodded her head in approval. He then looked at Griff and said, "How are you looking for your security duties tomorrow? Can you spare him?"

Griff replied, "We will manage. I'll get Judy to cover for the rounds I had planned for him. She needs to get out in the woods and get more familiar with the outlying areas of the property, anyway."

Evan looked at Jake and said, "Sure, that sounds like a great idea. Maybe we can even talk Mildred and Ollie into letting her come over to visit on occasion to socialize... when she feels up to it, that is."

Everyone agreed and chatted for a moment. They all enjoyed the sense of community that was building. At least in their part of the world, a feeling of normalcy was beginning to return, sans the modern conveniences of mass communication, supply chains, and residential power, of course.

Evan turned to the group and said, "Okay, then, I've got some chores to do, so I'm gonna get busy. Let's plan on the Thomas farm group leaving right after breakfast in the morning. We'll take the tractor and trailer again since we have a foursome. Everyone bring your pistols, including you, Jake. And actually, Jake, you can bring a rifle as well. Bring a VZ58 so that we will have common mags and ammo. You can shoot as well as anyone can. We might as well be as heavily armed as possible."

Jake replied with a huge smile from his sense of pride. He loved how he was beginning to be seen as one of the men, rather than just one of the kids. He was also anxious to meet Haley, as he, too, was desperate for some social interaction from a peer.

With that being said, everyone went on with his or her respective busy day. Homestead life, although rewarding, kept everyone quite busy. Nothing that benefitted their daily lives came without the investment of hard work.

Early the next morning, as everyone ate breakfast, Evan went over the travel plan with everyone. He ensured that they all had everything they needed, and he then briefed Judith and Peggy on what to expect and what to do if the unexpected were to occur. "Since there are five of us and we have the clothes to deliver, we will go ahead and burn into our fuel stores a little more and take the tractor and pull the flatbed trailer. I'll drive and Jason will use his scope to glass the areas up ahead. Jake can be the proverbial trunk monkey and keep an eye out behind us. You two ladies keep your eyes peeled as well. Since there are two of you, one can scan the woods and surrounding terrain to the left and the other can do the same on the right. We can't afford an ambush with so many of us away at once. If something were to happen to us, that would leave the manpower back here at the Homefront way too thin," he said.

"Why don't we just take a truck?" asked Peggy, being new to going out on a run.

"Those Cummins diesels are pretty loud and can be heard a long way off. The tractor is relatively quiet. Also, that motor on the tractor just sips fuel at idle so it will burn less into our fuel stores. We are trying to save the diesel for the trucks and the generator. The trucks are our emergency bug out vehicles and the generator, well, that's obvious. All we use gasoline for is the tractor, and at our rate of consumption, that is what we have more of to spare. Also, being an open-top flatbed trailer, if something were to happen, we could all jump off and run in any given direction, whereas the trucks are a little harder to egress in a hurry. The sheet metal doesn't provide any ballistic protection to speak of either, so it really just seems like a better idea to use the tractor for now. If things get sketchy in the future, perhaps we would use Jason's truck with the shielding he already has in place on his over-the-bed rack."

"Egress?" she asked.

"To get out of in a hurry," he replied.

"Oh, that's one of your terms like hand-railing," she replied.

"Yeah, I guess so. Don't worry; over time, you'll be a tactical momma and have all of this stuff down and will be teaching it all to Zack," he said with a smile.

She laughed in agreement and Jason added, "Yeah, we will need Zack and the boys to provide us security in our old age, if this stupid world doesn't get itself lined out by then."

"So if everyone is ready to go, let's get the show on the road," Evan said as he stood up. They all grabbed the stuff they were taking along and headed out to the tractor. Jason had his Remington as usual; Evan and Jake took along their VZ58s, and Peggy and Judith had their pistols and the clothing for Haley.

As everyone climbed aboard, Evan fired up the old tractor, and with a jerk of the clutch, off they went. Being the first time Peggy had been away from Zack since they rescued him from Newport, Kentucky, she felt uneasy but was excited to see the change of scenery for the day.

The first few miles were uneventful. It was a beautiful fall day, the air was chilly, and the leaves were beginning to turn. “I love this time of year,” said Judith.

“Me too,” said Peggy. “The fall colors are so beautiful.”

Jason said, “The only drawback is that after the pretty colored leaves fall off of the trees, it looks like a nuclear war zone with everything being dead. It also makes it damn near impossible to walk quietly through the woods with all of the crunchy leaves.”

“Leave it to a man to ruin the moment,” Judith said with a laugh.

“Yep, they always do,” replied Peggy.

Just then, a doe bolted across the road ahead of them. Evan stopped the tractor and shut off the motor. “Listen up,” he said. “That thing was running from something, judging from the way it tore across the road without paying us any mind.”

They all sat there quietly and heard a disturbance moving through the brush at a high rate of speed. Just then two large mutt dogs, one with characteristics similar to a Rottweiler, and one a little more lean and hairy like a German Shepherd—both obviously mixes—came bolting out of the woods in pursuit of the deer. The first dog ran right across the road as if it didn’t notice the tractor full of people. The second one slid to a stop in the middle of the road and turned to face the tractor. It was obviously malnourished. It was so lean its ribs were all in clear view and its hair had been falling out in patches. It had a possessed look on its face. Nothing at all like a well-adjusted dog one would meet in the park. Evan had shouldered his VZ and held his aim on the dog. The dog’s hackles rose as it took an aggressive posture.

“Smoke it,” said Jason with a calm whisper.

"Not if I don't have to," Evan said calmly. "I don't want to pop off a shot out here and give our movement away for miles. Everyone just remain still and calm."

The dog began to back away, never letting down its guard. As it neared the side of the road, it turned and darted off into the woods to rejoin the pursuit.

"We need to start bringing Molly's crossbow along with us for silent shots," Evan said, relieved that the situation with the dog worked itself out.

"Or I need to start bringing my can," Jason said, referring to the suppressor he has back at the Homefront for the threaded barrel on his rifle. "That thing looked feral."

"Feral?" asked Peggy.

"A feral animal is a domestic animal that lives in the wild and has reacquainted itself with life without humans," he replied. "Feral dogs have been known to attack and kill people quite often. They no longer look to humans as a source of food, but rather a food source. They attack livestock as well as people and can be very dangerous."

"Yeah, especially because people are used to dogs seeing themselves as subservient to humans and let their guard down," Evan added. "A feral dog may as well be a wolf, albeit not quite as capable as a wolf, but the premise is the same. I would say that over the past year, quite a few dogs have been abandoned by their owners who simply couldn't spare the food to feed them or their owners themselves didn't make it and they found themselves on their own. Either way, if you see a dog, don't think of it as merely a stray. You could find yourself in a world of hurt, these days, with that old mentality."

He then fired the tractor back up and said, "Well, let's get the heck out of here before they lose the deer and come back for us. I don't want to have to get into a gunfight with a pack of dogs today." They once again continued to the Thomas farm, but now they all kept a little better eye on their surroundings.

As they approached the Thomas farm, Evan dismounted the tractor and Jake took the controls. Following their standard operating procedure, Evan proceeded to the house alone to ensure the situation was secure before bringing everyone else up the driveway. Jason crept off into the woods to cover him with his .300 Win Mag while staying within sight of the tractor to cover Jake and the ladies, as well. Evan was met by Ollie and gave the signal for Jason to proceed with the others.

Ollie met Evan in the driveway and said, "How was the trip?"

"Good, except that we ran into a couple of wild looking dogs that crossed our path chasing a deer. It was a tense moment, but all is well. It definitely makes you think twice, though, about rustling bushes," he said with a laugh.

"Yep, I had to shoot a dog not too long ago," said Ollie. "It was raiding the chicken coop. It was a mangy looking old thing. I see you brought a few more people with you this time."

"Yes, sir. That's my son, Jake. He's near Haley's age, so we figured it might make her feel good to have other kids around. The young lady is Peggy. We've told you all about her, and, of course, you know Judith. She's here to give Haley her new clothes and make sure they all fit and don't need any alterations. She brought some sewing items just in case."

"Well, that's just wonderful," Ollie said.

As Jake brought the tractor to a stop, Ollie looked at him and said, "You must be their extra security." Jake just smiled. He was a little shy, as he had not been around many new people in quite some time. "Okay then, everybody, come on in. Mildred and Haley are around back on the screened-in porch," Ollie said, welcoming them all to his home.

As Judith, Peggy, and Jake visited with Haley and Mildred, Ollie looked at Evan and Jason and said, "Let's take a walk." He led the men back outside.

"Did you ever find those missing cows?" asked Evan.

"No, that's what I wanted to talk to you about," Ollie replied. "As a matter of fact, I'm missing four total now. I found some boot prints out in the back pasture that don't match anything of mine, and they don't look like yours either. I tracked them a little ways off in the woods. Someone has definitely been accessing the property on a fairly regular basis. There are tracks of a different degree of erosion so you can tell they've come and gone between rains. I didn't track 'em very far because, well, being by myself, I didn't want to accidentally catch 'em. If anything happened to me, Mildred and Haley would be sitting ducks."

"Have you seen any signs that they have been near the house?" asked Jason.

"No, thank God," Ollie replied. "For now, it looks like they have been staying out of sight of the house. I'll betcha that's where my missing cows are. Someone is rustling them, probably just right through the woods. It should be easy to track them—for several well-armed men, that is."

"Let's check it out then," Evan said. "I couldn't live with myself leaving here today with that kind of uncertainty for you guys. You need to know what's going on and they need to be stopped."

"I'm game," added Jason.

"Well, let's do it then. I'll tell Mildred we're gonna go out and check the fence line so that they don't expect us back anytime soon," Ollie said as he walked towards the house.

Jason looked at Evan and said, "Why is it that every time things seem to stabilize, we get thrown a curveball?"

"I know what you mean," Evan replied. "As soon as we start feeling like a safe, little community, something comes up. But then again, it will probably take quite a while to shake everything out... if it is going to shake out, that is. That or we just build a fence around all of our combined properties and live like it's a zombie apocalypse."

"Sadly, zombies would be much easier to deal with, or aliens," Jason replied.

Evan chuckled and smiled, remembering the situation they were in the last time Jason said something like that. Just then, Ollie came out of the house with his Ruger American Rifle slung over his shoulder and the .45 that Evan had given him on his side. Evan looked at him and said, "Do you always go checking the fence line armed for battle?"

"Oh, she knows I was fibbing to keep the kids from worrying," replied Ollie. "That woman knows what I'm gonna say before I say it."

"Funny how that works," replied Evan.

"Yep, and if you don't say what they thought you would say, they just change your mind for you," added Jason as all three of the men chuckled.

Ollie walked over to his old red Massey Ferguson tractor, which had no implements attached at the time and fired it up. "Climb on, boys. Each one of you stand on a lower link. We ain't goin' far. You won't fall off." Evan and Jason looked at each other, shrugged, and hopped on. Each of them stepped up on a lower link of the three-point hydraulic hitch and leaned back on their respective fender. Ollie let go of the clutch and with a lurch, they were off. Ollie drove them out past the barn and beyond his back pasture. He pulled up alongside the tree line and came to a stop, shutting off the motor. Ollie looked at Jason and Evan and said, "Right over there is where I found their footprints."

Evan and Jason hopped off the hitch and followed Ollie up the tree line, quietly observing the area as they walked. They knew they were not sneaking up on anyone due to the sound of the tractor's engine, but there was still no reason to be reckless. "Right there, there they are," said Ollie, pointing to the ground.

Jason kneeled down and inspected the tracks. “Looks like several sets of boots to me,” he said. “These look like old G.I. issue jungle boots and so do these over here, but they are from different sized boots. This one over here looks like a more modern hiking boot. At a glance, I’d say you have three trespassers, at the least.”

“It looks to me like they were coming and going through the creek. You can see their tracks come out again on the other side,” said Ollie, pointing into the woods across the creek.

“Well... there’s only one way to get an answer without sitting here for days,” Evan said. “Let’s follow them.”

Chapter 14: Road to Recovery

Nate was awoken by a local woman volunteering as a nurse's aide. "Hello, my name is Lucinda. I'm here to bring you something for your pain and to see if you need anything."

"Thank you, ma'am," Nate responded. "Any idea when a doctor or someone may be by? I've got a lot of questions."

"I'll go and ask your brother. He's checking on a few of the other patients now," she said as she handed him a couple of pills and a glass of water. "This is for the pain and the swelling. I think your brother is going to bring you some antibiotics also. They are worried about the possibility of your leg getting infected considering the situation they found you in. Nothing to worry about though, it's just a routine precaution."

"Thank you, ma'am. You're too kind," he said returning her smile. He swallowed his pills, laid his head back down on the pillow, and stared at the ceiling for a while. A lot had happened over the past few days. Everything in his world had been both accomplished and turned upside down simultaneously. He now had his brother, but his body was not the same as it once was, and he was not sure where his brother's heart would lead him. He found himself feeling depressed and, for the first time in the past year, his mission in life was uncertain. In the state he was in, he was not even sure if he could make the journey alone to Virginia. He had, of course, seen many people deal with an amputation and overcome every challenge that came before them afterward. Unfortunately, he had no idea what his limits would be now, so things were just harder to imagine.

After about an hour had passed, Luke entered the room with a young lady in her late twenties to her early thirties. She was an attractive strawberry blonde whose smile lit up the room. "This is Doctor Stewart," Luke said. "She's the one who put your busted butt back together."

"Thank you, ma'am," Nate said as he reached out to shake her hand.

"My privilege, Mr. Hoskins," she replied.

"That's the first time anyone has called me Mr. Hoskins in a long time... if ever, actually," said Nate. "When I joined the Navy, I was too young to be a Mr. As I got older, since I was enlisted, I didn't warrant a Mr. or a Sir; I was always Petty Officer or hey Sailor."

She grinned at his jokes and said, "How does your leg feel today?"

"There is some dull pain... and it kinda feels like it is still there," he responded.

"Yes, that is normal. It's called a phantom pain or a phantom sensation," she replied.

"I think I saw that episode of M*A*S*H when I was a kid," he said with a grin.

"Well, at least you are in good spirits," she said. "Other than that, your temperature is a little high. That's normal at this point as your body fights off any infection trying to set in. We would like to get you up and about as soon as possible to avoid pneumonia or any other complications. Do you feel like you can use crutches?"

"Yes, ma'am; I feel up to that for sure," Nate replied. "I'd rather hobble to the restroom than use a bedpan."

"Well, good, that's the attitude we like to hear," she said with a chuckle. "Your brother tells me you have made quite the journey to get here."

"You could say that," Nate replied. "So, how long am I stuck here? In bed, that is."

"As long as an infection doesn't set in and your wound heals quickly, we should have you on a prosthesis in a couple of weeks if we can find you one," said Dr. Stewart. "With things the way they are these days, we don't really have access to a typical medical supply chain, but we do have a few supporters who used to work for several prosthetics manufacturers here in Texas. Prior to the collapse, due to our business-friendly environment in the state, we were blessed with the fact that we had sixty-one manufacturers in Texas that made prosthetics. One thing that has made our efforts here with the TSG so successful is that we have sought out key people who used to work in such industries and created partnerships in order to have them provide us with support in exchange for a mutually beneficial relationship. What that is varies, but our Texans are generally patriotic people and believe in what we are doing. Anyway, we will take some measurements and make an estimate of what you will need and try to get something in the works for you. In some cases, we have some previously issued units that we can get even sooner if the measurements work out. They are nothing fancy, but they are functional. Your brother is a pretty popular fellow around here, so maybe with it being you, we can pull a few strings." She said this last part as she shared a flirtatious look with Luke.

"Great! I've got to get back on the road as soon as I can," he said as he looked at his brother, who looked away and avoided eye contact.

"That sort of attitude is exactly what will get you on the road to recovery as soon as possible. Keep it up," she said. "If you don't have any more questions, I'll be on my way. It was great talking to you. I'll be back in the next day or two to see how you are doing."

"Okay, thank you very much, ma'am. It's a God-send to get this kind of care in today's world," Nate said as he reached out to shake her hand.

Doctor Stewart left the room and Luke took a seat next to his brother. He sat staring at the floor with his elbows on his knees while wringing his hands. "So... is she one of the reasons you are torn about leaving?" asked Nate.

"Not exactly... well... maybe," Luke stuttered. "It's not exactly like I can just turn right around and come right back if we get all the way there and can't find Mom and Dad. I've got a good thing here, and I can see things possibly working out with her. It's not like back in the day when I could just call her up. If I walk out that door, I may never see her again."

"That may be true, but if you don't go, you'll likely never see our parents again. I thought our family was inseparable. I don't know what you've gone through to change how you see things now, but you're not the Lucas Hoskins I expected to find," said Nate in a disappointed tone.

Luke just sat there wringing his hands while continuing to stare at the floor. "What's your plan?" Luke asked.

"Well, I had always pictured us working that out together. Now, with my leg the way it is and being on my own... well... I guess I had better start putting something together. I've got a few weeks to get it all worked out I suppose," replied Nate.

"Well, if you need anything let me know," Luke said as he stood up.

"I could obviously use some suitable clothes," Nate responded. "I doubt they kept my blood-covered stuff. Also, my pack if they still have it somewhere. I could use some maps or an atlas to start my planning. Oh, and what about my guns? I had a Beretta M9 and a shotgun. The M9 was on my hip, but the shotgun was somewhere in the front of the Humvee at the time of the crash."

Luke took out a pen and some scratch paper and started jotting down everything that Nate was saying. After he finished his list, he put it in his shirt pocket and said, "I'll see what I can find out. The first time I saw you, you were already stripped down, so I'm not sure where your things are." Luke then turned to leave the room. Halfway to the door, he paused for a moment, turned to face Nate, stuttered, and then said, "Never mind."

"What is it?" asked Nate.

"Nothing. I've got to get going. I'll be back later this evening," Luke said as he left the room.

Nate laid his head back into the pillow and thought to himself, *now what?*

Chapter 15: Rustlers

It was decided they would attempt to track on foot whoever was accessing the Thomas farm. Evan said, "I think we should split up and cover a wider swath looking for signs. Perhaps one directly over the hot trail while the others hang back and off to the side, hand railing the course to the left and the right. They may not have been using the exact path every time and we don't want to miss anything."

I agree," said Jason. "I'll take point and use my scope to look up ahead on the trail. Let's move in bounds. I'll advance, stop, and glass the area, then I'll signal for you two to follow and then you two can advance on each side accordingly. We want to take our time and be thorough while simultaneously thinking defensively. We don't want to stumble across someone that may be coming back this way."

"You fellas just tell me what you want me to do and I'll do it," said Ollie.

"Jason's gonna be up front, I'll offset the trail to the right, then you hang back a bit to the left," Evan said. "We'll keep that bound unless Jason has us rally on him, or unless something goes down."

"Okay, then, I'll keep my eyes on you two," said Ollie.

Jason slipped into the woods and followed the trail until he was almost out of sight. He glassed the area up ahead with his scope for a few moments and then motioned for Evan and Ollie to proceed. Evan handrailed the trail off to the right, and Ollie followed to the left. They occasionally saw a squirrel in a tree, and at one point, they flushed out a grouse on accident. Aside from that, it remained mostly quiet and uneventful as they ascended a long, gradual hill following the trail. The woods were heavy with brush and fresh, crisp, fallen leaves, making stealthy travel a challenge. They continued this bound through the woods until reaching a ridgeline. Jason gave the signal to rally on the ridge. Evan and Ollie worked their way up the hill and joined him in a well-hidden position to survey the terrain that gradually descended in front of them.

"What's up?" asked Evan.

"Is this your fence, Ollie?" asked Jason, holding up the end of a cut strand of barbed wire fencing.

"Sure as hell is," Ollie replied. "Looks like it's not been cut long. The ends aren't as rusted as the rest."

"There are also hoof prints through here coming from that way," Jason said as he pointed along the ridgeline heading towards Ollie's farm.

"They must have been keeping a watch on the place through the access point we followed while someone else led the stolen cattle up this way and then off of the property down through here," added Evan. "Were does this end up, Ollie?"

"There's a creek at the bottom and on the other side is an old mining road that leads up to the old coal mine behind the Murphy place," Ollie said. "You can get to a lot of the properties from that road if you didn't mind a hike in the woods to come in the back way."

"You mean like they are doing here?" said Jason.

"Yes, just like them sons-a-bitches are doing here," replied Ollie with a scowl on his face.

"Well, let's keep going to follow this out," said Jason. "We have got to get to the bottom of this or you won't be able to sleep at night."

"Right behind you," said Ollie with a feisty voice.

They continued a little farther through the woods, now following the livestock trail as well as the human prints. Coming up to another rise in the terrain, Jason gave the down signal, followed by rally on me, and quiet. Evan and Ollie followed his signals and moved into Jason's position to join him.

"I thought I saw movement up ahead. We'll just lie low for a minute and watch," Jason said as Evan and Ollie moved in close to him behind a cluster of trees and brush.

Evan took out his binoculars and scanned the area as well. As he panned from right to left, he saw movement and stopped. He scanned the area, trying to get a better look, but his binoculars were at their maximum useful range. "Jason, look towards that big rock with the downed tree lying across it," Evan whispered.

Jason dialed back the zoom on his scope to get a wider field of view in order to find Evan's possible target. "Okay, got it," Jason said as he acquired the rock in his scope.

"Okay, now go just about ten feet to the right of that," said Evan. "You see the shiny spot?"

"Yep, got it," Jason said as he reached up and dialed more zoom into his Nightforce scope. "Holy hell, those are sunglasses. The sun is hitting them just right to make a nice, shiny reflection for us. Looks like they are on a ball cap... yep, just moved. It's a man. Looks like he's lying back against a tree. I can't see much beyond that. There are just too many branches and too much brush in the way."

"That SOB is probably lying low until nightfall before he comes on down to the pasture," said Ollie, getting more and more irritated about the intrusion onto his land and herd.

"That, or he's supposed to be a lookout for someone else," added Jason.

"Let's go introduce ourselves," Ollie said with a serious tone.

"Let's try and pinch him in," said Evan. "Jason, do you have your handheld?"

"Yep," replied Jason as he pulled it out of his cargo pocket.

"Good," Evan said. "Ollie, you cover this angle. If we spook him and he runs this way, you can stop him. Preferably of his own free and breathing will. We need intel, so we need him talking. I'll swing wide right. Jason, you swing wide left. We'll both circle around and pinch him in. Earpieces for the radios only. No gunfire unless necessary. We don't know who else is out here and don't want to call them in on us. Once in position and we can see the entire situation, we'll work out a plan."

"Roger Roger," said Jason as he proceeded off to the left, concealing himself behind the terrain until reaching a suitable spot to begin his arc around and through the woods and down into the descending terrain below.

"Keep your eyes peeled," Evan said to Ollie as he followed a similar path around to the right of their person of interest.

Evan crept through the woods. With every inch closer to the man, it seemed as if the woods got quieter and the sounds he made walking on the organic debris that layered the forest floor got louder. As Evan got into position behind the man, ninety degrees to Ollie's perspective, he heard Jason whisper over the radio that he was in position directly across from him.

Just as Evan began to key the mic to work out a plan with Jason, they were startled by the thundering boom from Ollie's powerful .30-06 rifle. The man they had been sneaking up on leapt to his feet and began to run up the hill towards Ollie. They could now see that he was carrying an AR-15 and a load-bearing chest rig containing numerous magazines. As the man reached for a radio on his belt, Evan leapt up, pointed his VZ58 at the man's back, and yelled, "Drop the weapon! Drop the weapon!"

The man spun around, bringing the rifle into position, and as Evan began to squeeze the trigger, one of Jason's .300 Win Mag rounds ripped through the man's side, dropping him to the ground. As he fell, the round in the chamber of his AR-15 rifle was fired, narrowly missing Evan as he heard the round whiz by his head.

Evan and Jason both sprinted up the hill towards Ollie's position. As they reached the ridge, they saw Ollie frantically pointing and yelling, "Towards the house! There was another man! He's running towards the house!"

Evan and Jason both sprinted through the woods towards the Thomas home. All Evan could think about was the women and children at the house. *Hopefully, Jake was able to hear the shots off in the distance*, he thought as he dodged tree branches, trying to gain on the man. Just then, he heard Ollie's rifle fire again. He turned his head back to look in Jason's direction and yelled, "Go help Ollie! I'll cover the house!"

Jason diverted his run back up the hill towards Ollie. *I'm a sitting duck for an ambush right now*, thought Evan as he frantically ran down the hill. *All that guy has to do is duck off into the brush where I can't see him and cut me to pieces as I run by*. As he neared the pasture, the brush began to thin out to open his field of view. He was able to see the man, who was wearing the old style desert camouflage from the Gulf War era, running across the field towards the barn. Evan broke out into the field, running at a full sprint. He was gaining on the man but wasn't going to be able to catch him before reaching the barn, or even worse if he continued for the house. *Who knows how much observing these guys have done to know our force strength*, Evan thought. *I can't risk it.*

He slid to a stop, raised his rifle into position and fired. "Damn it!" he said aloud as he realized he missed. He was breathing so heavily, it was difficult to stabilize the short barrel of the VZ58 for a steady shot at what was at least one hundred and fifty yards. Holding his breath, he fired another shot as the man passed the barn and headed for the house. "Shit!" he yelled aloud as he missed again. He calmed and steadied himself, took a little more lead on the target, and fired a third shot. He waited what seemed like a second of flight time for the bullet to impact, and with a thud, the man hit the ground face first, limp like a rag doll, and slid to a stop.

Evan took off running again towards the house, not knowing what may have transpired while they were gone. As he approached the downed trespasser, he visually verified a wound in the center of the man's back. He kicked the gun clear of the man for good measure and then resumed his run towards the house. Jake observed the events unfold and ran out onto the back deck with his own rifle in hand. Exhausted and out of breath from his extended run, he mustered just enough wind to yell to Jake, "Keep everyone inside. Get them in the basement and then stand watch from the first floor. I'll be back!"

He turned to run back to Jason and Ollie. As he began a winded jog, he heard Jason over the radio say in a steady, monotone voice, "Ollie is down... we lost him. Is the house secure?"

Evan dropped to his knees in the middle of the pasture and pounded his fist into the ground in a fit of rage and sorrow. He turned and saw Mildred standing on the deck, watching him with a blank look on her face. It was as if she knew. He yelled, "Jake!" and Jake took Mildred by the hand and pulled her into the house. He got back up and began his jog back up the hill towards Jason. He said, "Secure and on my way. Are you secure?"

"Can't make any promises, but it seems to be. I'll cover you the best I can," replied Jason.

Evan made his way back into the woods towards Jason's position. He recklessly jogged back up the hill, without taking caution to keep his head on a swivel to scan his surroundings. He was exhausted and emotionally numb. As he approached Jason's position, he saw Ollie laid out flat on his back.

Jason was kneeling over him with his hat in his hand. He looked up at Evan and said, "There must have been another one down the hill that we didn't see. He must have advanced on Ollie as we abandoned him here to head for the house. You look like hell. Sit here and rest for a minute while I go down and see if I can get some intel off of the one down at the bottom," Jason said as he wiped a tear from his eye. He got up to head down the hill, slipping off into the bushes to take an indirect approach, just in case the third individual was still in the area.

Evan sat down on the ground with his back against a tree. He took his hat off and slumped over as his fatigue and emotions overcame him all at once. Ollie's death would, without question, leave a terrible hole in the group. A thousand questions swirled around in his head as he let it all soak in. What about Mildred and Haley? What about the cattle? There was no way an elderly woman and a young girl could work this place on their own, even without the threat of thieves and rustlers. *Oh well,* he thought. *There will be time to hammer all that out later. Right now, he and Jason have some work to do.*

He collected his composure, stood up, walked over to the ridge, and glassed the area below with his binoculars. He picked up Ollie's .30-06 and used it to cover Jason who was still downhill, assessing the situation. Ollie's powerful .30-06 with its scope would do much better at covering Jason from a distance. His VZ58 was a fine weapon for close-quarters fighting, but he could not afford any more misses today if a situation arose.

He watched through the scope of the rifle and saw Jason collect the gear from the downed intruder, including his rifle. Jason put the load-bearing vest on and threw the extra rifle over his shoulder with the sling and slipped back into the concealment of the heavy woods to make his way back up the hill. Once he got back up to Evan, he said, "I haven't got a clue who those guys might be. There was nothing identifiable on that one."

"I don't like Jake and the ladies being down there alone," Evan said while scanning the surrounding woods anxiously.

"You take Ollie's rifle and that other gear you collected and get down to the farmhouse to help keep watch. I'll carry Ollie out. We can't leave him here."

"Roger that," Jason replied. "Are you sure you don't want me to do that?" asked Jason. "You've got to be exhausted after running down to the house and back."

"That's why I want you to go. You'll get there faster. I can stop and rest with him if need be. I'd just feel better if there was another gun at the house right away," replied Evan as he knelt down next to his dear friend Ollie.

"Roger that then; I'm on it!" Jason said as he began a jog down the hill in the direction of the farm.

"Well, old friend, what do we do now?" Evan said aloud as if Ollie could hear him. "Don't worry, though; we will take good care of Mildred and Haley and help protect their inheritance. You're all a part of our family now." Evan's eyes welled up with tears and he cried for the loss of his friend.

Chapter 16: Unbreakable Bonds

It had been a little more than a week since Nate awoke in the makeshift hospital to his new reality. He had been getting out of bed and using crutches extensively, trying to stay mobile. He also began exercising as much as he felt he could. He considered himself to be his own physical therapist, as only he knew the rigors he would soon have to put his body through. Having made the treacherous journey this far in perfect condition, he knew his challenges for the rest of his journey would seem even more daunting now. He made a vow to himself to not let the loss of his lower leg slow him down.

Luke continued to visit Nate every day. Nate no longer mentioned his brother coming along to complete his journey. Without that pressure, Luke felt more relaxed with Nate and his visits got longer each day. They were beginning to feel like brothers again.

Luke stopped by for his daily visit and asked, "Feel up to a game of horse?"

"You've got a basketball?" replied Nate.

"Sure do," Luke said. "There's an old hoop out back. It doesn't have a net, but it works."

"Heck, you were a sore loser when I had two legs. How are you gonna handle it when I beat you with only one?" asked Nate with a smirk on his face.

"You know the more smack talk you do, the more it will sting when I win," Luke said, returning the look.

"Game on then, little brother!" Nate said as he hopped around on one leg to taunt Luke.

The two brothers went out back to the alley court, which was nestled between two of the buildings fenced off for TSG hospital use. "Same rules as back in the day, and you can take the first shot," Luke said as he bounce-passed Nate the ball.

"I don't need charity, little brother," Nate said, refusing the ball and bouncing it back to him. "It's your court; you shoot first."

"Okay then," Luke said as he took his first shot. The ball easily went into the hoop. "If there was a net, it would have been nothin' but *swoosh*!"

Nate reached out with a crutch to redirect the rebound back to him. Once he grabbed the ball, he tossed his crutch on the ground, hopped over into the position of Luke's shot, and easily put the ball into the hoop. "You could at least try," he said looking at his younger brother.

"If you insist." Luke walked back a little further and shot again. This time his ball bounced off the rim and was a miss.

"Uh oh... you've given me the keys. Now I'm gonna drive away," Nate remarked as he lobbed a shot from his position. "*Swoosh!*" he said in an exaggerated manner as his ball easily made it in the basket.

Luke got the rebound and dribbled the ball as he walked. "Yeah, well, just don't crash like you usually do," he said, referring to Nate's less than stellar teenage driving record.

"Boom! That's an H little brother!" Nate exclaimed as Luke's shot bounced off the rim.

"Yeah, yeah, we've got a long way to go till it's over."

For the next several shots, the brothers traded shots and insults, both men with hits and misses. They were now neck-and-neck and Nate just made a shot and said, "Well, little brother, you're at H-O-R-S. If you miss this one, that's the game. You wanna make it interesting?"

"What did you have in mind?" Luke replied.

"If you make this one, I'll never give you a hard time or try to pressure you into going with me again," Nate said as he bounce-passed the ball to Luke.

"And what if I miss?"

"You go with me—when I'm ready to travel, of course."

Luke stood there for a minute and said, "You always were a competitive jerk. Deal."

Without even taking the time to aim, Luke took his shot. To Nate, it seemed as if the ball flew through the air in slow motion. As the ball neared the hoop, Nate saw that it was not even close. It missed by over four feet. Nate looked at Luke with bewilderment and Luke said, "A bet's a bet. I guess I have to go now."

Nate stood there momentarily speechless. "Are you sure?" he finally asked.

"Yes... yes, I am," Luke said.

"What about Doctor Stewart?"

"Rachel and I were talking last night..."

"So her name is Rachel?" Nate interrupted. "We were never properly introduced. She's still Doctor Stewart to me."

"Yes, it's Rachel Stewart," Luke said. "I've been a jerk. It took her to show me that. She told me that I was upside down in my priorities. She said that any man who doesn't put family first, isn't the kind of man she would be interested in. If it's meant to be, I would find my family, help them out, and then come back to her. She said she didn't want a man full of regrets and should haves."

"That's a classy lady," Nate said. He smiled sarcastically. "She's obviously way too good for you."

"Ha ha... but touché, I guess," Luke replied. "She's even gonna help us out. She took our info with Mom and Dad's info and is going to have the word put out over the wire that we are looking for them."

"We have wires?" Nate asked sarcastically.

"Well, it's HAM over the air stuff, I believe. Some medical network," Luke said.

"That's cool, I guess. Now hand me my damn crutches. I don't wanna hop around on one leg all day. This acting tougher than you is tiresome," Nate said as he leaned against the side of the building.

Luke picked up Nate's crutches. As he handed them to him, he jerked them away as if he was messing around. Nate reached for them, lost his balance, and fell into Luke's arms. The two immediately bear hugged each other as Nate said, "It's good to have you back, brother."

Chapter 17: Heartbreak

Back at the Thomas Farm, Evan shook off his emotions and wiped his tears from his eyes. “Game face,” he said aloud to himself. “No time for heartaches. I’ve got a job to do.” He grabbed Ollie by the hands, pulled him up, threw him over his shoulders into a fireman’s carry, and started his hump down the hill. *If any of those bastards are still out here, I’m a sitting duck*, he thought to himself as he kept his eyes scanning for threats as he negotiated the thick woods. *I can’t really walk quietly and I can’t get to my gun in a hurry. Oh well, I might as well stop worrying about it and just get it done.*

After a tiring hike down the mountain, stopping to lean against a tree on occasion to rest, Evan made it back to Ollie’s pasture. He took a quick scan of the area before exposing himself. He could see Jason on the back porch in the distance, standing guard over the house. *Jason must have Jake standing watch out front,* he thought. Considering it safe, he stepped out into the field to expose himself to Jason’s watchful eye. He reached into his pocket and clicked his mic on his radio to get Jason’s attention.

As he walked into view, the back door of the house flew open and Mildred ran out, screaming and crying, with Peggy trying to hold her back, to no avail. Evan swallowed the large lump of emotion in his throat and kept walking across the field towards the house. As Mildred got close, he knelt on the ground and gently laid her dear husband on the grass. He stood up, removed his hat, and placed it over his heart. He then took a few steps back to give her room.

She collapsed on top of Ollie with a sorrowful cry like Evan had never heard before. Of all the horrible suffering he had witnessed over the past year, he had never seen the likes of what Mildred was going through. He could not contain himself and began to cry as well. He looked to the porch and saw Judith consoling Haley, who was also breaking down into a sorrowful cry. *That poor girl,* he thought. *As soon as she is returned to normalcy after the hell she endured, her new family has already been shattered.*

Jason walked out to Evan and said, "I'll stay with her for a while. Go make sure Jake is okay. He was pretty worried about you."

"Okay, man; thanks," Evan replied as he patted Jason on the shoulder and walked towards the house. His body began to dump its adrenaline and his true fatigue started to set in. He was completely wiped out. He made it to the porch, exchanged nods with Peggy and Judith, who had their hands full with Haley and went on into the house.

Jake was in the living room in the front of the housekeeping a vigilant watch out the window in the direction of the front driveway. He saw his dad enter the room, ran right to him, and gave him a big hug. "I'm okay, I'm okay," Evan said.

"So what's going to happen now?" Jake asked.

"I think we are going to be spending the night here tonight and then will begin to deal with things tomorrow. Mildred is in no condition to travel and it's gonna be getting late soon. Keep standing watch here for now. I'm gonna get on Ollie's CB radio and try and reach the Homefront," Evan said as he patted Jake on the shoulder and walked into the other room.

Just around the corner from the living room was Ollie's den. It was finished in fine woods and had furniture and shelving that Ollie had made by hand. It was a level of craftsmanship that you just didn't see anymore. The walls were covered with mounted hunting and fishing trophies, as well as photographs of fond memories of his life with Mildred and their children. Over on his desk, he had an area where he would hand tie his own fishing flies. It looked as if he had been working on some lately.

To the right of his fly-fishing activities was his old base station CB radio. He had talked to Ollie over that radio from the Homefront many times, and now the airwaves will be missing that old familiar voice. Evan sat down in Ollie's chair and reluctantly flipped the switch, turning it on. He sat there for a moment in silence and then keyed up the mic and said, "Anybody at the Homefront?" All he heard was white noise and static. He adjusted the squelch on the radio to quiet the noise and tried again. "Anyone on the Homefront?"

This time he heard Sarah answer, "Yep, we are here and all is well. How did the clothes fit Haley?" she asked.

He paused for a moment. "Something has happened. We are all fine, but Ollie was killed. We are going to have to spend the night here and make our way back to the Homefront in the morning with the addition of Mildred and Haley. Can you please get Griff?"

"Oh my God," she said. "What happened?"

"I'd rather not go over the details over the radio, but I need to relay some info to Griff."

"Okay, just a minute," she said.

After about five minutes, Griff's voice came over the radio. "What happened, Ev?"

"We ran into some hostiles while checking up on something. They use scouts and lookouts," replied Evan. Using a pre-arranged phrase to order a total lock down of the Homefront Evan said, "Release the dogs." He then discreetly notified Griff that when he called back, they would be given the details of their movement via code. This was done in order to prevent the potential hostiles in the area from setting up an ambush with their own information. "We will communicate more DC at time 1," he said.

"Roger that; the dogs are loose," replied Griff.

The discreet communications they had chosen to use was simple book code. With book code, each person involved has exactly the same book to use as a base for the code. The communicator then sends a word on a page in the book as the page number, line number, and word order on that line. An example would be 201-10-5. The recipient of the message would then go to page 201, count down ten lines, and then over five words. The fifth word would be added to the decoded message. For relaying time discreetly, at both the Homefront and on their person, they carried a chart of all twenty-four hours of the day, followed by a random number assigned to the hour. In this case, the intended communication time of "time 1" could be decoded by simply looking for the one on the chart and seeing 0700 next to it. The numbers assigned to each time were in random order so that a pattern could not be followed. In addition, they had an odd day/even day chart so that if 0700's code were compromised, the next day it would be different in another attempt to avoid being patterned. To further dissect the clock, time 1.5 would then be 0730 in this example and so on. This was a very simple way to help secure their communications during a potential hostile event.

Evan put the mic down and started to turn the radio off. He paused when he realized that they might need to receive transmissions from the Homefront. He didn't want to drain the batteries that Ollie had been using to power the radio via solar charging, but if something went down back home, he wanted to know. He followed the direction of the power cables to their source, which was just down the hall, where Ollie had them mounted in a rack in a closet. He opened the closet and saw four large, heavy equipment batteries. "Well done, Ollie," he said aloud to himself. "This will do." With that, he left the radio on and went out to check on the others.

On his way outside, Evan passed back through the living room where he saw Jake dutifully standing watch in the front of the house while Judith was on the sofa holding and comforting Haley. He stepped out onto the back porch where Peggy sat, watching Mildred mourn her dead husband off in the distance. "Where's Jason?" he asked.

"He's up there," she said, pointing towards the top of the barn.

There Jason stood, on the very top of the barn with his binoculars in hand; he scanned the property, keeping a vigilant watch over Mildred below.

"So what now?" Peggy asked.

"Well, I guess we stay here tonight and try to get Mildred and Haley over to our place in the morning. Then we'll have to figure out the cattle situation."

"I can't stay here tonight!" exclaimed Peggy. "Zack won't be able to make it through the night without me. His nightmares have been getting worse and worse."

"He may have a rough, tear-filled night, but he has Molly, Sarah, and Judy to take care of him. He will be fine. Mildred, on the other hand, won't. She needs to be emotionally stable to make the trip, and I'm sure she has loose ends to tie up around here."

"Yeah, you're right. I'm sorry," Peggy said. "I'll go out there and sit with her for a while. Just in case she needs anything."

"That sounds good," he replied. "I'll go work this out with Jason." They both stood and walked away.

Evan entered the barn, climbed up into the loft, and scurried up to the roof via an old, rickety ladder. As he climbed up on the roof, he said, "How's it going?"

"No signs of trouble that I've seen," replied Jason. "I guess we're spending the night here, huh?"

"That's what I figured," answered Evan. "Once Mildred is stabilized, we can ask her what needs to be taken care of before we leave. The way I see it, Mildred and Haley need to stay with us for a while. Unless some sort of order is restored, it won't be safe for them all alone here. Not to mention the fact that she has her hands full running a household and taking care of a young girl and probably can't handle the additional workload of the cows alone."

"I was thinking about that too," said Jason. "How many head do they have?"

"Maybe forty or so? That's a guess, but somewhere close to that," replied Evan.

"Well, it would be insane to keep splitting our group up, leaving the Homefront short staffed just to come over here and work the cattle on a regular basis," Jason said. "I think we need to move them to our place. If, of course, that's what Mildred wants."

"A cattle drive? Us driving cattle would be just like the movie *City Slickers*," said Evan with his sneaky grin. "But then again, there are more people around here than just us and we need to band together to put a stop to this crap anyway. We need to arrange a meeting with our trading partners."

"You mean the confederacy," Jason interrupted.

"Yes... as Ollie put it, our confederacy," Evan said as they both looked down from the roof at him and Mildred below.

Later that evening after Mildred regained her composure, Evan and Jason discussed with her their thoughts. She agreed and told them she just could not stay there right now, anyway, and that Haley needed the safety of the Homefront. Evan and Jason took Ollie's body and wrapped it neatly in fresh bed sheets, and then again with plastic sheeting and placed him in the cool root cellar until they could arrange a proper community burial.

Judith and Peggy decided to cook dinner for everyone, as it had been a long and tiresome day. While they were cooking, Evan looked at Jason and said, "We never checked that guy."

"What guy?" Jason asked.

"The one that I dropped running to the house. He's still out in the back pasture," Evan replied.

"Well, dang, old man—you're slipping!" said Jason. "Let's get to it then."

Evan and Jason slipped out of the house quietly, leaving Jake in charge of standing watch. Evan and Jason both always carried a small flashlight with rechargeable batteries. They had served them well over the past year; however, the batteries were beginning to fade and were no longer holding a charge, as they should. "Looks like we are going to have to revert to caveman torches before long," Evan said, referring to the weakness of his light.

"Yep, I was thinking the same thing. We had better figure something out before these things are useless. It sure would be easier if this was a zombie apocalypse."

"How do you figure that?" asked Evan.

"Everyone would be eaten and there would be no form of society at all. We could just go to the empty malls and stores and take what we need. Here, we still have to be civil. Being civil just holds you back," said Jason in a joking manner.

"Yeah, well, if this was a zombie apocalypse, the dead guy we are walking out to search in the dark would be trying to eat us by now," Evan replied.

"You have a point there," replied Jason.

As they approached the man, Evan shined his light on him while Jason went through his pockets. He pulled a Glock 9mm out of his holster and put it aside; he then pulled out three magazines, all still fully loaded and placed them with the gun. As he searched the man's pockets, he pulled out a pack of Marlboro reds and said, "Hmmm."

"What?" asked Evan.

"Oh, the guy up by the ridge also had two packs of these in his pockets," replied Jason. "You would think by now cigarette supplies would be running thin without resupply in over a year. I seriously doubt these guys were preppers and just happened to be stocked up on smokes for the apocalypse." Jason stood up and collected the pistol and magazines. "Where was his rifle?"

"Oh, I think it fell right over there when he dropped." Evan shined his flashlight in the direction he was referring to. "Oh, there it is," he said, pointing.

Jason went over to the rifle and picked it up. "A Ruger Mini-30. At least it's a common round to the VZs and SKSs."

"Yep, let's get back to the house," Evan said. "I don't want the ladies to worry."

As the men returned to the house, Peggy and Judith prepared some pan-fried beef with onions and fried potatoes for dinner. Being a cattle farm, there was no shortage of beef, and the potatoes and onions were from Mildred's own garden. As they sat down to eat and said grace, they all felt guilty, as Mildred was still too distraught to join them. She just sat on her bedroom floor at the foot of her and Ollie's bed, sorting through old photos that she had kept in a box.

Judith went to check on her. She knocked gently on the door and asked, "May I join you?"

"Of course, dear," replied Mildred.

Judith sat down next to her and said, "I don't think I've ever told you this, but I too lost my husband, and it was that horrible thing that brought me into this loving, caring, and courageous group. My husband and I were lost at sea in our sailboat, *The Little Angel* after the attacks began. I ran into these people out at sea on an old yacht. They were fleeing the troubles of what they were facing on land just as we were. Anyway, my husband had a heart attack and was dying. I was alone and helpless. I have no doubt in my mind that God put them before me to save me. They risked their own lives to get my husband help, but he unfortunately didn't make it. They took me in as one of their own and dragged me half-way across the country, and here I am with them today. Peggy in there has a similar story, although it was her parents she lost. I guess what I'm saying is that today is, without a doubt, the worst day of your life; but you're not alone, and as long as these good people are around, you will never have to go through anything alone again. I truly consider them my guardian angels."

Mildred leaned over and gave her a big hug. Through her tears, she said, "Thank you very much; thank all of you, oh, so very much."

That night, Evan and Jason took turns keeping watch over the others. Jake volunteered to take a shift, but Evan insisted he get some sleep and thanked him for what he had already done.

Luckily, that night was uneventful, with the occasional noise from a farm animal to break the silent monotony. The next morning after everyone awoke, Peggy and Judith made breakfast; thankfully, Mildred was doing a little better and joined them. After breakfast, at seven o'clock sharp, Evan got on the radio and called the Homefront. "Good morning," he said over the radio on their selected channel.

"Good morning, love," replied Molly. Evan got a huge smile on his face just from hearing her voice.

"I assume everything is okay there?" he asked.

"Yes, just anxiously awaiting your return and worried about you all," Molly replied.

"Tell Griff to stay sharp and we will be there by time 4," Evan said. "Oh, and we will have a few additional homesteaders for a while."

"I figured as much. Judy, Sarah and I are working on that now," she assured him.

"Well, we've got a lot to do, so stay safe and we'll be seeing you. I love you," he said.

“I love you too,” Molly lovingly replied. And with that, they both got off the air and went on with the business at hand.

Chapter 18: Preparations

Back in Texas, Nate's recovery had been going well. His mission in life did not allow him time to be held back by an injury, at least not if he could help it. After he and his brother had emotionally reunited on the basketball court, his spirits were high and his hope to reunite with his mother and father was once again soaring.

Every day, he followed a workout regimen to get his body prepared for what could be a long and grueling road ahead. Having already traversed half of the country in its collapsed state, he knew not to take anything for granted and that any weakness would be uncovered and would hinder his goals.

When he was not exercising his body, he was exercising his mind. Luke had acquired some geographic and topographic maps of the regions of the country that they would likely be traveling. He studied the maps in great detail and plotted several possible routes. He also accounted for diversions from each route along the way at different points, in the event that they needed to modify or completely change their route due to the local conditions. After all, most of the country was still out of power and mass communications of any sort had yet to be reestablished due to the continued political infighting and the instability of society. Given these factors, they were simply unable to know the conditions of the country along their route, and therefore needed several alternative options.

Nate had also been studying the state of the union as best he could with the information he could glean from the TSG folks. From what he gathered, from both confirmed reports, as well as hearsay, the country was still in a total state of disrepair and in many cases was getting worse. Washington D.C. had been brought back to a reasonable state of normalcy in regards to utilities and the general rule of law. The federal government was using the military to augment the local police and had established checkpoints to control the travel of everyone in and out of the city. The D.C. area occasionally had an act of violence that was blamed on "homegrown right-wing insurgents," as the administration referred to anyone that opposed their new level of oppressive rule. Many questioned these as false flag events designed to keep tensions high and to justify the heavy-handed tactics being used to rid themselves of opposition, as no one was ever caught in the act. The only arrests made were after-the-fact raids on the homes of political opponents who usually did not survive to argue their case.

He also learned that the emergency powers enacted via executive order also allowed the president to seize and redirect food assets to the urban populations that he had attained direct control of and where his support was the strongest. Basically, if you comply, you will eat. If you resist, your supplies will be slow to come, if at all, and will be lacking sufficiency to feed the local population, leading to hunger and desperation. This tactic has been used to get resistant populations to submit repeatedly throughout history. If the loyal population centers are living well, people tend to give in to the will of the oppressor to be among those who are favored.

The most disturbing news that Nate learned was that the federal government had been engaging in armed conflicts with some of the resistant states' National Guard and organized militia forces. Some drone attacks on opposition leaders had even been reported. Even more disturbing were reports that, due to the weakened state of the federally controlled armed forces because of the mass desertions, the president was calling in "UN Peace Keepers" to help quell the open resistance to his heavy-handed rule.

The timing of these outside forces being requested also coincided with the president's announcement that, due to the current state of the nation, no further national elections would be held until total order was restored. The reports also stated that the congress was no longer functioning in a constitutional manner, as the senators and representatives who opposed the presidential dictates were either arrested on insurgency charges and held without trial or had fled the capitol to their home states. Only the loyalists remained, and were now nothing more than a rubber stamp for the president. This partisan rubber stamp congress gave his dictates legitimacy with the remaining world powers.

Nate wondered if there was collusion between the president's administration and the remaining world powers to bring America to its knees in order to form a world government. Many of the people he had talked to who had first-hand accounts of some of the reports were inclined to believe it was possible. What once was a concept that only the most extreme conspiracy theorists could believe, was becoming more likely by the day.

During his brother's visits, Nate would brief him on his proposed routes of travel, as well as the events going on around the country from the reports he had collected. After today's update, Luke said, "Dang, brother, you should have been an intel analyst instead of an MP."

"Well, little brother, unlike you who always knew you wanted to be a doctor, some of us didn't know what we wanted to be when we grew up so we just fell into things. Heck, I probably wouldn't really want to know what was going on at the level of a spook though. I don't think I could keep my mouth shut. I would just be another whistleblower accused of treason," Nate replied.

Luke looked at him with a confused look and said, "Spook?"

“Oh, yeah that’s a Navy term for people in the intelligence community,” Nate explained.

Luke laughed and said, “Yeah, probably so. Anyway, I have a surprise for you.”

“What’s that?” Nate asked curiously.

“Bring it on in,” Luke yelled to the hallway.

In walked Doctor Stewart with a lower leg prosthesis for Nate. “It’s about time you guys stopped talking politics long enough for me to bring this thing in. I was getting tired of waiting in the hall,” Doctor Stewart said with a smile. “Your brother here wanted to be all dramatic about it.” She winked at Luke. “Anyway, normally we would fit you with a preparatory prosthesis, and then move you on to a permanent one over time. That is because your stump will go through some physiological changes as time passes, most notably losing some mass and becoming smaller. You, of course, are a man on a mission, so we simply don’t have that luxury of time. I pulled some strings with one of the local gentleman who was a prosthetist before the collapse and he made this one to the best of his ability to be permanent for you. It has quite a bit of adjustability to it, and he included numerous stump socks, as well, to help you adjust the fit as things change over time.”

Nate reached out, took the device, and said, “Thank you so much. I can’t wait to get up and around on it.”

“Let’s see how it fits,” she said.

For the next half hour, she explained the basics to him and explained the proper care of his stump during its use, as well as the general care and maintenance of the prosthesis. She had him don and remove it several times to make sure he could adequately secure it to his leg without causing any problems with improper fit. “I’ve got one of our TSG guys that uses a prosthesis similar to this scheduled to come by and pay you a visit tomorrow,” she said. “You’ll do much better getting his first-hand accounts of what to expect than from me simply reading from a manual. I encourage you to get up and around on it as much as you can today—with a cane, of course—until it becomes second nature. That way you may come up with some specific questions to ask, based on your initial experience with it."

Nate immediately hopped up out of bed, though a little unsteadily at first, and began to experiment with the way it felt and the way he would now have to concentrate on his gait to get it to function properly. He started off holding on to things but was soon able to let go and experiment with his balance. "I'll be up to traveling before you know it, Luke," Nate said.

Luke and Rachel left Nate to experiment with his new leg in private. Luke knew that his brother worked better that way. Knowing people were watching him stumble around would just hurt his pride and hinder his learning. Luke also felt that he needed to be spending as much time as possible with Rachel, as he could feel their departure for the East Coast rapidly approaching. He knew Nate wouldn't need much time to acclimate to his new leg before he would be dragging him out the door.

That night, Luke and Rachel spent some much-needed quality time together. They made hopeful plans for the future, and to an extent, enjoyed the bliss of their intentional disregard for the cold hard truths that surrounded them.

The next morning, Nate was visited by TSG Corporal Johnny Reid. Corporal Reid showed up bright and early, knocked on the door, and entered Nate's room and introduced himself. "Johnny Reid is the name, I hear you are the brother of Doc Stewart's sweetheart."

"Is that what they call Luke around here?" replied Nate with a laugh.

"Yep, but that's just out of jealousy," Reid said with a smile as he took off his hat and took a seat. "She's a fine woman, and not too bad on the eyes either. Any dirty grunt around here would feel like the king of the world to be picked by her."

"Yep, I imagine so," replied Nate as he started to feel bad about pressuring Luke into leaving such a good situation for the danger and uncertainty that lies ahead.

"So you've joined the club, I hear," said Reid.

"Club?" Nate said in a curious tone. "What club would that be?"

Reid rolled up his right pant leg and said, "This club."

"Oh yeah." Nate moved his bed covers and swung to the side of the bed, revealing his amputation. "Rachel... uh, Doc Stewart just brought me this yesterday evening," Nate said as he picked up the prosthesis and handed it to Reid.

"Yeah, this thing is made real good," said Corporal Reid as he inspected it. "This thing ought to last quite a while. So, you got any questions or concerns?"

"I'm not sure quite what to ask," Nate replied. "I've messed around with it some. I guess I just need to get used to it so that I can trust putting all of my weight on it. Right now, I'm obviously favoring my good leg and putting a majority of my weight on it, and when I do put my weight on the prosthesis, I find myself trying to get back to my good leg as quick as I can."

"That will come with time. For now, though, I recommend you consciously distribute your weight as evenly as possible. If you spend a majority of your time with uneven weight distribution, it will cause you other problems down the road. Back problems being one example of that."

The two men spent the better part of the next two hours walking up and down the halls. Reid shared some of his pointers and helped point out some of what he felt were Nate's issues. It was a real help to have him there. Nate was a self-motivated individual, but some lessons are best learned from someone with first-hand experience, and Nate did not have any time for setbacks.

"Well, I have to get back to work," said Corporal Reid as he looked at his watch. "I've got a supply run later this evening and have some briefing and preps to do. You take care of that leg and it will take care of you," he said as he turned to leave the room.

"Thanks again!" said Nate enthusiastically.

"No problem, man. Oh, and good luck on your trip; but to be honest, if you being able to hang with Sergeant Wilson and his pack of wolves is any indication, you are one tough son of a gun and I'm sure you'll make out okay."

"I didn't feel tough compared to those guys," Nate replied.

"Yeah, they had that effect on people. They are sure as hell gonna be missed around here. Take care of the Doc's sweetheart," he said with a smile as he turned and left the room.

Chapter 19: A Community's Strength

After the horrible events that unfolded at the Thomas farm, Evan, Jason, Peggy, Judith, and now Mildred and Haley, all made it back safely to the Homefront. Molly set up temporary accommodations for Mildred and Haley in the basement, and the two were welcomed into the home with the loving embrace of everyone there. While the women were focused on getting the two newcomers settled in, Evan, Jason, and Griff discussed the matters at hand.

Evan and Jason gave Griff a debrief on everything that had occurred on the Thomas farm. They shared every detail in order to help bring him into the thought process for how to proceed with the two problems they now saw before them. First, they needed to better secure the Homefront from any similar hostile intruders. Second, they needed to secure and care for Mildred's cattle. Not only were the cattle Mildred's property, but they were also an important source of milk and meat, as well as a critical barter item with the other cooperative homesteads.

"First things first," said Griff. "We need to secure this place and we need to do it now. We don't want that kind of thing to go down again. Mildred and Ollie were pretty much alone out there, so there was no way Ollie could have kept a perfect watch on one hundred and fifty acres by himself. Those guys were able to slip in and out undetected for who knows how long, gathering intel and sizing up their prey before you guys stumbled on to them and threw a wrench into the works. Unlike their situation, we've got the advantage of numbers here, so we need to put together a better strategy than what we currently have."

"What do you suggest?" asked Jason.

"Well, I think we need two watchstanders at a time. One on the inner perimeter, covering the home and the surrounding structures. The other watch-stander should be on the outer perimeter, consisting of the property line and surrounding roads, and, of course, the access road."

"There is an awful lot of outer perimeter to cover for just one person," added Evan.

"Yes, that's not the ideal staffing, but it's what we have," Griff replied. "At least that way, even if we don't observe a threat directly, we may be able to see signs of their presence, such as footprints and the like so that we can take preemptive action before things start to turn up missing or worse. Also, we could intervene before the intruders were able to get overly familiar with our situation like happened at the Thomas place. It's impossible to know just how long those guys had been getting in and out of there before Ollie noticed."

Evan stood there scratching his chin and said, "That's a good point. Ollie had mentioned that he thought some cows might have been missing before we even made the trip out to the Murphy place. If we would have realized that he had intruders sooner, we may have been able to prevent what happened."

"I think we should split the watch up like this," explained Jason. "There are three of us men, four if you count Greg, and five with Jake. Whether we include Jake or not is up for debate, but I think Greg definitely needs to be in the mix."

"Agreed," responded Griff.

"The men can take the outer watch. We can have a random roving foot patrol who looks for signs of entry onto the property, with some tree stand observations thrown in as well. Basically, rove searching the ground from treestand to treestand, and then spend some time in each stand, making sit-and-wait style observations. The women, which would be five without Mildred, and I don't think we should include her just yet, can rotate the inner perimeter watch. They can make occasional rounds of the home and the structures in the immediate vicinity, as well as monitor the cameras from the inside. That's a fairly even spread. We can have three eight-hour watches per day. I know that seems tedious, but considering that now two of the properties, the Murphy place, and the Thomas place, have had fatal confrontations with intruders, I don't think our convenience really needs to be at the top of the priority list."

"I agree, and I think Jake is old enough and responsible enough to be put into the rotation," added Evan. "We can't spread ourselves too thin. We still have a lot of work that needs to be done around here just to feed and clothe ourselves, in addition to protecting ourselves."

"Yeah, we can discuss the particulars later, but for now I think this is the game plan we need to pursue," concluded Griff.

"Well, I think that's settled then, but what about Mildred's place?" asked Jason

"I think we need to drive the cattle over here for sure. There is no way we have the staffing to cover two properties," Evan said. "We need to relay what happened to Ollie to the other homesteads, anyway. When we do, I was thinking we should solicit volunteers to help us relocate Mildred's herd. With two homesteads being hit, we all need to band together when things like this occur. If we don't share intel and manpower, over time, we will be picked off one by one by every band of thieves, looters, or psychos that come along."

Later that evening, Evan spoke with Mildred about all of the options that he, Jason, and Griff had discussed. He assured her that the cattle would always be hers, regardless of their location, and all of her property would be treated as such. She thanked the men for being so willing to help her and Haley through this ordeal and told them that whatever they thought was the best course of action was fine by her.

"Ollie always made these kinds of decisions," she said. "He was the man of the house and ran the farm; I simply ran the inside of the home all these years. I'm not in a state of mind to be making any big decisions right now. Maybe someday, but as of now, I'll defer those types of things to you gentlemen—if that's okay with you, of course."

"Yes, ma'am; of course. Not only are you dear friends who we also consider family, but we are all in this mess together and we will never let you down," Evan said as he tipped his hat to Mildred.

The next morning, Evan and Jason began their routine scheduled barter run. They stopped first at the Thomas farm. They made a quick patrol of the property and found it to still be undisturbed from how they had left it the day before. They also counted the cattle and came up with forty-four in total. In addition, Mildred had ten chickens, two goats, and a pig that they had bartered for that she was fattening up.

"We can put some stake sides on the flatbed trailer and pull the rest of these critters behind the tractor. I guess," said Jason as he calculated what Mildred would need to move right away. "I think if we disconnect the main part of the chicken coop from its run, we should be able to get the entire coop on the trailer, which we will need, as Molly's coop is pretty crowded as it is. Not to mention the fact that Mildred may want to keep her birds separate from Molly's. We can always come back and take down the fence later to rebuild her chicken run."

"Great idea," Evan replied. "We are gonna need some help with the cattle though. Daryl Moses is quite the horseman, so we need to get him on board for sure. Lloyd has a horse or two at his place as well."

"And most importantly, Jimmy Lewis can donate some moonshine to calm our nerves during this evolution," said Jason with a smirk on his face.

"Heck, it may be the cattle that need a swig of shine," replied Evan with a chuckle. "I doubt any of them have ever stepped a hoof off of this property."

"Isn't Linda Cox an equestrian as well?" asked Jason.

"I believe so. When I took Molly over there to get some fabric, it seems like there was a bunch of old pictures on the wall from some sort of equestrian competitions from when she was younger. Maybe she would still be up for the task."

"Well, it wouldn't hurt to ask," said Jason.

"I agree," Evan said as he looked up at the sun. "Let's get on with our rounds. The day is burning and we need to get all of this hammered down to get these animals moved as soon as possible. This place isn't gonna stay unmolested for long. Not if those guys had any friends who are still out there."

With that being said, they loaded up what Ollie and Mildred had already promised in barter to other homesteads and continued to the next destination. Over the course of the day, they retold the horrible story of what had happened at the Thomas farm to each and every homestead. They wanted everyone to not only feel the need to chip in and help for the sake of their little community, but they also wanted to express to them the dangers that they all faced if they didn't stand together on this and any other security issue that may arise in the future.

As they told the story to Linda Cox, she looked a bit disturbed and said, "Just the other day, my dogs went nuts and chased something off into the woods from behind the house. One of them didn't come back. I thought I heard a gunshot off in the distance but didn't know if it was someone hunting or something unrelated, so I simply dismissed it. But now that you say that, it seems a little more suspicious. And then the next day, one of the Muncie boys showed up here. I believe it was the middle one... I think he said his name was Joe. He came by with a man I had never seen around here before. As Joe, or whatever his name was, talked to me and seemed to try to keep my attention at the door, the other man stood back a little farther and kept looking around the property. It just didn't feel right. I had the other dogs in the house at the time and they were getting pretty aggressive. You could tell they didn't want me to step outside. They wedged themselves between me and the screen door while I talked to Joe."

"What did they want?" asked Jason.

"Oh yeah," she continued. "Joe said they were just looking for work in the area and asked if I had any odd jobs that needed to be done. They said they were hungry and would work for food. I thought that a bit odd, as they both seemed well fed. Most people around here have shed their extra weight over the past year, but these men seemed to be doing just fine. A little odd for someone who said they were hungry and looking for food I thought."

"Who was the friend?" asked Evan.

"He never introduced us. He just always said we but never said who the other man was. He just stood back about ten feet during the entire conversation. Either he was afraid of the dogs or afraid of me and the shotgun I had leaned up against the opened door."

"That, or he needed to stand back where he could get a better view and take mental notes of the property," added Jason. "I tell you one thing that is odd; of all the other homesteads we have talked to, not one of them have had those men come around looking for odd jobs. If they were truly looking for work, don't you think they would be going around to all of the homesteads to advertise their services?"

"Oh come on, guys, now you're making me nervous," Linda said.

"Nervous is good," said Evan. "It will help you keep your wits about you. We can't assume the Thomas farm problem is isolated and will go away. We have to stick together until we are sure it's over. If you would like to join us tomorrow when we move Mildred's cattle, we would love to have you. We could use someone with your horse skills. Jason and I are handy, but we aren't ranchers."

"Who else is going?" she asked.

Evan pulled out his handwritten notes and said, "So far, Robert Brooks, Lloyd Smith, and Daryl Moses will be on horseback. If you came along, that would give us two on each side. Charlie Blanchard and Jimmy Lewis are both bringing an ATV. I'll be driving my old Ford tractor pulling a trailer with some of Mildred's belongings up front, and Jason will be driving Ollie's Massey Ferguson tractor, pulling a livestock trailer in the rear. We are also going to be using the trailers on the tractors as security platforms. I'll be armed as will Jason, and Will Bailey and Billy Skidmore have both volunteered to ride shotgun. We'll put one on each trailer. They can focus on being the security lookouts while you folks on the horses and ATVs can focus on keeping the herd moving along and intact."

"With a representative from most of the homesteads present, we'll also be talking about a way to come up with a joint security strategy," added Jason. "We need to get some sort of area-wide patrol going so that we can figure out if the Thomas farm thieves are still in the area."

"Well count me in then!" she said with excitement. "I could use a day away, and I definitely want to be involved with whatever you guys discuss about patrolling the area. I'm starting to not feel so good about living alone out here."

"We'll get a handle on this if we all pull together. Just do us a favor and call us on the CB anytime something suspicious happens and don't go outside unarmed," Evan said. He then proceeded to explain to her the meetup point and the time for the group to get together the next morning. He and Jason then loaded up some of the clothing items that Linda had made or repaired for barter so that they could deliver them to the other homesteads on their next pass through. Once they had her things all loaded up, they got on their way. Tomorrow was going to be a long day, and they wanted to make sure to get back to the Homefront in time to get everything ready before nightfall.

Chapter 20: Contact

Nate had now been on his new prosthesis for several weeks and had continued with his physical fitness and rehabilitation plan. He was feeling strong and getting anxious to go. He could tell that his brother was still torn, wanting and needing to help him try to reunite their family, yet did not want to leave Rachel behind in Texas during such uncertain times.

Nate had acquired nearly everything he personally needed for the journey and would question Luke about his own readiness almost every time they met. Luke was staying in a barracks type facility across town with several other TSG soldiers and medical personnel. Luke had reassured him that his location was secure and well guarded, but Nate still worried about Luke's safety while traveling from his quarters to the medical facility, especially after what had happened to him and his band of TSG escorts.

Nate had just finished his breakfast and was starting to go a little stir-crazy. His room was in the center of the facility and had no windows to look outside. The TSG medical and security personnel, who ran the facility, insisted that he not leave the grounds without an escort, as he did not have the security credentials to return. He was, after all, still an outsider, even though the TSG's hospitality made him feel as if he was one of their own.

To occupy his mind, he decided to unpack his backpack and inventory his supplies as he had done many times before. This exercise in readiness was mostly a time killer for him, but it also helped add reality to his plan of continuing his journey that sometimes just seemed like a faraway dream. As he began to unpack his bag, his brother came into the room more excited than Nate can remember seeing him throughout this entire ordeal.

"Nate! You're not going to believe this!" he said frantically.

"What? Believe what?" Nate said as he sprang to his feet with confidence on his new leg.

"It's Mom! Remember when I said Rachel put out an information request over the radio?" Luke asked with excitement.

"Yeah, yeah, now what is it?" insisted Nate.

"Well, there is a group called the Survivors' Locator Network run by volunteer HAM radio operators," Luke said. "You can call in the name of a person or persons you are looking for while leaving your own name to help be found by them as well. They add to and subtract from the list daily based on new reports. Sometimes they are able to put together a match of people seeking each other. That's what Rachel did! She gave them Mom and Dad's info with ours as the seekers. She just got word from them that they got a match! Mom is out there somewhere looking for us!" Luke exclaimed as he put his arms around Nate and began to cry. "All this time I've tried to act tough and block everything out that's not standing right in front of me. I didn't want to face the pain of having lost you or our parents so I just focused on the here and now. I'm sorry for being a jerk. You were right all along, Nate. You always are," Luke said as he held his brother and cried.

Nate did not know what to say. He was speechless. Was this really happening, or was this just another of the myriad dreams he has had where he quickly awakens to his sad reality? After a moment of letting it all sink in, the brothers relaxed their emotional embrace and Nate asked, "So where is she? What about Dad?"

"There wasn't much info to start. All they had was that Judith Hoskins of Norfolk, Virginia, was seeking sons Nathan and Lucas Hoskins. Her current location was simply

Tennessee. There wasn't anything specific. There was nothing about Dad," Luke replied.

"Tennessee? What are they doing in Tennessee?" replied Nate.

"Who knows?" answered Luke as he shrugged his shoulders. "I'm just glad they aren't out to sea on *The Little Angel*. That would have made them damn near impossible to find. Not to mention the fact that we should consider it a blessing since Tennessee is one state closer. It's also a fairly stable area, which, of course, is probably why they went there."

"So what now?" asked Nate. "Do they know about us?

"Our info was on there," said Luke. "I'm assuming they will radio their point of contact with our info. I asked Rachel to have them update our status and to request their specific location as well as to let them know that we would be on the move to them as soon as we have it."

"Luke," Nate said in a serious tone.

"Yeah, what?" he replied.

"Before we get too excited about finding them, we need to realize something and prepare ourselves," Nate said in a serious tone.

"Prepare ourselves for what?" Luke again asked.

Nate looked him in the eyes and said, "There was no mention of Dad. Don't you think she would have put Bill and Judith Hoskins if they were both looking for us? Dad had a heart condition. It has been an exceedingly stressful year, and you know as well as anyone our current medical supply situation. You can barely get the drugs you need for your patients, and that's with the support of the entire state of Texas. Dad may not have had those kinds of resources, and he can't be far from his pills."

Luke just stood there quietly for a moment, realizing the legitimacy of Nate's concerns and said, "Well, brother, I hope that for once you're not the one who is always right."

Chapter 21: Moving On

The next morning on the Homefront, everyone was busy with the preparations for the move of Mildred's livestock. Griff had volunteered to stand watch at the Homefront, as well as to begin construction of a temporary holding pen for the cattle. They had decided on an area where the cattle could graze until they got adequate fencing up for a larger, more permanent area, and Griff wanted to have it done before the cattle arrived. Once they got everything settled in, they would gather the necessary materials, some of which would have to be sourced from the Thomas farm's existing fence, and begin construction of an area more suited for free grazing.

Going on the run to the Thomas farm from the Homefront was Evan, Jason, Mildred, and Judith. Being her closest peer and having been there when tragedy struck, Judith had become Mildred's close friend. She knew that Mildred might have a tough time going through her and Ollie's things, so she wanted to be with her to lend her support. For security reasons, it was decided that the others should stay on the Homefront, in addition to helping Griff get the livestock area ready for the arrival of the animals.

They said their goodbyes and good lucks as Evan fired up the old Ford tractor and Jason attached the hitch. Jason helped Mildred and Judith aboard the trailer and then Jason climbed up himself. Sarah walked over to the trailer as Jason leaned down and gave him a kiss. She handed him his rifle and pack and wished him luck. Molly and Evan said their goodbyes and she lifted each of the girls up to Evan, who was sitting up in the driver's seat, and they each gave him a hug and kiss. He slid his rifle into the homemade scabbard that he recently made and mounted to the inside of the tractor's rear fender. Molly and the girls stepped back while everyone at the Homefront waved and wished them all good luck with the cattle and for a safe trip. Evan let out on the clutch, and with a jerk, away they went.

The trip to the Thomas farm was uneventful. It was a beautiful fall morning without a cloud in the sky. It was cool but comfortable. *The perfect day to drive the cattle,* Evan thought as he scanned the area for threats. Mildred and Judith gazed at the changing color of the leaves and the beautiful rays of light that shined down through the branches. Mildred thought that perhaps God was showing them favor after all they had already gone through.

Upon arrival at the Thomas farm, Evan stopped just short of rounding the corner to the driveway, keeping the tractor behind the visual cover of the surrounding foliage.

He shut the engine off to listen to their surroundings as Jason hopped off the trailer and darted off into the woods to get an assessment of the situation before exposing themselves on the open driveway. After a few moments, they heard the bushes rustle and Jason popped out, gave Evan a thumbs up, and climbed back up on the flatbed trailer.

"A few of the others are already here," Jason said.

With that, Evan fired up the tractor, popped it in gear, and proceeded to the driveway. Upon reaching the house, they saw several horses tied up to the deck railing and one ATV parked next to the house. Linda Cox and Charlie Blanchard walked out to the trailer to say good morning. Jason hopped down from the trailer and gave Judith a hand climbing down as Charlie helped Mildred.

Linda walked up to Mildred and gave her a big hug. "It's wonderful to see you again," she said. "I only wish it was under different circumstances."

"Thank you, Linda," Mildred said as she reached out and took her hand. "My life will never be the same without Ollie, but at least he had the good sense to befriend this wonderful group of people or I would be all alone and helpless. They have been a godsend."

The two women exchanged a hug and then Mildred introduced Judith and Linda, who had never met in person. With a smile, Linda said, "So I finally get to meet the woman behind the voice on the CB radio. Thank you so much for all of the daily updates from your HAM radio. I look forward to hearing your updates every morning as I have my tea."

"What kind of tea do you have?" asked Judith. "We ran out of tea a few months ago, but we still have some bulk coffee stores."

"Oh, it's an herbal tea that I make myself and then sweeten and thicken it up with honey from my bees."

Mildred, Judith, and Linda walked up to the porch as they discussed Linda's tea recipe.

Charlie looked at Evan and Jason, pointed down the driveway, and said, "There comes Daryl Moses. That makes all four horses. I gave Will Bailey a ride and Lloyd brought Billy Skidmore. That makes everyone but Jimmy Lewis on the other ATV."

"Where are the others?" asked Jason.

"Oh, they're around back gathering the herd. We got here kind of early," Charlie said.

"I guess that's the storekeeper in you," said Evan with a laugh.

"Yeah, that and we're excited to finally be involved with a community again," he replied. "I probably speak for more than myself to say I was going nuts never leaving my own property. Not to mention the fact that if I ever need help, I know you will all be there for me."

"You've got that right," said Jason.

"Well, gentlemen, let's gather the men. We've got an important job to do before we get started," said Evan.

"What's that?" asked Charlie.

"We've got to bury Ollie," Evan replied. "I talked to Mildred about it last night and she has a place all picked out. She wants him buried here as she plans to return someday when things settle down. We will get the grave prepared and then gather the women and have a small ceremony. I would have preferred to get everyone in the community together for a real service, but we can't risk getting everyone out and leave our homes empty and undefended with all things considered."

Charlie and Jason nodded in agreement. Just as they started to turn and walk around to the back of the property to get the others, Charlie stopped and said, "Well, I'll be damned."

Evan and Jason turned to see what Charlie was staring at and saw Jimmy Lewis walking up the driveway on foot.

"What the heck is he doing on foot? I thought he was bringing an ATV," said Jason.

"Well, let's go see," said Evan.

The three men walked down the driveway and met Jimmy halfway. Charlie said, "Jimmy, are you okay? Where's your quad?"

"Ah, guys, I'm so sorry," Jimmy replied. "When I agreed to bring my quad, I didn't realize I was down to my last bit of gas. I didn't want to back out and let you all down, so I assumed I had enough to get here. I was hoping to borrow enough to get the job done and get home. I ran out about a mile and a half down the road. I'm sorry guys."

"Oh, that's okay, Jimmy; don't sweat it," Evan said. "You're here and that's what matters. Charlie, Ollie has a few gas cans in his shop out back. Why don't you grab one and give Jimmy a ride to go rescue his quad before it grows legs and walks off?

We'll get everything else done. We won't start the ceremony without you."

"Will do. Let's get on it," he said to Jimmy as the two men walked towards Ollie's shop.

Evan and Jason met up with the rest of the men out in the back pasture and went over the plan. "Hey, Jason," Evan said.

"Yeah, boss," Jason replied.

"Can you run and see if there is any fuel in that old excavator Ollie has in the barn? If so, see if you can get it up and running. We can use that to dig the grave if it runs."

"Roger Roger," Jason said as he headed off to the barn.

Evan then turned to Will Bailey and said, "Will, since you're our resident woodworker, do you think you can look around in Ollie's shop and find some hand tools, screws, and nails to put together a coffin? He has tons of wood lying around since he seemed to never throw anything away. Don't sweat the hinges; we can just nail it shut. It will be a proper burial with a casket, and he wouldn't have wanted anything fancy."

"Sure thing; that won't take me long at all," Will replied as he headed off to complete his task.

"I'll give you a hand, Will," Daryl said, following along behind.

Jason returned from the barn after a few minutes and said, "There is fuel in the excavator, but the battery is dead. I found some jumper cables. If you wanna bring the tractor over, we'll try to get it going."

"Sure, I'll bring it over," Evan said as he began to walk towards the tractor.

In the home, Judith, Linda, and Mildred were going through the important things that Mildred wanted to take to the Homefront for safe keeping. She planned to return to her home someday but did not want to risk losing her prize possessions while it sat uninhabited and mostly unguarded.

Mildred sifted through her photos and scrapbooks, detailing her and Ollie's wonderful lives together. Even though their worldly lives together had been cut short by this tragedy, she still considered herself the luckiest woman in the world to have been married to a man of Ollie's caliber. To her, no matter what society used to measure a man, whether it be his career, his level of education, his finances or his social status, Ollie set the standard for her. No level of achievement in a man-made society could ever measure the worth of Oliver Thomas.

Meanwhile, Evan and Jason had gotten the excavator running and started digging Ollie's final resting place. They were burying him exactly where Mildred said he would want to be—underneath a majestic magnolia tree, up on a hill where he and Mildred had shared many summer evenings. The view of their property was breathtaking from there, and she knew that is where he would want to spend eternity.

As they completed the grave, Will Bailey came up the hill and said, "I've got the coffin ready. It's rough around the edges, but it's made from planks from Ollie's own barn so I'm sure he'd approve."

"Knowing Ollie, he wouldn't have wanted it any other way," said Evan.

"It's down by the cellar," Will added. "I assumed you would want to get him all squared away there."

"That's perfect," Evan replied. "Let's go get everything ready, then let's give him one last ride on that old Massey Ferguson. We can hook his trailer to his tractor to get him up here. Then we'll go and get Mildred and Judith when everything is in place."

Jason took the excavator back to the barn and the other men went on down to the cellar, got Ollie positioned in the coffin, and loaded it onto the trailer. Evan drove the tractor, pulling Ollie along on the trailer, up to the magnolia tree on the hill. As he shut the tractor down and climbed off, he saw

Charlie and Jimmy round the corner of the house on their ATVs. They saw him up on the hill and rode up to him. Evan caught the two men up on what they had accomplished while they were retrieving Jimmy's ATV. He then said, "Why don't you two gentlemen go down to the house and ask the ladies if they would like a ride up here and tell them we are about ready."

"Of course. C'mon, Jimmy," Charlie said as the two began to ride down towards the house.

Jason made it back up the hill from the barn and joined Evan as he stood there admiring the view. "I can see why they loved this spot," Jason said.

"Yep, it's understandable why this was their special place," replied Evan. "I guess we should get Lloyd, Billy, and Robert to take a break from the herd if they can, to be a part of this. If you'll go get them, I'll ask Mildred how she wants to handle everything."

With a nod, Jason began his walk to the back pasture. While he was off rounding up the men, Charlie and Jimmy came from the house with Mildred, Linda, and Judith. Judith rode on the back of Charlie's seat, Mildred on Jimmy's, and Linda sat on the front of Jimmy's cargo rack with her feet dangling off. She was dressed to herd cattle so it was not an inconvenience to her at all.

As they arrived at the top of the hill, all of the men present took off their hats and placed them over their hearts as Mildred slowly walked over to the casket. She gently rubbed her hand down the full length of the casket as she walked. She seemed to be lost in her own memories for a moment. It was then that Jason returned with the other men.

"Well, it looks like we are all here," Evan said.

The men surrounded the casket and lifted it off the trailer. Mildred laid a beautiful handpicked bouquet of flowers from her and Ollie's own flower garden on top of the casket and nodded for the men to proceed. They lowered him into the ground with straps from the trailer and then took a few paces back.

"Would anyone like to say a few words?" Evan asked.

"You do it," said Mildred to Evan. "You and Jason have spent more time with Ollie, other than myself, than anyone lately. I know he, or rather we, look upon you two as sons and not merely neighbors."

"I would be honored, ma'am," he said. Evan took a step forward and began. "I know I speak for all of us when I say that the value of a man is not defined by what he does for himself, but rather what he gives of himself to others. Ollie was a veteran of Korea. He was a combat veteran who survived things of which most of us, even in the current state of things, will never have to endure. You could see the strength he must have had during those times in his daily life here. Not only was he an extremely loyal and devoted husband and father, but he was a protector and a guardian of others. It was Ollie that insisted we check on Isaac Murphy, even when the danger was staring us in the face. He pushed forward through a hail of bullets to rescue me from a pinned-down position, putting himself at great risk. If not for Ollie's insistence to put ourselves in that position to help a friend, we would not have found young Haley. He then showed another side of his strength when he took in Haley, who had been through a hell on earth, and gave her a wonderful home and a family. No, the value of a man—a real man—cannot be measured in things, but is measured, instead, in the lasting impression that he has made as a role model for other men to follow. To the women in his life, he is an example of what should be expected of a man if he is to be worthy of her. No pile of gold left behind to heirs will ever be equal to what Ollie has left behind in hearts. I just hope that someday Molly will look at me with the love and admiration that Mildred has for Ollie, and that other men will use the strength of my character as a goal to live up to, as I do of Ollie's. We are all blessed to have known him."

"Amen," said everyone softly as Evan stepped back.

Mildred then said, "Thank you, Evan. Thank you all for everything you have done and continue to do for us. The greatest thing Ollie has left me, besides the wonderful memories, is the love I feel from each of you here today. Ollie's memory will live on not just in my heart, but also in your hearts, as well as young Haley's. Thank you for this wonderful moment on this beautiful day. If God keeps me around for a while, I will spend many an evening under this tree, celebrating in the memories of my wonderful life. This is a gift you have all given me here today."

There was not a dry eye in the crowd. Everyone mourned the loss of Ollie, but even in death, he had managed to give them resolve. It was unspoken, but everyone in the community felt as if they were now strengthened, and that they would all be a lot closer now, as a real community, not just a trading confederacy.

Chapter 22: The Observer

After the ceremony and the burial was complete, the group got on with the task at hand, which was relocating Mildred and her livestock to their temporary new home at the Homefront. As Mildred and Judith were escorted back to the house by Charlie and Jimmy, Linda and the rest of the men stood around in a circle, going over the game plan. As Robert Brooks finished giving his recommendations as to how to best move the cattle as a herd, Jason interjected and said, "Sounds great; now you guys go pretend you're doing that while Evan and I deal with something."

The men started to get confused and Jason continued, "Don't look around. Keep standing here as if everything is normal while I explain. Earlier I saw a glint of light halfway up the ridge directly in front of me. Don't turn and look!" he reiterated. "I'm sure we are getting glassed. Whoever it is, isn't very schooled in the art of surveillance, or they would realize the angle of the sun to their location would cause reflections of light that give their position away. My guess is, whoever was taking the cattle and shot Ollie hasn't moved on just because they lost a few buddies. This herd is priceless in a hungry world."

"What's the plan?" asked Evan pretending to continue with the business at hand.

Jason then proceeded to say, "Let's have Charlie and Jimmy stay with Mildred and Judith while everyone else tends to the herd. Evan and I will slip away while we pretend to be working in the cellar, and then we will head for the woods where the observer is. We will split up and try to pinch him in while he is busy watching you guys deal with the cattle. Since we can probably assume the herd is their primary target, they will more than likely be focusing on what you're doing. Act as normal as you can and don't look that way. We don't want them to realize that we are on to them. If you hear a gunshot, sprint for cover. It may be them shooting at you, it may be them shooting at us, it may be us shooting at them, or us simply trying to warn you. In any case, be conscious of your surroundings and have a place in mind to take cover at all times."

Everyone nodded in agreement and Robert Brooks said, "Okay, men, let's move some cattle."

As the main group went back to the pasture to tend to the herd, Evan and Jason went to the barn. Once inside, they placed their rifles, which had been in the barn while they were working, albeit a tactical error to have been without them, inside the empty space within an old pallet. They then carried the pallet in plain view over to the cellar, which was built into the hillside and surrounded by tree branches. The shade of the trees and the subterranean architecture gave the cellar its cool storage qualities, and in this situation, it gave Evan and Jason the concealment needed to slip off into the woods.

"Hopefully they'll just think we are dragging an old pallet over here for random reasons and will lose interest and turn their attention back to the herd," Jason said.

"Unless they think we brought a pallet over here because there are bulk items of potential value in the cellar that we would need a pallet to move," Evan replied.

"True," Jason said. He then nudged the rifles out of the pallet with his foot, sliding them onto the ground. Once the rifles were out of the pallet, he took a nearby axe and began to knock the pallet apart in plain view. As he popped a board loose, he would stack the wood neatly as if he were merely using the pallet for scrap wood. As he was putting on this show for any potential hostile observer, Evan slipped off into the woods with his VZ58 and Jason's Remington. Jason then leaned the axe against a tree and sat down as if he was simply taking a break.

After a few moments, he thought to himself that surely the observer had lost interest by now and had looked away. With that hope in mind, he slowly got up and walked into the woods, out of sight.

He met up with Evan, got his rifle, and said, "Okay, you go straight up and over the hill. Come back around to where you think you would be behind him to block a direct escape. I'll give you a few minutes to get in place, and then I'll creep up the hill and go at him horizontally. I'll either get him in sight, in which case I'll make it up as I go or he'll get bumped like a bedded down deer and you can do whatever you need to do."

"We need intel, so if at all possible, keep him breathing, which I know is asking a lot from you," said Evan with a smirk on his face.

"I can only do what he will let me do," Jason replied. "It's hard to merely wound with a .300 Win Mag, though," he said as he grinned back.

"Dude, you get more jacked up by the day," Evan said jokingly.

"It's called battle-hardened, my brother; jacked up is what the thugs become," Jason replied.

"Okay, get on with it, funny man," Evan replied in jest with Jason's familiar, "Roger Roger."

"Keep it up and I might miss and let him head your way," Jason replied as he slipped off into the woods towards the observer.

Evan laughed and headed up the hill. He found a well-worn game trail and used it to make good time up the hill without making too much noise. As he crested the ridge, he began to move horizontally towards the last known position of the observer, on the backside of the hill out of sight. As he moved across the hill, he found boot prints. Some older, but some fairly fresh. They led up over the hill to the approximate location of the observer. He also found a cigarette butt that appeared to have not been there long, as it wasn't weathered at all and was warm to the touch. He wondered if this was a routine observation point that the intruders used to try to pattern Ollie's movements and to estimate force strength on the farm. He thought that surely they had seen him and Jason there multiple times, always armed, which may explain why they were lying low before their encounter.

As Jason moved ever so slowly and quietly towards the observer, he got a glimpse of the man through his scope. He couldn't get a clear view of the man's face, as he too was using the scope on his rifle to watch the men working below. It appeared to be a lever action rifle, perhaps a .30-30 or the like. *Not much range with that from his position*, Jason thought to himself. He truly must only be on lookout or something. *"Hmmm, leave him breathing,"* Jason said to himself as he adjusted the windage and elevation on his riflescope for a very well placed shot. With a light touch of the trigger, followed by a sharp boom from his muzzle, the intruder's rifle slammed into his face while shattering into shards of metal and wood. Jason had aimed for the man's rifle with the intent of taking him out of the fight without killing him. The impact shoved the scope of the man's rifle into his right eye, nearly blinding him. As blood poured down his face from the impact as well as the shrapnel from the shattered rifle and the impacting bullet, he dropped the gun and began to sprint up the hill towards Evan in retreat.

Down below, the men working the herd immediately dove for cover as directed as soon as they heard Jason's shot ring out across the valley. They remained behind cover for the time being, not knowing who fired the shot.

As the man ran up the hill towards the ridge, Evan could hear him clumsily running through the brush making tremendous noise while crunching through the dead autumn leaves in haste. Evan ducked down behind some vegetation, and as the man approached him, he came out of nowhere with the metal folding butt stock of the VZ58 and smashed the man across the face, knocking him back onto the ground. The man landed on his back with several broken teeth and a spray of blood flying out of his now busted mouth. Evan immediately jumped on the man with one foot on his throat and the barrel of his rifle pressed so hard into the man's forehead that the AK style slant muzzle break was cutting into his skin.

"Move and die," Evan said in a voice full of rage.

Just then, Jason emerged from the woods saying, "Ev, it's me!"

"I'm on him," Evan replied.

"That worked like a charm," Jason said, referring to his intentional shot into the man's rifle.

"What did?" Evan asked.

"Oh, I'll explain later," he replied.

While Evan held the man on the ground with his boot and rifle, he asked him, "What the hell are you doing here?"

The man could barely talk with a swollen mouth full of blood. Jason removed the man's side-arm from his waistband, as he was carrying a small .38 snub nose revolver.

"You had better bring a lot more gun than that if you're gonna be invading other people's homesteads these days," Jason said. "There is no 911 we have to call... no cops to explain where we get the fertilizer we use in our gardens or our slop for the pigs, so speak up when he talks to you, or our pigs are gonna get meat tonight," Jason said as he kicked the man in the side.

"You blew out my eye. I can't see out of my eye!" the man whined as he writhed in pain beneath Evan's boot, spitting blood as he spoke.

Jason searched the rest of the man's pockets and the small daypack he was carrying. He had several packs of Marlboro red package cigarettes, the same kind found on the other invaders, as well as a hand-drawn map of the property.

"Phillip Morris must be doing well in the collapse," Jason said. "There sure hasn't been a shortage of smokes around here lately."

"Speak up," Evan demanded. "Who are you with?"

"Just a bunch of guys that got together after it all fell apart," the man said.

"Just a bunch of guys that got together to do what?" Evan replied as he felt his rage grow. It took everything he had to keep himself from stomping the man's throat in. "Got together to rape, pillage, loot, rob? You saw an opportunity and you took it, didn't you?"

"We just do what we have to do like everyone else. It's dog eat dog. Nothing personal, just survival," he said.

"Well, I've got news for you, scumbag," said Evan as he gritted his teeth and bore down harder on the man's forehead with his rifle. "You bit the wrong dog. I don't know how many people you have hurt or killed in the past year, but it's over. Your group killed a dear friend of ours while looting his property. That's not gonna stand unanswered. You can tell us everything you know and we will let you go, as long as you promise not to hook back up with them and clean yourself up, or you can die right here and be our pig slop. Your choice," Evan said as he put more pressure on the man's throat, nearly closing off his windpipe.

The man stayed silent and struggled under Evan's boot. After a moment, Jason pulled out his knife, bent down, and cut the man's shirt open, leaving a shallow cut on the man's stomach.

"Should I gut him here like an elk or drag him out and do it in the barn like a deer?" asked Jason.

“I don’t feel like dragging him out heavy, so let’s do it here,” Evan said in a nonchalant manner. “He’ll be a lot lighter without his guts.”

“Roger that,” said Jason as he began to pierce the man’s flesh with his knife just above his navel.

“Noooo! No, please don’t—I’ll talk, I’ll talk!” the man replied with panic in his voice.

“How many are there of you total?” asked Evan.

“About fourteen, I think. I’ve never counted,” the man said.

“Where are you staying? Where are you guys holding up while you rob us?”

“With a guy named Frank. We met him working a deal on the smokes,” the man said.

“Frank Muncie?” Evan asked.

“I think we never really use last names. He’s got a couple younger brothers there too,” said the man as he struggled to breathe.

“What deal?” Evan asked relaxing his boot now that the man was talking.

“Frank had come into a truckload of smokes on another deal. He wanted to trade them all for a girl. He said there weren't any good women around here,” the man said.

While trying to contain his rage, Evan said, “So you traded a girl for smokes?”

“Yeah,” he answered.

“Where is the girl now?” Evan calmly asked with an unimaginable rage growing inside.

“She was black, and he said he didn’t like dark meat, so when he was done with her, he gave her to the other guys and...”

“And what?” Evan demanded.

The man began to realize he had said too much for his own good. “Well, some of the other guys, not me, were a little too rough with her and she didn’t make it,” he said hesitantly.

"You mean you killed her?" Jason shouted.

"Not me man, not me, the other guys," he said.

"Isn't it funny how the guy spilling the beans is always innocent," Evan said to Jason.

"Yep, ironic," Jason replied.

"I've had about as much of this piece of trash as I can stomach. Let's take him back down to the barn," Evan said.

"I thought you said you were gonna let me go!" the man demanded.

"Oh, we will, and we will give you the same consideration you gave her," Evan replied. "Jason, paracord his feet. I'll get his hands," Evan said as they tied the man up and gagged him.

They dragged him down the hill feet first, over rocks and thorns and anything in their path. He attempted to scream the entire way down the hill, as he was lacerated and bruised all over due to the rough treatment. Evan and Jason weren't intentionally being cruel to the man; they had just stopped seeing him and his kind as human. He and his group were a threat to them and every other decent person who they may choose to target next.

When they got back down the hill, they signaled for the others to join them. They dragged the man across the field and around behind the barn.

"Holy hell, what did you do to him?" asked Robert Brooks.

"He tripped and fell... a few hundred times," said Jason.

Evan and Jason then went on to explain everything they had seen and what was going on at the Muncie place. They shared with the others the disgusting details of their vicious behavior and left it up to the group to decide what to do with him. A few ideas were tossed around, such as simply killing him on the spot or letting him return to warn the others to move on.

Evan then said, "Gentleman, there is only one way to deal with this kind of thing right now. There is no law enforcement to turn him over to; there is no jail to put him in. He signed on with those raping and murdering scumbags, who killed Ollie, by the way, because he is like them. No decent human being could be part of that sort of thing. We can't rehabilitate him, and we can't detain him. I only see one answer. Is it the most civilized answer? No, it's not. Do I wish things were different? Yes, of course I do. In a different time or place, I would simply turn him over to the police, but we simply do not have that option."

"I've got an idea that will send a very clear message to his partners in crime," said Daryl Moses.

"What's that?" Charlie Blanchard asked.

"Well, let's send them a very strong message, get some payback, and reduce their numbers all at the same time," he said.

"Now you're talking," said Jason. "Let's hear it."

Chapter 23: The Trojan Horse

Back in Texas, Nate and Luke were both feeling as if the world was finally coming together for them. After receiving the news over the radio that their mother was actively looking for them, Luke joined Nate in sharing the planning and preparations for the trip. They truly felt like brothers again. Luke now visited Nate every evening to help him with his physical therapy and fitness plan. Afterward, they would discuss the trip. Nate shared all of his lessons learned from his journey to Texas and how those lessons may apply in the rest of the journey to Tennessee. At this point, however, their planning was incomplete, as they did not know where in Tennessee she was located.

As Luke came by for his evening visit, Nate asked, “Any word from Mom?”

“No, I checked with the station radio operator,” replied Luke. “She said the Survivors’ Locator Network has no way of contacting individuals on the list; they simply wait for them to check in from time to time, at which point they relay any messages they have in que for them. She checks in on our behalf daily now but says they haven’t received anything from the other end in a week.”

“Man, I can’t wait to get a location. Then it’s just a little bit of final planning and we’re off!” said Nate.

“Are you sure your leg is up to whatever may come, including extended hikes over rough terrain?” asked Luke.

“As ready as ever,” Nate confidently responded. “It’s not like it’s a pirate’s peg leg. This thing works pretty well once you learn to trust it. Besides, it gives me a fifty percent less chance of dying from a snake bite while hiking through the woods than you.”

“Touché, brother,” Luke said with a grin. “I can already see this is going to be quite the adventure with you.”

“So how are things going with Rachel?” Nate asked changing the subject.

“It’s going great except for the leaving part. We’ve been spending as much time together as we can. She knows I’m not going to just run off and forget about her. She also feels much better knowing that Mom now has access to a HAM radio. We can keep in touch that way and not lose each other.”

Just then, a loud explosion rocked the compound. The lights went dark as the generator shut down. “What the hell?” exclaimed Nate as he jumped out of bed to see what was going on. Unfortunately, in the chaos of the situation, he leapt out of bed out of reflex, not remembering that he had relaxed the adjustments on his prosthesis. Having just finished his workout, he was trying to give his leg some much-needed blood flow. The loose fit caused him to lose his footing and he went crashing to the floor. Gunfire erupted outside of the building as the smell of smoke and fire began to creep into his room. In the confusion and the darkness, Nate struggled to get his prosthesis squared away so that he could get up and be ready for whatever may come.

Luke ran to his side and tried to help him get himself together with a pen light that he always carried in his pocket for patient use. “Are you okay?” he asked in a panic.

“Yeah, I’m fine. Grab my pack—it’s got my 9mm in the top,” Nate said as he got his leg donned properly and got to his feet. Luke handed him his pack and Nate immediately reached inside to retrieve his Beretta M9. He snapped the paddle holster onto his belt and racked a round into the chamber, readying himself in the event the facility was overrun. “What the hell was that?” he asked Luke as he went over to the door to listen for movement in the hallway.

"We've been hit before. Usually just harassing fire, an IED, or car bomb on the street. That sounded like it was inside the building, though." They could still hear gunfire outside as Luke said, "They also don't usually stay in the engagement after contact. They must be stepping it up a bit. Can you see what's going on in the hallway?" he asked.

Nate cracked the door open and looked around. "I don't see or hear anything, so I'm gonna check it out," he said. As he looked out into the dark, smoke-filled hallway, he could hear yelling off in the distance, but nothing in their immediate area.

"Nate, we've got to get to Rachel," Luke said with a worried tone.

"Where would she be right now?" Nate asked.

"Probably the triage room just off of the main ward. She was on shift when I came down here. It's straight down the hall to the double doors, then just a little ways down on the right," Luke said.

"Where's your sidearm?" asked Nate.

"In my locker, just past the ward," he replied.

"Seriously?" Nate said in a frustrated manner. "C'mon man. Step it up. We are in the homestretch. Don't get lazy on me now."

"I know, I know; you can bitch at me later. Let's get to the triage," replied Luke.

"Okay, then cover behind me. We'll stick to the left when going down the hall to set us up for the double door opening on the left," said Nate as he proceeded into the hall. Luke followed closely behind, shining his light in their direction of travel as necessary.

Upon reaching the double doors, Nate looked through the window on the door and said, "I can see some light coming from the ward, but that's it."

"They have standby battery-powered lights for when the generator is shut down," Luke replied. "Do you see any movement?"

"No, but it looks like someone is down in the hall," Nate said. "They are moving around but appear to be incapacitated. You go help and I'll follow along and cover you."

Without hesitation, Luke ran down the hallway and began to attend to the wounded man while Nate scanned the triage area for threats and survivors. "He's alive, just banged up," Luke said. "C'mon, Mr. Walker, snap out of it," said Luke to the man.

"It's a mess in here, no survivors," said Nate reluctantly as he cleared the triage.

Luke leapt to his feet and ran into the room only to be horrified by the carnage. There was blood and the battered, dismembered, and charred remains of several of the medical staff personnel and patients. He looked frantically for any survivors, but alas, there were none to be found. He thankfully did not see any signs of Rachel among the horror scene that only moments before was their bustling triage unit.

"He's waking up!" yelled Nate from the hall.

Luke rushed back out to the hallway to care for Nick Walker, a retired firefighter who had been a TSG medical volunteer. "You're okay, Mr. Walker. You look like you got out of there just in time to miss most of the blast but got caught up in the concussion from it. You took a good hit, but you seem intact. Can you talk? Are you having any pain?" Luke asked him.

"My head... oh, my head hurts, and my ears are ringing and are very painful, other than that, I think I just got the wind knocked out of me," he responded wincing in pain as he moved his jaw.

"What in the hell happened?" asked Luke.

Mr. Walker struggled with ear pain for a moment and then composed himself enough to explain. He said, “Someone dropped off a wounded man at the front entrance who was bleeding heavily from the abdomen. The people who dropped him off just sped away. We could see that he would die without our help, so we rushed him in to get him assessed by Doc Stewart, hoping that she could possibly save him. She was in the restroom when we brought him in, so Lucinda cut open his shirt to look at the wound. His abdomen was covered with bloody cloth bandages. As she tried to remove them, Kyle saw a wire that was tied to the bandages pull at something inside of him. He was crudely stitched together, and I guess Kyle realized it was a bomb lodged inside the man and screamed for us to get out, but it was too late. I just happened to be on my way out to get some fluids for his IV when I heard Kyle scream. I turned out of reflex, saw the wire in the man’s stomach, and dove for the door before it all went dark.”

“So Doctor Stewart wasn’t in there for sure?” Luke asked frantically.

“She had gone to the restroom is all I know,” Mr. Walker repeated.

“Stay here with him,” Luke said to Nate as he got up and ran down the hall.

Luke busted through the double doors into the other hallway as he ran to find Rachel when TSG security personnel entered the hall yelling, “On the floor! On the floor now! Hands out to the side and empty!”

The men pointed their M4 carbines at him while another TSG soldier frisked him and shined a light in his face. “He’s ours, let him up!” the soldier yelled.

Luke got up from the floor and pointed at Nate and Mr. Walker who now had the attention of the security personnel and said, “Those two are good! The one on the floor is hurt and I’m looking for Doc Stewart.”

Just then, a woman's voice yelled out from down the darkened hallway, "Lucas!"

Luke turned to see Rachel running to him. She grabbed him in an emotional embrace and began crying. She said, "I went to Nate's room after the explosion and you two were gone. I was so afraid something had happened to you. Oh, thank God you're okay," she said as she wiped the tears from her face. It was then that she turned and looked down the other hall to see Nate kneeling down with Mr. Walker lying on the floor and the triage unit's door blown off of the hinges. She yelled out, "Oh my God, no!" and ran to the triage. She looked in the room at the blood and carnage and collapsed to her knees. Her coworkers and the patient were killed and were barely recognizable. She put her hands to her face and began to cry.

One of the TSG soldiers looked at Luke and said, "When the confusion hit from the bomb going off inside the building, our guys out front standing watch at the entry point were ambushed with a barrage of automatic fire. One is confirmed dead, the other is critical. We need you and the Doc ASAP!" the soldier said.

"We're on it," said Luke as he jogged over to Rachel as she knelt on the floor just outside of the triage. "Rachel," he said as he leaned over and put his hand gently on her shoulder. "An injured soldier needs us. I know it's hard to put this horrible stuff aside and just go right back to work, but that's all too often what we must do. Another horrible tragedy could happen in someone else's life if we don't."

She wiped away the tears and nodded in agreement, still too choked up to speak. They stood up and rushed to follow the TSG personnel to the fallen soldier. The other security personnel on the scene had dragged the wounded soldier inside during the firefight. A trail of blood led from where he fell after being shot all the way into the building to where he was now lying on the floor in the middle of an administrative office. Another TSG soldier had been applying pressure to his wounds while they waited for Luke and Doctor Stewart to arrive.

As they entered the room, Luke rushed to his side, knelt in front of him, and started gathering vital signs while Rachel got an assessment of his wounds. His liver had been pierced, as had one of his lungs. He had a severe sucking chest wound and could barely breathe as he choked and gasped for air as his lungs filled with blood. Rachel ordered Luke to treat the chest wound with a vent flap while she assessed further. She found another wound in his lower abdomen. Her eyes filled with tears as she thought to herself, *how did he last this long*?

She looked at Luke and just said, "Morphine... give him two hundred and fifty milligrams of morphine."

Luke looked at her with confusion, as that high of a dosage would simply put him to sleep, with no chance of ever waking up. He could see it in her eyes that there was no chance of saving him.

"Ease his pain," she said. "Those are my orders."

He nodded and grabbed the morphine out of the medical bag that one of the other soldiers who had been administering first aid had already brought to the scene. He gave the dosage as ordered, and as the dying soldier slipped off to sleep for the very last time, Rachel broke down into an inconsolable cry. She looked up at the other soldiers and through the tears, mouthed the words, "I'm sorry." She had seen death and suffering before, but today had simply pushed her over the edge. She was a new doctor and had volunteered her services with the TSG, in part because it was the patriotic thing to do for her state, but also for the experience. This, however, was much more than she had bargained for.

While they were tending to the dying soldier, Nate was directed to return to his quarters. He did so reluctantly and just sat in the dark, waiting for word from Luke. After about an hour, the generator kicked back on and with it, the lights.

Nate eventually fell asleep, fully dressed and with his 9mm lying on his chest. He awoke the next morning to a sad and somber scene. The friendly smiles of the local volunteer nurses and medical assistants simply were not there. The only people there were the surviving security staff from the previous day who were just now being relieved by the next watch rotation.

At around nine in the morning, Luke finally arrived at Nate's room. The two brothers exchanged their thoughts about the previous night's attack for a while, and out of nowhere, Luke changed the subject. "It's time we get going, and Rachel is coming with us."

"What? Seriously, that's great... uh... I mean, I guess. What caused her to decide to go?" said Nate pleased with the news but a bit confused.

"She said she can't handle the trauma," Luke said. "She nearly had a nervous breakdown last night. She's fresh out of medical school. She would merely be an intern in any other reality, but because of the limited resources, they just threw her into this job and hoped for the best."

"But she did so well with my amputation," Nate said.

"Well, actually, you were out of it for most of that, so I guess you don't remember," Luke explained. "Doctor Patel actually performed your operation; she merely assisted and did the in-person follow-ups with you."

"Who's Doctor Patel?" Nate asked.

"He stops by from time to time to check up on the place. Luckily for you, he was in town when you were brought in. He's been getting progress reports from Rachel over the radio. He says you're ready to go," said Luke as he patted Nate on the shoulder. "Good timing, too, I might add. You'd have to go, anyway, since they are shutting this place down. After last night's attack, the city leaders don't want to host us anymore, and since the Governor doesn't want us to seem like an occupying force, we've gotta go. So... long story short, she's decided to go with us. She doesn't want to simply be reassigned to another war torn town and not know if we will ever see each other again. Besides, she figures they will probably need a doctor wherever we end up, anyway."

"Well," Nate said, "I'm sorry it's under these circumstances, but I'm glad. I was really starting to feel like a jerk for dragging you away from her."

"So back to the plan," Luke said, changing the subject. "I asked the HAM operator here to send one more message to the Survivors' Locator Network for us. I told them to tell Mom and Dad that their sons are leaving Texas and heading for Tennessee. ETA unknown. Please leave specific location information for the next contact."

"That should do it," replied Nate. "But how do we make further contact if we are leaving our HAM setup here behind?"

"Oh, she also gave me a list of HAM operators who are friendly to TSG personnel that are located along our potential routes of travel," Luke added, "And one more thing–I may have found us safe passage into Mississippi, which could cut off a lot of time."

"How is that?" Nate asked. "And from what I remember, safe passage is hard to come by around here."

"Texas, Louisiana, and Mississippi all have an unwritten defensive alliance," Luke explained. "They loan and trade resources to one another and share intel. The TSG has a C-130 heading to Tupelo, and I may have gotten us a ride."

"Wow, little brother, and here I thought I was the one leading this reckless expedition into the unknown," joked Nate.

"Oh, you are," Luke said. "That's as far as I can get us on my connections, the rest is up to you."

Chapter 24: Resolve

Back in Tennessee on the Thomas farm, Daryl had proposed an idea to the rest of the group on how to deal with the member of the murderous group that they had been holding as a prisoner. "So what exactly is our goal here?" he asked. "Is it simply to run the vermin off so that other people will be raped, robbed, or killed in their wake? Is it merely revenge? Or do we want to fix this situation permanently? As Evan said, we just don't have a way to deal with this guy, or their entire group, in a peaceful and legal manner. I also truly believe that if we just run them off or let them go, we will be facilitating more of the horrendous crimes of which they are already guilty. I would call them animals, but I have a deep respect for animals. They are monsters. They need to be dealt with as such."

"What do you propose?" asked Evan.

"Yeah, are you suggesting that we just kill them all?" responded Billy Skidmore with skepticism. "Like we could even do that without taking casualties ourselves. Just look at Ollie, and that's just from meeting them in the woods."

Daryl stroked his beard as he said, "True, if we met them in a head-on battle or an assault, chances are we would suffer casualties as well. That's not something I'm suggesting. In the area where we do have an advantage is freedom of movement and the element of surprise. If we are all in on this together, we can move about freely, using each homestead as a lookout. As far as the element of surprise goes, we know who they are. We know where they live. We know how they think. They, on the other hand, see us as individuals and assume we don't know much about them. They probably also see themselves as the wolves and us the sheep. I see it quite differently. They are the wolves, but we are the bears."

"I like where you are going with this," said Jason.

"The one thing we do need is anonymity," added Daryl. "We need them to believe that there is an organized group—not necessarily associated with any of the homesteads—keeping an eye on the area. We don't want reprisals while we are dealing with them. We want them to feel on the run and intimidated, not empowered to take revenge. We need to basically seem like a group of secret guardians for the area."

"I like that concept," said Evan. "That could actually work for us in the future too. It would give people some sort of feeling that there is a law around here, even if the law can't readily be identified. People behave a lot better when they know there will be consequences for their actions."

"So how do you propose we deal with these guys?" asked Charlie.

"Well," Daryl said, "I think we can snipe at them for one. Jason has that fancy rifle there that he seems to be pretty handy with at long ranges. I've got a Savage Model 12 LRP in 6.5 Creedmoor that I can knock the tits off a fly with at one thousand yards. What do you guys have in long-range stuff?"

"Evan's got a fifty," added Jason.

"A .50 BMG?" asked Daryl.

"Yeah, it's one of those single shot bolt-action uppers made to mate up with an AR-15 lower," Evan replied. "It came in pretty dang handy to Griff last year when the Homefront came under attack before Jason and I got here."

Jimmy spoke up and said, "I don't have anything as tacti-cool as a fifty, but I do have a 7mm Rem Mag with a good scope. It may not bust down walls at one thousand yards, but it will drop thin-skinned two-legged game at that range."

"See guys, with those four rifles we could do some serious harassing fire to whittle them away or just to soften them up," Daryl said. "And to set the tone, I have a special gift I could make for them."

"What's that?" asked Robert.

"A flint bomb," said Daryl with a smile.

"A what?" several people asked.

"A flint bomb," he said. "It's simple, really. It's no secret that I make my own black powder, and I have quite a bit of it. I have plenty to spare for a special occasion such as today. Black powder is very explosive compared to modern smokeless gunpowder. If we mix a couple pounds of it with some nails and other debris and put it in some sort of container, we would have an anti-personnel bomb."

"What would you use for the ignition source?" asked Jason with a very intrigued look on his face.

"Simple," he said. "A lock from an old style flintlock rifle. They are so simple to use for something like this. When you pull the trigger on a cocked flintlock rifle, the hammer falls striking the frizzen. The piece of flint held in place on the hammer creates a spark against the frizzen that ignites the powder in the flash pan. In this case, it just sparks, igniting the surrounding black powder. All we have to do is to mount a flintlock mechanism into the powder container, cock it, then tie a line or string to the trigger. Once the trigger is tripped, by whatever method we deem appropriate, it goes... BOOM! Goodbye to anyone in the area."

"I'm glad you're on our side, Daryl," Jason joked. "That's genius."

"Not genius at all. When you're single and into gunpowder as a hobby, you have a lot of time on your hands to think things up," Daryl replied.

"So just how do we get them in position for your bomb?" asked Charlie.

"A backpack," replied Daryl. "You know... jihadist style."

"And just who is the jihadist?" once again asked Charlie.

"Your observer over there, of course," said Daryl as he pointed to the man Evan and Jason had captured.

Everyone got silent for a moment at the thought of Daryl's suggestion. They were serious when they were discussing it earlier, but all of a sudden when you put a human face on any destructive act, it puts the reality back into the situation. The jovial mood was now extinguished, but that did not change the fact that they intended to end this situation permanently. They would not be sheep in their own homes.

"You guys, this just doesn't feel right," said Robert.

"Well, what else do you propose?" asked Daryl. "Look, like we have said several times, we can't deal with them, and we can't just turn them loose on the men, women, and children the next town over either. Are you willing to let someone in your family die because you tried to be fair with these guys and they won?"

After a moment of silence, Robert said, "No, you're right Daryl. I just can't believe it has come to this."

Evan spoke up and said, "Robert, most of you folks around here are lucky, with the exception of Isaac Murphy and Ollie, of course. We, on the other hand, have faced this sort of menace over and over. Many of us at the Homefront were in the New York City area when everything went down. We had a long and bumpy road to get back to Tennessee. We lost some great people along the way, and we had to do things that in any other time or place simply would not have even been an option on the table. But you know what? If we didn't, none of us would be here. As Jason here put it to us back then, you have to be aggressive enough, soon enough, to deal with the situation. If you expect things to work themselves out any other way than to cause heartache for yourself or others, you're sadly mistaken. I, for one, believe that not one life of any member of our families is worth risking out of concern that whatever we do to them may not be fair. Well, nothing is fair right now, but I'm not going to sit on the sidelines and wait for one of those murdering, raping, monsters to hurt one of my children or loved ones. I vow right here, to be aggressive enough, right now, to end this."

"Me too," said Jason.

"And me," added Daryl.

"Count me in," said Charlie.

"Let's do it," said Jimmy.

"I'm in," said Billy.

"You're right. Let's get it done," said Robert as he came to terms with their new reality.

"So let's get back to the anonymous nature of the task at hand," Daryl said, getting back on track. "I think it may add a little intimidation factor if we go by a group name like we were saying. We need them to not know who it is or what our total force strength may be. Personally, I like *The Guardians*."

"That does have a nice ring to it," Evan said. "And it sums things up a little better than if we were a militia or the like since we do not intend to be a formal unit, but rather a secret group of men who merely stand watch over our fellow neighbors," he said.

"Not to mention the fact that there has been so much anti-militia propaganda put out by the administration, that using a name associated with a militia is like volunteering for the next drone strike," Jason added.

The men just chuckled in agreement and then Evan said, "Okay fellas, let's get back to the task at hand. Let's get our friend here down in the basement of the main house where we can lock him up good and secure while we move the cattle and Mildred's things. While we are doing that, Daryl, why don't you head back to your place, whip up your flint bomb, and then meet us at the Homefront. We will work on a finalized plan from there on how to get the ball rolling."

Everyone agreed and Evan and Jason volunteered to deal with the prisoner while the others got back to the herd. They put the man into a large wheelbarrow and wheeled him to the lower basement entrance to the house. They did not want to take him through the upstairs, as the women were present and they would prefer to keep the dirty details to themselves if at all possible. Once they got him to the basement, which had a very secure door that could be locked from the outside, they gagged him and tied him securely to a chair inside of the utility closet. They then tied the chair to a support beam going from the floor to the ceiling.

"We will be back," Evan said to the man as he and Jason began to walk out of the room. Before they exited, he turned to the man and said, "At least you had better hope we come back. If your friends out there ambush us and take us out, we won't be able to come back for you and it will take you quite some time to starve to death down here." He then turned around and walked out, slamming and locking the door behind him.

As Evan and Jason left the house via the downstairs basement door, Mildred yelled down to them from the screened in porch above. "What were you two doing down there?" she said in a suspicious voice.

"Just putting some things away for later," he said.

"Was that a gunshot I heard about an hour ago?" she asked.

"Yes, ma'am, it was," he replied. "Jason saw something, and he had to deal with it. It's taken care of now, we will explain more when we get to the house, but the sun will be across the sky before we know it so we have to get back to the cattle."

"Okay," she said reluctantly. "We have everything ready to go in here."

"Great, we'll help you load it all up just before we hit the road," he said.

"Oh, nonsense; we aren't helpless just because we are women. Where do you want us to put it? We will go ahead and load it all up."

"Well, I guess you can put it on the flatbed attached to the Ford. We will probably use your trailer hooked to your Massey Ferguson to load the smaller animals," he said.

"It just sounds so weird you referring to it as my tractor instead of Ollie's. But you're right, of course. I'll get used to it eventually," she said as she stepped back into the house.

Evan felt guilty about not being completely up-front with her, but they had a job to do and they did not have time to keep debating everyone about it. Besides, he sort of felt like she could see right through him and understood, just like when Ollie would bend things a little bit in order to say it in front of Haley or other guests. *She is an amazing woman and no man would ever beat her in a game of wits,* Evan thought to himself as he and Jason walked off to join the other men.

Chapter 25: Tupelo Bound

After Luke left Nate's room to go check on Rachel, Nate went through his things one more time. He sure wished he would have gotten his shotgun back after his accident. He felt vulnerable starting out on such a journey with nothing more than a handgun. He knew the odds of getting all the way to Tennessee without getting into some sort of altercation were slim to none.

After he got his things arranged, he pulled out his map of the area and tried to plan a route but realized that until they hear something more specific about his mother's whereabouts, he really had no idea which direction to go from Tupelo. *Oh well. Surely, they will have a HAM setup in Tupelo at the guard base there,* he thought.

Luke returned to Nate's room about an hour later. He had a bedroll and some MREs. "I've got some stuff for you for the trip."

"Thanks, the MREs will really come in handy, but I've already got a sleeping bag," Nate said.

"You'll like this sleeping bag," replied Luke as he placed it on Nate's bed and rolled it open.

As he rolled it open, he exposed two Colt M4 carbines. The uppers and lowers were separated at the takedown pins in order to get them to fit inside of a sleeping bag for discreet travel until they reached Tupelo. Once on their own, they could quickly be reassembled.

Nate smiled and said, "You never cease to amaze me, little brother. Where did you score these?"

"They are packing up and breaking this place down right now to get ready for the move," Luke explained. "That sort of makes it easy. I was only able to get six thirty-round magazines of 5.56mm ball ammo for them, but that should do the job for anything short of an all-out battle. We can each carry three mags, plus you've got your Beretta."

"That's way better than what I thought we would have, so no complaints from me," Nate responded. "So what are the details of the flight? When do we leave?"

"The TSG C-130 leaves Corpus Christi at 0600. There is a convoy heading down this evening to reallocate some of our medical supplies. Some of the supplies are going to the TSG Operational Support Center there while the rest of our stuff is going to San Antonio."

"Isn't that far enough south to be on cartel turf?" asked Nate. "I've not had good luck with your convoys so far."

"We still have a firm grip on the coastal towns like Corpus Christi. It's the inland to the western parts of southern Texas where we have lost some ground," Luke Explained.

"Oh, okay," replied Nate. "Sounds good to me. I'm ready anytime."

"I'm gonna go and help Rachel get her stuff together," said Luke as he turned to leave the room. "Meet us at the front of the building around 1630. They want to be on the road by 1700, as Corpus Christi is pretty desperate for our supplies."

"See you then, brother!" said Nate.

The day seemed to drag on forever as Nate waited for 1630 to roll around. He had already checked and double-checked that he had everything, so he occupied his time studying his maps of Tennessee, wondering where his mother—and hopefully his father—might be. On the one hand, he hoped they were in the western part of the state just to shorten the trip; however, he knew Memphis had completely broken down amidst the chaos of the collapse, and that it was far from a safe place to be. *Without power and city services, it must be a total hellhole by now,* he thought, *probably just like every other major metropolitan area where gangs now rule the streets.* East Tennessee, although farther away, provided the most promise as it was much more rural and had the mountains and the outdoor resources to be life sustaining.

After a long day of waiting and planning, it was finally 1600. *Close enough*, Nate thought. He had to get out of that room he had been in for weeks before he went stir-crazy. He threw his pack on his back and walked to the front of the facility. It was as busy as a beehive there. The remaining personnel not on guard duty were loading the remaining supplies onto the trucks.

The NCO in charge of the evolution, a grizzled looking staff sergeant, yelled aloud, "What's not on the truck by 1700 stays! We've gotta roll. Prioritize folks. Medicine, weapons, ammo, food, and then everything else... in that order!"

Nate stood off to the side out of the way and thought, *I sure hope they don't want to search my bags, with two of their M4s rolled up in my sleeping bag*. Just as he finished the thought, Luke and Rachel arrived, each with their pack on and wearing multi-cam BDUs.

"This is the first time I've seen you out of your scrubs," said Nate to Rachel.

"Yeah, well, there are not a lot of reasons for a girl to get all dressed up around here," she said jokingly.

"I'm glad you're coming with us," he said with a smile. "I would have only been taking half of my brother otherwise." She just smiled and blushed in response.

They stacked their packs neatly out of the way and helped with the loading effort. There were two M35 2 1/2 ton trucks and three Humvees for the convoy. At about ten minutes before five o'clock, everything was all loaded up and lashed down tight. The staff sergeant walked around double-checking everything, and when he was satisfied, he said loudly, "Last chance for a piss or a smoke! We roll in ten!" He then walked over to Rachel, Luke, and Nate and said, "You must be Doc Stewart and her medical team."

"That's right, Staff Sergeant; where will we be sitting?" she asked

"In the back of the first M35 truck," he said. "We made sure to leave some room in there. It's a tight fit, but it's only an hour and a half to two hours max to Corpus Christi."

"Oh, that will be fine. Thank you very much," she replied.

As he walked off, Nate looked at her and Luke with a grin and said, "Medical team, huh?"

"Whatever it takes, brother," Luke replied with a smile.

The convoy personnel milled around, took care of their last few personal items, and then began to mount up. A security detail was posted at key positions around the front gate of the facility, as well as along the street of the intended route of the convoy.

As they took their seats in the back of the truck, Nate looked around at all of the cargo packed in tightly around them and said, "At least all of this stuff will give us a certain level of ballistic protection. That's better than the fabric top, alone, I guess," he said.

His statement seemed to make Rachel nervous as she bowed her head and said a little prayer. She had not spent much time outside of the TSG's major facilities, and the thought of being ambushed or attacked, like had happened with their convoys so many times before, terrified her. Some of the casualties she had seen during her time in Victoria had been casualties from direct combat operations; however, a large percentage of her patients had been victims of IEDs, snipers, and roadside ambush attacks.

"Don't worry," Luke said, trying to comfort her. "We've got pretty good control over the coastline. We'll make it to Corpus Christi just fine."

She just squeezed Luke's hand in response. Her timidness made Nate worry how she would handle the nearly unavoidable conflicts they would come across during their journey, as well as the uncomfortable conditions they would be facing. He knew they would be sleeping outside on what was becoming increasingly colder nights, as fall had begun to show signs of an early winter.

As the trucks fired up their diesel engines, the main doors to the facility were opened and the M35s and Humvees began their potentially treacherous journey to Corpus Christi. “Well, here we go,” said Nate. “This will be my first flight since it all began. How about you two?” Nate said, trying to get Rachel’s mind off of what she could not see or control outside of the truck.

“I’ve taken a TSG flight in some sort of little propeller airplane they have,” Rachel replied. “I had to do some training with the TSG Medical Department in Austin. They flew me from College Station to Austin and then back. It was really weird. It was a night flight, and nearly all of the lights on the ground were dark. That was also near the beginning, when power outages were probably at their worst. It seemed like someone had just unplugged America.”

Just then, the truck struck a large bump in the road and swerved to the side and back. Nate’s heart skipped a beat. He expected to hear explosions or gunshots erupt at any moment.

“Relax, Nate,” Luke said. “There hasn’t been any work done on the roads around here for over a year. It was probably just a pot-hole.”

Embarrassed that he flinched, Nate said, “Yeah, I know. It’s my first time out of the medical center since my night from hell. I’ll be fine.”

Rachel put her head on Luke’s shoulder and soon feel asleep. She had not slept since the attack and was completely exhausted. Every so often, she would hear a noise or feel a bump and she would be startled awake but would quickly drift off back to sleep.

The first hour of the drive was uneventful. As they approached the town of Woodsboro while traveling on Highway 77, the convoy came to an abrupt stop. Rachel awoke and looked at Luke and asked, “What is it? What’s going on?”

He answered, “I’m not sure. What is it Nate?” he asked as Nate positioned himself to look out of the back of the truck’s canvas cover.

“I can’t see from here,” Nate said. “Several of the guys from the Humvee behind us got out with their weapons and moved up ahead of us. There must be something blocking the road.”

As Nate finished his sentence, Staff Sergeant Miller, the NCOIC of the convoy, came around behind the truck and said, “There is a broken down van in the road up ahead. Our escorts are checking it out. If it looks questionable, we will have to turn around and backtrack to avoid getting too close. Just stay in here until given further instructions from me or one of my guys.”

“Will do,” said Nate.

Staff Sergeant Miller then joined his security detail ahead of the trucks. He went up to Corporal Hayes, who was using a high-powered Leupold 12-40x60mm spotting scope to assess the situation up ahead, and said, “What do we have?”

“We have what appears to be a broken axle. It’s one of those GM corporate axles that holds the axle, wheel, and all in with a c-clip. If you snap an axle shaft, the wheel, axle, and all come out of the housing. That would be hard to fake,” said Hayes.

“Potential threats?” Miller then asked.

“Two Hispanic adult males,” he said. “Oh, and it looks like there may be one or two more occupants in the van that I can’t get in my field of view.”

“It’s a long damn way back to where we can detour around this,” Miller said in frustration. “Still, it seems too fishy. Gasoline is damn near impossible to get these days for your average person. They are a long way out here to be burning fuel like that with no place to resupply."

"It looks like the two visible adult males at the van are arguing about something and pointing this way," interrupted Corporal Hayes. "No, wait. One of them is walking toward us now."

"Weapons?" asked Staff Sergeant Miller.

"Negative," Hayes replied. "At least nothing I can see."

"Well, damn it! We don't want to be taking unfamiliar detours after dark with this load. You guys keep your eyes and guns on the people at the van and the surrounding area. I'm gonna make contact."

"Roger that," replied Hayes.

As Staff Sergeant Miller began to walk towards the man coming towards them, the man paused momentarily and then continued. He met with the man about seventy-five yards ahead of the convoy. "¡Hola!" he said to the man. "Are you having some trouble?" he asked.

"Howdy. We sure are, as a matter of fact," the man said with a deep southern American accent. "Who are you with?" he asked.

"The Texas State Guard," Staff Sergeant Miller replied.

"Oh thank God," the man said, relieved. "My brother was afraid you might be federal; from what we've heard, you are better off if you can avoid them. They've been confiscating weapons from people and detaining others. My name is Lonnie Martinez. The other man at the van is Jeff, my brother. My wife, Celia, and little boy, Matthew, are with us too."

"Where are you headed?" Staff Sergeant Miller asked.

"San Buenaventura Mexico," Lonnie replied. "We held out in Louisiana as long as we could, hoping things would get better, but that just doesn't seem to be happening. Our family, our extended family that is, has a ranch down there. We're hoping to hook up with them to ride this thing out."

"Where are you planning on getting fuel?" asked Miller. "How did you get this far for that matter?"

"Natural gas!" he said proudly. "I worked for Louisiana LP in Alexandria before we went out of business shortly after the collapse. This was one of our service vans. They were all set up to run on our own natural gas. You'd be amazed at all of the abandoned homes you can find with tanks still full of gas. If it's an abandoned house, I just tap into it. If not, we offer barter for some. I've got everything I need to tap into any line or tank I find along the way."

"Sir, that is the smartest thing I've ever heard," said Staff Sergeant Miller. "Would it be too much to ask to allow me to take a quick look at your vehicle? We've had our fair share of bad encounters, and before I bring my people by your vehicle, I'd feel better if I got a closer look."

"Absolutely," Mr. Martinez said. "Come with me."

The two men turned and walked together towards the van. The convoy security personnel watched closely through their optics for signals from Staff Sergeant Miller. As the men approached the van, Corporal Hayes said to the others, "I see movement in the vehicle."

"On it," replied Private Hicks, who zoomed in on the target with the Leupold Mark 4 mounted on his DMR rifle (designated marksman rifle).

As he glassed the target area, he zeroed in on the movement within the vehicle, ready to engage if so ordered by Corporal Hayes. Corporal Hayes zoomed the magnification of his scope to 10x, and through the open rear door of the disabled van, he could see the person inside pick up a Kalashnikov pattern rifle. He shouted, "AK! They've got an AK!" The DMR fired at the figure with the gun in the van, dropping the person with one shot. Staff Sergeant Miller turned to face the convoy frantically waving his arms and began to scream NO as Lonnie's brother, in a fit of rage, drew a concealed handgun and fired two rounds into Miller's back, dropping him to the pavement.

The TSG security detail opened fire on the van, bullets ripping through the thin sheet metal and shattering the glass. Mr. Martinez was hit several times while trying to shield his dying wife's body from the hail of gunfire. His brother picked up a rifle to return fire, but before he got a shot off he was cut down as well.

When all movement around the vehicle stopped, Corporal Hayes ordered a cease-fire. He and Private Hicks ran towards the vehicle to check on Staff Sergeant Miller, who was struggling to breathe, lying face down in a pool of his own blood.

"You stupid sons of bitches," he said through the pain. "You slaughtered an innocent family. They were good people. She was simply getting the gun out so that I could see it in plain view. I'll see you all in hell," he said as his last breath slipped through his mouth.

"Holy shit man! Holy freakin' shit!" Private Hicks said as he looked inside the van to clear it of any potential threats. "We killed a little kid and his mother!" he yelled out as he dropped to his knees in tears. "We murdered an entire freakin' family!"

"Shut up man! Shut your mouth. Nobody has to know," said Corporal Hayes as he tried to calm private Hicks down. "We can just tell everyone they were a legitimate threat. No one has to know..."

"I'll know, you son of a bitch! I'll know it for the rest of my damned life," Hicks said as he stood up and walked up to Corporal Hayes, drew his sidearm, and fired at point-blank range into Corporal Hayes' head, killing him instantly. He then turned the gun on himself, firing a shot into the side of his own head as tears streamed down his face.

Staff Sergeant Miller, Corporal Hayes, Private Hicks, and the entire Martinez family now lay dead, where just a few moments before, a promising young family was on their way to reunite with relatives. The remaining TSG personnel all just stood there in shock. They could not believe what they had just been a part of and what they had just witnessed.

Nate, Luke, and Rachel had been taking cover on the floor of the truck bed in which they were riding since the gunfire began. One of the TSG soldiers ran to the back of the truck and pulled the canopy back and in a panic said, “We need you, Doc, we need you bad.”

Luke grabbed Rachel by the arm and said, “Let’s go!” and helped her down from the back of the truck. The TSG soldier led them to the van where Rachel nearly fainted from the horrific scene. When she saw the dead child, who had been clearly killed by the TSG’s own gunfire, she screamed, “Oh my God! What have you done? What the hell happened here?”

“I don’t know, I don’t know,” the frantic soldier said. “It must have been a mistake. Miller tried to wave us off as the gunfire started, but Hayes and Hicks just kept shooting! I didn’t do any of it! I swear!”

Rachel dropped to her knees and began to cry as Luke checked the bodies for signs of life, just in case they had a survivor. He looked at her and shook his head no.

Rachel put her hands over her face and started crying and yelling, “Why, why, why in God’s name does this keep happening? Will the killing ever stop? Will the death and misery ever stop? I just don’t get it. I just don’t understand. This was a family with a child, for God’s sake!” She then broke down into a deep, sorrowful cry with her hands covering her face.

Nate climbed out of the back of the truck and joined them up at the van. He walked up to them and saw the horrible scene. “Dear God,” he said aloud. He said a quick prayer to himself and then walked over to the soldier who had accompanied Rachel and Luke to the van.

Two of the other soldiers from the convoy joined them as well, with the rest remaining at their trucks, as is standard operating procedure. Luke looked at the three confused soldiers standing there and said, "Who's the senior man now?"

"I am," replied a young Vietnamese-American soldier. "I'm Corporal Nguyen. It was Staff Sergeant Miller, Corporal Hayes, and then me."

"Well, what's done here is done," Luke said. "Doctor Stewart and her team have to get to Corpus Christi with the medical supplies. I think you should take charge, get the bodies on the trucks, and get a move on. With reduced manning, our defensive capabilities are lacking so we need to get off the road ASAP. Especially before someone gets word we've already been hit once. They'll circle like sharks with fresh blood in the water."

"Agreed and on it," he said as he instructed the two men at the scene to begin to secure the area while he jogged back to the convoy to coordinate with the other soldiers.

The vehicles in the convoy simultaneously started their engines and crept up alongside the bullet-riddled van. Corporal Nguyen had a few of the men set up a security perimeter while the others, with the help of Nate, Luke, and Rachel, began to bag the bodies for transport. The slain family was loaded into the back of one of the M35s while the dead TSG soldiers were loaded into the other. Nate, Rachel, and Luke would now be splitting up and occupying the three empty Humvee seats left vacant by the event.

Nate rode with Corporal Nguyen, as Private Hicks had previously occupied his passenger seat. The rear of the Humvee was in the cargo configuration and was loaded to capacity, leaving only enough room for the two men up front.

"How much farther?" asked Nate.

"About a half hour or so," replied Nguyen.

After a few moments of silence, Nate said, "I was in the Navy when it all started. Were you regular active duty before?"

"Yeah, I joined the regular Army to get my citizenship. I was based at Fort Bliss and left when everyone around me started bailing out. I joined the Texas National Guard, which soon became the State Guard because some of my buddies did, and I really didn't have anywhere else to go. These guys have been like family to me; it's just been getting pretty rough around here lately. I grew up in Vietnam and always dreamed of coming to America where everyone had opportunity and had all of the comforts the world had to offer. Now I wish I had stayed at home in Vietnam. If they are in the same situation over there as we are over here, things didn't really change that much. They are already used to getting by with a lot of work and very few things. Now I just see Americans as being spoiled and soft, unable to cope with hardship."

"Yeah, this ordeal is sorting out the wheat from the chaff, I guess," Nate said in agreement. "The people that don't have what it takes will either die, turn to crime or turn to the government for handouts in exchange for loyalty. The free rides are definitely over."

After a few more dusty but uneventful miles, they arrived at the TSG Operating Base that was being run out of the Corpus Christi airport. As Nguyen pulled up to the gate in the lead vehicle, he said to Nate, "Well, it looks like I have got some explaining to do. I'm sure they expect Staff Sergeant Miller to be the point of contact."

He stepped out of the vehicle and approached the gate guard. Nate watched as he spoke with the other soldier, who then made a radio call that was quickly responded to with the arrival of an armed security detail. Nguyen explained himself to the senior man and then the responding security team was dispatched to search the vehicles.

Oh great, Nate thought. *They're gonna find the M4s and bust me for theft and for trying to sneak them on base for sure.* His nerves were on edge as a soldier came up to his door and asked him to step out of the vehicle. As he swung his prosthetic leg out of the Humvee to get out, the soldier saw it below his pant leg and said, "Are you TSG or a Vet?"

"I'm a Vet," Nate replied, "but the drug cartels took the leg, not the oil cartels."

The soldier gave him an approving grin and said, "Who are you with now?"

"I'm traveling with Doctor Stewart as part of her medical team," he said confidently.

"Oh, okay. Carry on then," the soldier said as he moved on to the next truck in the convoy. After their search of the convoy, Nguyen returned to the Humvee and led the convoy inside of the secure area of the base.

Once inside, and after a thorough debriefing on the events that took place during the trip from Victoria to Corpus Christi, Rachel coordinated with her contacts in Corpus Christi and she was given lodging for the night for herself, Nate, and Luke. They were then escorted to their guest lodging where they would wait out the night until their flight departed the next day. Their lodging was formerly a commercial hotel converted to a barracks, located adjacent to the airport property. As they were saying their goodnights, Nate jokingly said, "Enjoy your beds and your morning shower. We may not get another for a while."

Chapter 26: The Drive

With Mildred's important items and clothes loaded up on the trailer that would be pulled by Evan's tractor, there was just enough room for Judith, Peggy, and Mildred, and for their security detail to ride aboard it as well. Will, Bailey, and Billy Skidmore rode shotgun for Evan's trailer to provide security during the drive. The two were armed with an M16A2 clone AR-15 and a Norinco SKS respectively. The original plan was to have Billy provide cover from the rear on Jason's trailer, but once they realized Mildred had an enclosed livestock trailer that they could tow with a drawbar attached to the three-point hitch of the tractor, there was no longer a suitable place for him to ride, given the configuration. They felt this worked out just fine as it provided more protection for the women up front.

The four on horseback had gathered the herd just behind Evan. Jason was on Mildred's Massey Ferguson, positioned behind the cattle, with the smaller livestock loaded into the livestock trailer that he had in tow. Charlie on his ATV took point while Jimmy took the rear position. Both of the men on the ATVs were armed and had their rifles handy so they could respond quickly to any potential threat.

As Evan received word from Jason via their handheld radios that the rear was all formed up and ready to go, he gave Charlie, who was on the lead ATV, the thumbs up and Charlie led the drive off of Mildred's property. It took Charlie and Evan a few moments to learn how to match the pace of the cattle, but within a short distance, they had it all working smoothly. As they began to turn onto the country road from her property, Mildred looked back at her and Ollie's beautiful home that they vowed to live in until they died. *If the Lord is willing*, she thought, *I'll return home someday to live until I fulfill my end of the bargain.*

The first few miles were relatively smooth. The occasional cow had to be turned back into the herd by one of the horses, but they were making good time overall. As they wound down the country road, they were bordered on one side by a steep and heavily wooded hillside going nearly straight up in places. To their right was a ledge that led twenty or so feet down to a creek with heavily wooded banks below. The cattle had been reasonably easy to manage so far, as they were moving through a funnel that did not give them many options but to follow straight ahead. Although Evan and Jason appreciated this for the control it gave them over the cattle, their experiences over the past year made them wary of this type of topography, as it was also ideal for ambushes and sniping. It would not be the first time they had rounded the corner and found a roadblock designed to entrap travelers in the kill zone of a shooter.

After a few more miles, they came upon an opening in the terrain where a side road led off to the right. The road was Yellow Ridge Road and was used to access the properties to the east side of their alliance. As they came to the opening, some of the cattle that were not accustomed to being driven, began to stray off to the sides in an attempt to graze. The riders on horseback did a fairly good job of getting them back in line, but as none of them were experienced at moving cattle the old fashioned way, one heifer managed to slip through and head up Yellow Ridge Road, around the corner, out of sight before they could stop her.

Seeing that the cow needed to be turned back, Linda Cox yelled, "I'll get her." She turned and rode off around the corner to intercept the stray. As she ran her horse at a quick pace, she rounded the corner to see the heifer go just out of sight and around the next bend. *Damn it*, Linda thought. She sure did not expect to have to get this far away from the group. She looked back over her shoulder to see if anyone else had come along to help, and as she turned to look back in front of her, she saw a man standing in the ditch alongside the road with a rifle pointed directly at her. She immediately pulled back as hard as she could on the reins to bring her horse to a sliding stop and began to turn in order to escape back to the safety of the group.

"Go! Go! Go!" she yelled aloud to her horse while kicking her boots into his sides.

As she turned broadside to the man while desperately trying to get the horse turned around, he yelled, "Off the horse!"

She ignored his commands and when coming full turn, another man jumped out of the woods and attempted to grab the reins of her horse. She plowed through the man, knocking him down and out of the way. As she began to pull away, she heard a shot. It was immediately followed by the sound of the bullet as it whizzed by her head, just barely missing her. She then heard another shot, followed rapidly by a third. On the third shot, she felt a violent thump on her back, followed by a deep pain and the inability to breathe. Linda rode faster than she ever had before, rounding the two corners and rejoining the main road. Once back on the main road, she saw that the group had moved on past the open area. She continued running her horse as hard as she could towards the safety of her friends. As she gained on them, Jimmy saw her riding at a frantic pace and yelled to Jason to stop the herd. He then turned his ATV broadside to the road for cover, dismounted, and aimed his rifle behind Linda to cover her in case she was being pursued.

As she reached the group and brought her horse to a stop, Jason yelled, "What is it? What happened?"

She couldn't answer; she was still unable to breathe and was getting light-headed. As she tried to climb down off her horse, she fell to the ground. Jason jumped off the tractor and ran over to her, as did Daryl, who nearly leapt off his horse to help. The others tried to maintain control of the herd that had become spooked by all of the commotion.

As Linda struggled to breathe, everything began to get quiet and fade to gray as she lay there helplessly looking up at Jason and Daryl. The next thing she knew, she was coughing as she struggled to get air and awoke looking up at Mildred and Judith. “Linda, Linda dear, wake up,” she heard Mildred say.

“Was I shot? Was I shot?” she asked in pain.

“It appears that you were, my dear,” answered Mildred. “But luckily for you, that pack on your back had lots of stuff in it and it looks like your metal mess kit and a few other things together saved your life. Your back is bruised up pretty bad, though. You may have a few broken ribs from the impact.”

Linda looked around and started to sit up, but the pain was so severe she had to lie back down. When she tried to sit up, she realized she was lying on the flatbed trailer being pulled by Evan. “Where’s my horse?” she said. “Is he okay?”

“He’s fine,” said Judith. “Daryl tied him up to the livestock trailer and he is following along nicely.”

After a few more miles, they rounded the corner onto the gravel road leading to the Homefront. “We are in the home stretch now,” Mildred said to Linda with a smile. As the herd was directed away from the house towards their new temporary home, Evan turned the tractor, leaving the rest of the group to deliver the women to the home.

Evan climbed down from the tractor, where Molly and the kids met him and gave him all sorts of hugs and kisses in their excitement for his safe return. “Let’s get Linda in the house,” he said. “She’s a little banged up.” Molly, Sarah, and Judy then helped her down and led her into the house.

Peggy asked Griff's wife, Judy, "Where is Zack?" She had hoped and somewhat expected him to be running to her open arms.

"He's in the hall closet again," she replied.

"What do you mean again?" asked Peggy.

"Ever since you left to go on that run, he has been hiding," Judy replied. "Griff got him to come out once to eat, but other than that, he seems to be content to just sit in there.

Peggy dropped what she was doing and ran off to find Zack. She felt like a horrible mother for leaving him in such a condition.

As Judith and Mildred walked into the house to start planning what to do with Mildred's important belongings, Haley ran to Mildred, gave her a huge hug, and began to cry. "Oh, thank God you're home. I was so afraid I would lose another family."

Mildred held her tight as her heart was warmed by the fact that Haley considered her family. She had always thought that if Ollie died, she would want to join him soon after, but now young Haley had given her something to live for.

After putting the tractor away, Evan walked into the house to talk to Linda about what had happened. She explained how she had gone after a stray cow and was confronted. She also told him that the men fit the same basic demographic as the gang out at the Muncie place and how they had tried to capture her.

"Well, you get some rest," he said. "A lot is about to go down around here, and since you live alone, you may want to stick around this place until it all blows over."

Chapter 27: The Flight

The morning came early for Nate as he had tossed and turned all night, thinking about how much closer he would be to his mother and father the very next day. He tried to keep a positive attitude that both of his parents would be found in good health, but in the uncertain and dangerous world they now occupied, he felt that he needed to keep realistic expectations that things simply may not work out. After all, he didn't even know the location from where his mother had made contact with the Survivors' Locator Network, other than that at the time she was somewhere in the state of Tennessee. He would not give up hope. No matter how dark things had gotten during his journey over the past year, he was always able to keep moving forward.

It was 0300 in the morning. Nate got up early and double-checked his gear, making sure the Colt M4 carbines that were broken down and rolled up in his pack were still secure. They only had to remain hidden for one more leg of the journey, so he did not want loose gear to give it away now. He showered and shaved, thankful that the accommodations granted to him by the TSG had electricity and running water. He did not know the next time this luxury would be available.

At 0400, he met Luke and Rachel in the lobby for their escort to the aircraft. Everyone was early, as they knew the importance of getting on this flight. Rachel's medical contacts within the TSG would soon start to wear thin as they discovered she was no longer serving as a part of their team.

A young TSG Airman from what was formerly the Texas Air National Guard met them in the lobby at 0350 for their 0400 escort. "Are you folks the Stewart team?" he asked.

Rachel spoke up and said, "Yes, I'm Doctor Stewart. I assume you are our escort to the aircraft?"

“Yes, ma’am. I’m Senior Airman Castillo. It’s kind of a long walk. There aren’t many outside vehicles allowed on the flight line for security reasons. I can try to find a cart for your bags if you like,” he replied.

“No, thanks. We’re traveling light with just our packs, so we can carry them,” Luke said.

“Oh, I guess I was expecting some medical gear or something,” he replied inquisitively.

“They have what we need where we are going,” added Luke.

“Of course,” Airman Castillo said, getting back to business. “I won’t waste any more of your time then. Just follow me, please.”

The group left the lodging facility and walked across the parking lot, into what was formerly the commercial passenger air terminal. As they walked through the old terminal, they arrived at a heavily guarded security checkpoint. Airman Castillo explained to the guards whom the group consisted of and where they were going. The senior guard on duty demanded their travel orders before they could proceed onto the terminal ramp.

“Only crew, passengers, and aircraft handling personnel are allowed onto the ramp, Airmen. You know that,” he said. “I’ve got no documentation on these people, so there is nothing I can do.”

“Well, I thought—” Airman Castillo attempted to speak as the guard interrupted him.

“You know better than that. If they’ve been reserved space on the flight, there will be written orders,” he said. “I can’t bend on that. You need to talk to the person who put you on this detail and get it sorted out,” the guard said.

A sinking feeling came over Nate. *Did we go through hell in the wrong direction just to miss our flight over an administrative procedure*? he thought to himself.

"Perhaps orders were left here for us," Rachel said in desperation. "This was all arranged on short notice over the radio."

Just then, a man called out from across the room, "Doctor Stewart!"

Rachel turned to see Doctor Leonard Stafford, a gray-haired man in his mid-sixties walking to the checkpoint from across the room. As he walked to the security checkpoint, he approached the desk and said, "I'm so sorry, I'm Colonel Stafford with the TSG Medical Corps. I arranged the flight for Doctor Stewart and her team. The whole thing was last minute, and I did not get the paperwork to the flight operations personnel in time for them to get it to Doctor Stewart prior to her arrival." He handed some forms to the sergeant in charge. "Here is a copy of my approved request."

While the Sergeant reviewed the paperwork, Doctor Stafford turned to Rachel and said, "I'm so glad I caught you before you left."

"It's good that you did. Otherwise, it was looking like we wouldn't have been allowed through," she replied.

"Yes, I'm sorry about that. Without the benefit of email and fax machines, sometimes just getting the administrative side of things accomplished these days can take some time. Anyway, I'm so sorry to hear about what happened in Victoria. They were such good people and did so many great things for us there."

"That's just the world we live in now, isn't it?" she said.

"For the time being, my dear, I'm afraid it is. So are you going to introduce me to these fine young gentlemen?" he asked, reaching out his hand to Nate and Luke.

"Oh, of course," she said. "This is Luke, and this is Nate."

Nate and Luke both reached out their hands and shook his, saying their pleasantries with a smile.

"I've heard a lot about you, Luke. I'm glad you're on her team now as well, Nate," he said with a wink. "You two take good care of Doctor Stewart while on your assignment in Tupelo."

"Everything looks legit, sir," said the sergeant as he returned Doctor Stafford's paperwork to him.

Doctor Stafford turned back to Rachel, gave her a hug, and said quietly, "You be careful out there in this messed up world. Don't make me regret this."

Their escort, Airman Castillo, then interrupted and said, "Ma'am, we had better get you to the plane. They won't wait for you."

"Yes, go, go!" Doctor Stafford said as he nudged them towards the checkpoint.

Rachel, Nate, and Luke picked up their packs and rushed through the entrance to the ramp where the C-130 crew was finalizing their pre-flight checks and preparations. As they ran for the plane, Rachel turned and looked back at Doctor Stafford, who was still on the other side of the checkpoint and mouthed the words, "Thank you." She then turned and ran to the plane, not looking back again.

As Doctor Stafford watched her board the plane with Nate and Luke, he prayed silently, *Lord, what have I done? Please watch over her during their journey. Please don't let her be just another tragedy in this messed up world.*

The crew of the C-130 rushed them to their seats and helped strap them in. The crew chief told them all of the standard safety briefing items and added, "The skies are still contested. The federal government still considers the airspace above the states to be a no-fly zone. We fly in opposition to that declaration. They have yet to take aggressive action for doing so, but, well, just so you know, there's always a first time for everything. We stay low to avoid radar as best we can so it will be a bumpy ride. Here are some sick sacks. Don't puke in my plane. I'm not your mother so I don't want to clean up after you," he said.

They closed the aircraft doors and the Allison turbine engines began to whine. With the *swoop swoop swoop* sound of the propellers spinning up to speed, the airplane came to life. Within minutes, they were taxiing out to the runway for takeoff. Once in the air, Nate could not believe it. He was beginning yet another chapter of his journey and was excited and apprehensive about what was yet to come. When he was just beginning his journey, his goals were so uncertain and so far away that it was easy to deal with things one day at a time, but now thoughts of the future were constantly bouncing around in his head.

As Nate's thoughts were keeping him occupied, he looked over and saw Rachel with her head on Luke's shoulder, sound asleep. Luke looked at him and smiled, as he had to sit there uncomfortably, holding her head in place as the near vertical seating position of the cargo plane jump-seats didn't allow for much else.

"I'm surprised she fell asleep on this loud, bumpy thing," Nate said.

"She was up all night worried sick," Luke replied. "Her nerves are shot after all of the things that have happened lately. She went to medical school with dreams of a small town family practice somewhere in the Midwest. She never planned to be a combat doc. That was just a timing thing. After she graduated medical school, however, it all began to unravel. The TNG was the only game in town, and it felt like the right thing to do. She just wasn't cut out for it."

"Well, maybe with God's grace, the two of you can have a little community family practice in Tennessee someday," Nate said with a smile.

"I wish I shared your optimism, brother," Luke said.

“I wouldn’t be here right now without optimism, my brother,” Nate said with a smile. “Sometimes there is nothing more powerful than faith in God and a little optimism.”

As the airplane began to descend and maneuver for the runway, a crewmember came over to them and said, “Time to wake her up and snug up your harness. We will be landing in a few moments.”

They complied and prepared themselves for landing. Rachel felt refreshed after her short, but much needed nap. As the aircraft touched down, a feeling of relief and uncertainty ran throughout each of them. They were relieved to be safely on the ground and one-step closer to their goals, but now they were at the end of their formal plan. Luke looked at Nate and said, “It’s all on you now, brother. You’re the experienced survivor. You’re in charge from here on out.”

Chapter 28: Connections

Things on the Homefront had been hectic to say the least. The other men who came along to help move the herd returned to their own homes to prepare for what would inevitably come. Linda, however, stayed at the Homefront. Given the fact that she lived alone, in her injured state she knew she would not be able to adequately defend herself if need be, especially given what they now knew about the Muncie boys and their new group.

The homesteaders had a lot of work to do fencing in the cattle as well as getting Mildred and Haley settled into the now overly crowded home. Greg and Jake were assigned the duties of completing the livestock fencing as well as keeping an eye on the herd while the men focused on the physical security of the property.

As the dust began to settle, Evan, Jason, and Griff got together in the backyard by the firepit to discuss what they should do next. "I think the first thing should be to organize and secure our group. We need to stay off the radio as best we can. Now that conflict has been initiated, they may very well be able to listen in on our CB communications. Any sort of request for a meeting over the air may as well be a request for an ambush," said Evan.

Jason and Griff both agreed and then Jason said, "I think we need to make our rounds to each of the homesteads to check on everyone and to set up a meeting. Word of mouth can be considered our only secure comms right now."

"I agree," Evan replied. "Griff, you've been stuck here at the Homefront doing your security thing for nearly every outing since this Muncie gang stuff started. Why don't you and

Jason go make the rounds this time and I'll stay and hold down the fort? Maybe you can evaluate the security situation and provide recommendations for some of the homes that you feel could use a hand."

"That sounds like a great idea," said Jason.

"Yeah, I can do that. I've been getting cabin fever, anyway," Griff said.

"Great," Evan said. "Before you go, let's get with Linda to see if she needs you to do anything or get anything from her place while you're out."

"Roger Roger," said Jason.

"Will do," replied Griff.

"Oh, and maybe you can swing by Mildred's and check on our houseguest. Maybe throw the dog a bone or something," Evan added.

"Will do," Jason replied. "We'll get an early start in the morning since it'll take most of the day."

With that, Evan, Jason, and Griff all got up and went back into the house to spend some quality time with their wives while Greg and Jake took care of the security duties. As they walked into the house, they could hear screaming and crying coming from the basement. They immediately ran downstairs to find Judith sitting at the HAM radio station nearly hyperventilating and crying. Peggy was with her and was holding her tight, but instead of distress, she had a huge smile on her face.

The men were confused and Evan said, "What's wrong? Is everything okay?"

"Yes, yes, oh my dear Lord, yes!" Judith said through the tears. "My sons... it's my sons... they are out there looking for me. They are okay. They are alive and on their way to find me," she said struggling to talk through what the men could now see were tears of joy.

Evan, Jason, and Griff were happy for her but confused as to how she may have heard this news.

Peggy looked at them and said, “It’s the Survivors’ Locator Network. She heard about them through there.”

Judith interrupted Peggy and said, “I’ll explain it to them. I’m sorry. I’m so sorry that I broke your rules. I knew better, but I couldn’t help myself. It was gnawing away at me knowing that I may still have some family out there somewhere. I didn’t want to be all alone in the world.”

“It’s okay, Judith, just catch us up on what you’re talking about,” Evan said in a calm and understanding voice.

“Well, you guys told me I could listen in on the HAM and then relay any news of the outside world to the other homesteads by way of our CB radios,” she explained. “That’s all I was doing, exactly as I was told. Then one day, I was listening to a man from Indiana reporting on how to contact the Survivors’ Locator Network. He was reading an advertisement for it over and over again for a few minutes. He explained that the Survivors’ Locator Network is run by a group of HAM operators who are with a church group based in Arkansas. They simply act as a collection point for information about people who are either looking for someone or trying to be found. They try to match people up. For example, I gave them my name and who I was looking for. Then the next time I call back, they tell me if they have any matches, and if they do, they give me their information. They found a match for me. It was both of my sons, Nathan and Lucas. They are in Texas and searching for me. They also must have been given my information because they left a second message saying they were on their way to Tennessee to find me.”

At this point, Evan, Jason, and Griff began to get a little uncomfortable. They were happy for her if this was true, but the thought of someone being able to get their location over the radio was troubling. Especially considering that the Homefront was raided by a group of well-armed and informed individuals early on in the collapse. Evan calmly asked, "What exactly did you put out about your location?"

"I didn't put any details on there. I only said Tennessee. I didn't say a town, a county, or even a region. Just the state," she replied.

Relieved to hear this, the men looked at each other and exhaled in relief. She then looked them in the eyes and said, "I'm so sorry. You have saved my life repeatedly, you took me in and cared for me when I was alone in the world, and I betrayed your trust. It was a spontaneous moment of excitement to think I may actually have a way to find my sons, to at least know if they were okay, or if I really was all alone in the world," she said in a defeated voice.

"Judith," Evan said as he put his hand on her shoulder and kneeled down to her as she sat in the chair at the desk. "You will never be alone in the world. We may not be related by blood, but everyone here in this home is family. We have gone through more in a year than a traditional family goes through in a lifetime, and we have never faltered in our devotion to each other. We have a special thing going on here, and you are just as important and special of a part of it as anyone else, shared DNA or not. But that aside, I'm so happy for you. I can only imagine the hole you must have been feeling in your heart, not knowing if your own children were even still alive. If my kids were older and off on their own when this all happened, I would have been devastated to not be able to even contact them. I hope I never have to know the pain you have had the strength to suffer through over the past year."

"That being said, I want you to know that there is nothing we wouldn't do to help you find your sons. We just have to be cautious in doing so. We don't want to lead another batch of looters here by putting out any information about our little piece of the world. We are better prepared and supplied than most and there are many people out there who would gladly come and kill us, or our loved ones, to get it. Heck, with the situation at the Muncie place, those types are literally just a few miles away. So please don't feel you have to hide something like this from us. Just let us know what's going on and we can all sit down together and try to figure out the best way to help you or anyone else here with exactly what they need."

Judith leaned over, gave Evan a hug, and said, "Thank you so much. You can't imagine how thankful I am to God every day because he led me here." She then stood up and gave both Jason and Griff hugs as well.

"So, what's the next step?" Evan asked. "What do we need to do next in regards to your sons?"

"Well, according to the last message they left with the network, they are on their way to Tennessee. I have no idea when they will check in next. I guess I just need to leave some sort of location for them to travel towards."

Evan looked at Jason and Griff. Griff said, "Let's give them a point, not too far from here, where they could get the rest of the information they need without giving away precisely where we are."

"That's a good idea," Jason replied. "How about the Baptist Church in Del Rio? They have their doors open to the public still."

"That's right," said Evan. "They have men from Del Rio, who stand watch over the place so that they don't get looted and ransacked. They have a women and children's shelter set up there, right?"

"Yep," Jason replied. "We could set the church up with an extra CB radio if they have a power source for it, and then get Charlie Blanchard's place to relay for us since he is the closest to town. He should be able to pick them up from there. The church could then just contact us when they arrive so that we can travel to town to escort them home."

"Heck, it wouldn't be a bad idea to have a radio relay going all the way to town anyway," added Griff. "They could call our group if they needed assistance as well as being able to give our homesteads early warning if something bad is moving through the area."

"When you two guys make your rounds tomorrow morning, talk to Charlie Blanchard about that first since he would be our relay," added Evan. "I think he is probably the most connected with anyone left in Del Rio anyway since he had the hardware store there."

"Will do," replied Griff.

"Thank you all so much," Judith said. "If you'll excuse me, I'm gonna run and tell the other ladies the good news," she said with a smile on her face and a glow about her that they had never seen before.

Evan went upstairs and when he caught a break in the women's very excited conversation about Judith and her sons, he asked, "Do you ladies know where Molly is?"

"Oh, she's out with the chickens," Sarah replied.

"Okay, thanks," he said as he turned to walk out of the house. As he went out the back door, Lilly and Sammy were playing on the swing set that he, Jason, and Griff had built over the course of the past summer. It was a beautiful evening; the sun was shining through the trees, the birds were singing, and there was a light fall breeze. It was cool enough for a jacket, but still comfortable outside.

As he approached the chicken coop, he slowed down to observe Molly. Life was so busy and hectic most of the time just trying to feed and protect everyone that it seemed he rarely found the time just to slow down, enjoy life, and observe all of the wonders that surrounded him. Molly was singing to herself as he slipped quietly into the coop, admiring her figure and her natural beauty. She heard his foot crunch on some fresh hay and chills went up her spine in fear. Almost afraid to turn around as his hand gently touched her shoulder, she froze for a second and then felt his breath on her neck as he began to kiss her behind the ear and put his arms around her. She melted into his arms and closed her eyes.

After a moment, she turned around and kissed him passionately, dropping her empty egg basket onto the ground and embracing him with both arms. She pulled back from him just to be able to look into his eyes and said, “Oh, how I’ve missed you. When is this all going to be over so that I can have my husband back?”

“I don’t know, beautiful,” he said. “I wish I did. Hopefully, things will calm down soon so that we can take a little more private time for ourselves. When our two new additions arrive, maybe we can divide up the responsibilities around here a little more and get the time we need.”

Molly pulled back slightly putting her hand on Evan’s chest and said, “Two new additions? What?”

“That’s what I was coming out here to tell you before you sidetracked me with your beauty,” he said as he kissed her again. “Judith made contact... sort of... with her two sons. They are on their way here from Texas to find her.”

“Oh my God!” she said jumping up and down like an excited pupil. “That’s so wonderful! Oh, I have to go talk to her,” she said as she ran out of the coop towards the house.

“I guess I should have kept that to myself for a few more minutes,” Evan said to himself with a chuckle as he began to follow her with a smile.

Chapter 29: Mississippi

Upon arrival at the Tupelo Regional Airport, which was now an operating base for the Mississippi National Guard that had also severed ties with the federal government, Nate, Luke, and Rachel were led inside what was formerly the passenger terminal for regional airline service in and out of the area. A tall African American gentleman wearing a Mississippi National Guard uniform came out to meet them. "Doctor Stewart, I presume?" he said, looking at the three.

"Yes, sir, that's me, and these men are my staff, Lucas, and Nathan Hoskins."

"Pleased to meet you," he said. "My name is Lieutenant Colonel Marcus Jackson. I'm the Officer in Charge of our operations here at the airport. My Texas counterparts didn't really tell me what you were doing here or if I needed to lend any assistance. I only received word that you would be arriving on this flight. Is there something you need from us here?"

"I assume you have a HAM radio somewhere on the property?" she asked.

"Why, yes we do," he replied.

"If you would be so kind as to let us use your radio, we will know more about our mission," she replied.

"You weren't briefed on your mission before you left?" Lt. Colonel Jackson asked.

"Unfortunately, all of the information wasn't available at the time of our departure," she replied.

"Hopefully we can help. Follow me. I'll take you to our communications office," he said as he turned and led them through the terminal.

Upon arrival at the communications office, Lt. Colonel Jackson introduced them to the station's radio operator, a civilian in his early fifties named Herbert Brock. “Herb here will help you out,” he said.

Rachel pulled a piece of paper out of her pocket containing information that she had gotten from the radio operator back in Victoria, Texas. She explained to Herb what they needed, and he dialed in the frequency and made the call. Herb was wearing a headset, preventing the rest of them from hearing the radio replies that he was receiving. He was scribbling something down on a piece of paper as he was receiving a reply. Nate and Luke were both nervous with anticipation as to what the message might be. Herb took off his headset and said, “Well, here ya go. Looks like your contact can be reached at the Del Rio Baptist Church in Del Rio, Tennessee.

Nate and Luke both couldn’t contain their excitement as they heard the news. Finally, they had a destination. They could now see the light at the end of the tunnel in the search for their parents. As Luke hugged and kissed Rachel in all of his excitement, Lt. Colonel Jackson said, “I take it this isn’t a Texas State Guard operation at all, is it?”

Rachel looked at him and said, “No, sir, not really. We are... well, were... TNG medical staff. I am Doctor Rachel Stewart and Luke here was a member of my staff. That part is true, but there is more to the story.”

“Go on,” he said.

Rachel then explained in detail what had transpired with the three of them over the past year, and how Nate had traveled so far just to find his brother so that they may reunite with their family. She went on to explain the bombing in Victoria, and how she had come to join them in their journey.

After she explained the situation in detail, Lt. Colonel Jackson just stood there rubbing his chin for a moment in silence, taking it all in. Nate worried that he may be upset that they traveled under the pretense of official state business. *Such a thing may be considered a crime by them*, he thought to himself.

Lt. Colonel Jackson finally broke his silence after a few moments of deliberation and said, “If there weren't people left in this world who would do anything for family, then there wouldn’t be a world left worth living in. What can I do to help?”

“Oh, thank you so much!” Nate said with relief. “If we could post a message on the Survivors’ Locator Network, that would be great.”

“Sure thing,” he responded. “Just let Herb here know what you need.”

Herb transmitted a message for their mother to report that they were now in Tupelo and on their way to Del Rio. They thanked Herb and Lt. Colonel Jackson for their help and their hospitality as Lt. Colonel Jackson proceeded to escort them out of the terminal. “So, how are you going to get to Del Rio?” he asked.

“We haven’t gotten that far in the planning process,” replied Nate. “All we knew before we arrived was that they were in Tennessee.”

“Well, you’re in luck that she’s in East Tennessee. From what we know, the eastern part of the state is relatively stable. There really isn’t any sort of government or law enforcement presence, but there are constitutionally minded militia groups, and other such citizens’ organizations that keep an eye on things in their local areas. Memphis, on the other hand, is a smoldering ruin ruled by gangs. You will want to steer clear of that end of the state.”

“Thanks for the info, sir,” replied Nate. “Do you have any routes that you could recommend?” he asked as he lifted up his pant leg to reveal his prosthetic leg. “I’d rather not hike all the way there if I can help it. This thing is still new to me.”

"Hmmm, well that definitely complicates things for you, doesn't it?" said Lt. Colonel Jackson. "Did that happen in the service?" he asked.

"I was in the Navy prior to everything falling apart, but I never saw combat. This happened while traveling with the Texas State Guard. Rachel, um, I mean Doctor Stewart here was one of the Docs that patched me up. She just happened to be dating my brother. Small world, huh?"

"I'd say so," replied Lt. Colonel Jackson. "Well, let me think for a minute." He rubbed his chin. "You're going to what part of Tennessee?"

"Del Rio, sir," Nate replied. "It's in East Tennessee, all the way on the other side of the state, according to my map."

"Well, you sure as hell can't walk that far," Lt. Colonel Jackson said as he continued his thoughts. "You could I guess, but I sure wouldn't recommend it. I'll tell you what, if you promise me one thing, if you promise to make this one thing a priority in your life, I'll source you some bicycles and give you a ride as far as the Mississippi border. I would get you a vehicle, but you'd never find enough fuel to get you there. If the TSG held Doctor Stewart and your brother in such high regard that they not only helped you find them, but got you all transportation on a flight to here, you must be good people."

"Yes, sir, what do you need?" Nate replied.

"Pay it forward," he said. "Not just once, but over and over again throughout life. This country is nearly down for the count and just waiting for the knockout bell to ring. If we are ever going to pull out of this chaos we are in and once again return to being a thriving and peaceful nation, it's going to take a lot of good people doing great things. Right now, our country is tearing itself apart. While the separate factions of government are fighting over who to blame and who gets control, the people are fighting each other for food, shelter, and security. The good are dying and the bad are getting worse.

Be the good that this country and our world so desperately need.

"If someone crosses your path and they won't make it without your help, then be there for them. Show them good still exists. I have two daughters out there somewhere who I haven't heard from since the collapse. Like you, I've got my information and theirs on the Survivors' Locator Network, but haven't heard a thing. I would give anything for them to cross paths with good people like you who may be yet another link in the chain for them to find their way home," Lt. Colonel Jackson said as he wiped a tear from his eye.

"I give you my word," Nate replied as he reached out to shake his hand. "I wouldn't be here today if it weren't for people doing just that. And I'll personally say a prayer for your family every day of my life. I know God is shining down on me, and I'll pray that he always shines on your family as well."

Chapter 30: Psychological Warfare

Early the next morning, Jason and Griff began to make their rounds. Being just the two of them, they took along simple daypacks and rode mountain bikes to conserve fuel and to operate quietly. Jason brought with him the AR-15 that he acquired during last year's struggle to escape New York during the initial days of the attacks leading to the collapse. He knew that they had a lot of ground to cover that day, so lugging his Remington 700 around while riding his bike was not something he wanted to deal with.

Griff also brought along an AR-15 from the Homefront's arsenal. With both men carrying the same weapon platform, the two would have ammunition and magazine interchangeability. Considering the recent events in the area, they simply couldn't rule out a gunfight and needed to be prepared for such an event at all times. In addition, they also brought along several cans of blaze-orange construction area ground-marking spray paint. They wanted to use the paint to leave a few warnings for the group at the Muncie place.

Their first stop was the Thomas farm. They proceeded with caution when approaching the home, using a tactical bound and moving as a team. They had no way of knowing if the Muncie gang had returned to the farm in their absence, or if they were once again observing the area. Once they reached the side of the house, they entered through the basement level, clearing the room as they entered with their AR-15s at high ready. As Jason got inside and verified that the room was clear, he gave Griff the signal and he followed him into the basement.

Once inside, they could hear movement inside the utility closet. Jason crept up close to the door and tried to listen to see if he could verify that it was their prisoner. He then took the butt of his rifle and rapped it against the door, startling the man inside. "I think it's still secure," he said. He then fished the key out of his pocket, unlocked it, and opened the door with a broom handle in order to remain clear of the door just in case.

Inside, they found their prisoner still secure. They were both surprised by the overwhelming stench of human waste that permeated the small space. "Aww, man, he crapped himself," Jason said, covering his mouth and nose with his undershirt.

"What other option did he have?" asked Griff.

"True, I guess we are new to the whole prisoner-taking thing," Jason replied. There were flies swarming about in the room. The two swatted at them with their hats, trying to get them out of the closet. "Man, I almost feel bad. It must be hell being locked up in here sitting in your own crap," added Jason.

The prisoner nodded his head as if to verify that it was. Griff just looked the man in the eye and said, "Just think about Ollie and the girl they gang raped and murdered, not to mention all of the victims we don't know, about and you'll quickly lose your sympathy."

"Point taken and agreed," replied Jason.

Jason then proceeded to remove his CamelBak from his daypack. He hung it from a water pipe going across the ceiling above the man's head and adjusted it to where the drinking tube would dangle in front of the man's face. He then looked the man dead in the eye. "This has water with some sugar and a few other things in it. Think of it as a homemade sports drink. I'm gonna take your gag off so that you can drink. Don't talk to me because I don't want to hear anything you have to say. We will have a twenty-four hour watch outside the basement from now on. If we hear one little peep, I'll personally come in here and cut your tongue out of your mouth," Jason said as he showed him his knife. "Do you understand?"

The man nodded yes and Jason removed the gag. The man immediately grabbed the drinking tube with his mouth and began guzzling down the drink, as he hadn't eaten or had anything to drink in a day and a half; his body was beginning to go into severe dehydration.

As Jason and Griff started to exit the room, Jason looked back at the man, again showing him his knife and said, "Not one peep." They closed the door, leaving him alone and once again in the darkness with nothing more than his thoughts to haunt him.

Before leaving the property, in both the front and backyards near the house, Jason and Griff wrote a warning in the grass with the blaze orange marking paint. It said, "WATCHED AND PROTECTED BY THE GUARDIANS."

After leaving the Thomas farm, Jason and Griff began to make their rounds to each of the other homesteads. They discussed with them some security concerns for each of the homes, as well as organizing a meeting at the Thomas farm the following morning. They asked that at least one person from each homestead attend, but specifically, anyone participating in the raid or raids on the Muncie place was requested to be there.

As they arrived at Linda Cox's home, they used extreme caution, knowing that the Muncie gang had already showed an interest in the place, as well as the fact that Linda was recovering at the Homefront and nobody was present to keep it secure. They knew it was the most likely place to encounter a threat.

As they watched the property from the tree line, Jason said to Griff, "Those sickos have already shown a penchant for abusing women. Knowing that Linda lives alone, and the fact that she is an attractive woman, makes her place a likely target."

"Yep, this isn't a good time for anyone to be living alone, especially a woman," Griff replied.

As Jason watched the front of the house with binoculars, Griff said, "I'm gonna move to a position where I can see the back of the place."

"Roger that," said Jason. "You've got your radio on, right?"

Griff double-checked and said, "Yep," as he slipped back into the woods.

Griff worked his way around the property and up onto the hill behind the house. He glassed the area with his binoculars for a few moments and caught movement through one of the windows. All he could tell was that a figure passed in front of her bedroom window, but he couldn't make out any other detail. "Movement inside," he whispered over the radio.

"Specifics?" queried Jason.

"Negative," Griff replied. "Just a figure in the bedroom."

"There's no telling what those sick bastards are doing in a lady's bedroom while she's away," responded Jason. "Sit tight for a while. We need to figure out if they are moving through or lying in wait."

"Wilco," replied Griff.

About an hour had gone by with no further movement or signs of the trespassers. Jason spoke up on the radio and said, "I'm coming to you."

"Roger that," replied Griff.

Jason made his way around the house through the woods until he arrived at Griff's position. As he slipped up to Griff, he quietly asked, "Anything new?"

"Negative," Griff replied. "How do you want to approach this?"

"If they are setting up to ambush her, waiting them out may take longer than we have," Jason said, itching to deal with the intruders. "I'll move up to the house; you cover me. I'll use my earpiece for the radio. If you see a threat that I don't see, let me know."

"Wilco," Griff replied.

Jason then moved towards the back of the house. He stopped just behind Linda's stack of firewood, where he could wait and listen for a moment. After a few moments of no movement or sounds from inside the house, he slipped around the woodpile and hugged the wall by the back door.

"Looks clear," said Griff quietly through Jason's earpiece.

Jason then reached over and slowly and silently turned the doorknob, finding it unlocked. He was pretty sure Linda would not have left it that way herself. Jason then gave Griff the "rally on me" hand signal.

Griff slipped out of the woods and moved into position along the back wall of the house with Jason. "What's up?" he whispered.

"Must be an ambush type situation," Jason replied. "If they were robbing the place, there would be some noise or movement by now. I think we should move in. We can't win a fight from the outside and we can't wait them out. If we wait too long, more of their buddies may show up."

Griff nodded in the affirmative and said quietly, "Concur. By the way, didn't Linda have dogs?"

"As a matter of fact, yes, but where they heck are they?" Jason replied.

Griff just shrugged in reply and said, "Hopefully we won't meet them inside the hard way."

"Yeah, right," replied Jason.

Jason eased the doorknob until it released, and he slowly opened the door. He was expecting a creak in the door but was pleasantly surprised to find it smooth and quiet. Jason then slipped into the kitchen, followed closely by Griff. "I want to draw them out. I would rather surprise *them* than the other way around. Position yourself out of plain sight under the table. I'm gonna simulate a homeowner's return."

He opened and closed the back door in a loud, casual manner and poured himself a glass of water from the kitchen faucet. Like the Homefront, Linda's home was on a well and she still had running water from her own water pump. The pump ran on demand and was powered by a solar array that charged twelve-volt, deep-cycle batteries. He took a drink of water and nonchalantly set the glass down on the counter top, intentionally making a sound when he did so. He then opened and closed a few cabinets and waited.

After a few moments of hearing no movement, Jason whispered into the radio, "They must be planning to jump her in the bedroom."

Griff nodded that he agreed. Jason then motioned for him to advance towards the bedroom and take up a position of cover. Griff complied, and once in position, Jason rattled a few dishes together and casually strolled towards the bedroom, being sure to make audible footsteps along the way. As he reached the bedroom, he casually turned the knob, pushed the door open, and then stepped back with his AR-15 at the high ready.

Almost immediately, the closet door swung open accompanied by a man's voice saying, "Welcome home bit—" *POP! POP!*

Before he could finish his sentence, Jason fired two shots from his rifle into the man's center mass, blasting him back inside the closet. Another man immediately rushed out of the adjoining bathroom, blasting a pump shotgun and racking shells as fast as he could. The thin sheetrock wall where Jason stood began to shatter as the buckshot ripped it to pieces. Jason dove to the floor to avoid the shots and the flying debris. As he fell, he felt multiple bee sting-like sensations pierce his hip and right leg. This opened up a target opportunity for Griff, who sent several rapid-fire shots into the shooter, dropping him to the floor.

Griff immediately jumped up and scanned the room for other intruders. When he was satisfied that the threats were neutralized, he ran over to Jason. “Talk to me,” he yelled.

“I think I was hit in the side of the leg,” replied Jason. “Sweep the house to make sure it’s clear, and then come back.”

“Wilco,” Griff said as he ran through the house, clearing each room.

When he was satisfied that the two downed intruders were the only threats, he ran back to Jason, who had already stripped off his pack and was removing his blood-soaked pants. Griff grabbed a towel, ran water over it, and took it back to Jason to clean up the blood so he could assess the situation. As he began to wipe away the blood, Griff said, “I think you lucked out. That looks like small rabbit-shot pellets, not buckshot.” He then went into the bedroom where the man wielding the shotgun now lay dead. He picked up a handful of the empty shotshell cases, took them into Jason, and said, “He had a mix, some double-aught buck, some short brass small game loads, and some bird loads.”

“Luck of the draw,” said Jason. “I’d have rather had a birdshot round, but I’ll take this over a slug any day,” he said with a grin, which was immediately followed by a grimace from pain.

Griff took off his pack and pulled out his first aid/trauma kit. He told Jason, “I’m just gonna cover the entire area with iodine and pick out any of the pellets that are visible.” He applied the iodine and began to pick out the shotshell pellets from Jason’s hip and leg. “Looks like most of it is just below the surface. But then again, small game loads are designed so that they don’t do too much damage to the meat of a small animal like a rabbit or squirrel. With your clothes, gear, and the indirect angle of fire, it just wasn’t able to get the job done.”

"Thank God. With no doctors on hand, I'd hate to see what a real wound would fester itself into," Jason replied.

After about fifteen minutes, Griff said, "Well, I think that's as good as I can get it." He then wiped Jason's leg down with iodine one more time. "I don't really have a way of wrapping this up since it's so widespread. I'll just put some small bandages where I can and that'll get you going for now."

"Works for me. We've got a lot of homes to visit yet today."

"Are you sure you are okay to keep going?"

"If I bail because of a little pain and give those SOBs one extra day before we deal with them, someone else could suffer for it," replied Jason. "What do you think would have happened to Linda if she came home today? I doubt they were here to take her TV and DVD player. She would have gone through hell before they finally killed her. I can't let a little pain drag this thing out another day."

"Amen to that," Griff said as he helped Jason to his feet.

Later that evening and back at the Homefront, Daryl Moses arrived on horseback with a packhorse in tow. Evan greeted him at the gate after being notified of his arrival via radio by Greg, who was on watch at the time. "Welcome to our little piece of heaven," he said.

"It's good to be here. I brought some goodies for you to check out," Daryl said as he dismounted. He shook Evan's hand and then walked back to the packhorse. He reached into one of the large saddlebags and pulled out a metal can. "Here, my good man, is a flint bomb." He handed it to Evan. "Don't worry, it's not charged with powder yet."

Evan looked it over and said, "This is simplistic genius."

Daryl then went on to explain how it all worked and discussed with him the ways they may choose to deploy it. "I've got three of them," he said. With a grin, he added, "We will make those guys think they are taking on artillery fire."

"You're having fun with this, aren't you?" Evan said jokingly.

Daryl chuckled and said, "I'd much rather not be having to do this, but since I do, I might as well put all of those years of being the weirdo who plays with gunpowder to good use."

He and Evan shared a good laugh and once again, Greg spoke up over the handheld radio. This time, he reported that Jason and Griff were returning. Evan and Daryl walked back to the front gate and met them, anxious to see how the day had gone.

Evan immediately saw Jason's bloody pants and said, "What the heck happened?"

"Linda had some admirers waiting on her in her bedroom. They are no longer a threat," Jason put it bluntly.

Griff added, "One of them looked like one of the younger Muncie boys. We took their shotgun, rifle, and ammo and hid it in the attic. We figured since the ambush was for Linda, she might as well get to keep the spoils if she wants them. Not to mention the fact that since we were on bikes, we just didn't have room for extra stuff. We left a warning for their buddies if they were to come looking as well."

"Warning?" queried Evan.

"We sat the bodies up in some old lawn chairs in the front yard in plain sight. Jason got the idea to leave a message for anyone who comes looking for them or to join in on their party at Linda's. He put a sign around their necks that says, 'We were hiding, but the Guardians found us.'"

"We went with that theme all day," added Jason. "At Mildred's place, we wrote a large warning on the ground with ground-marker paint, and then at every other home in the confederacy we left a warning for any trespassers about the Guardians. That's three more of their group since Ollie was killed—five total, counting that day. I'm not sure how many of them there are, but they should start feeling unwelcome in the area pretty soon."

"That was a good idea," said Daryl. "To make the predator feel like the prey, that is. That may reduce their willingness to get out and about while we get ourselves together to deal with them. Speaking of which, I brought my toys. What's the plan?"

Griff said, "Everyone who volunteered to be in on the first harassment raid is meeting tomorrow at noon at Mildred's farm. We will hammer out a plan and deal with our friend in the basement then."

"Excellent!" Daryl said. "Evan, if you don't mind, I'd like to spend the night in your barn or something tonight. I'd rather not do any extra traveling with the black powder, and then I'll just go to the farm with you in the morning from here," Daryl asked.

"Hell no, you ain't sleeping in my barn," Evan said. "No friend of mine will have to put up with that. You can put your bedroll down somewhere in the house with the rest of us. It's crowded, but it's warm and dry."

"You just gave me a flashback of Charlie in Delaware," Jason said with a smile. Charlie was a man they met soon after the collapse, during the journey back to their families. "You sounded just like him just now."

"I'll take that as a compliment," Evan said, returning the smile.

Chapter 31: Back on the Road

Back in Mississippi, Lt. Colonel Jackson followed through with his promise and sourced three mountain bikes for Nate, Rachel, and Luke's journey. He also bent the rules of the Mississippi Guard by allocating a pickup truck to give them a ride to the Mississippi/Alabama state line.

During the drive, he shared with them what he knew about the state of the country and the world. He explained to them that most free markets around the world had collapsed in the wake of the downfall of the U.S. financial system. The global economy, which was so touted by some as a good thing, simply meant that the financial house of cards was spread over a much larger part of the world. China, Russia, and their smaller alliance states seemed to be the only winners.

Prior to the collapse, China and Russia had been strong-handed in securing a competitive and secure position, while other nations, such as the United States, were distracted by engineered social issues and political agendas disguised as good causes. Those nations simply slid into a position of weakness that could not overcome the downturn felt worldwide. He explained that his biggest fear would be that China and Russia would eventually begin to call in our debts, and that our current administration, which has proven itself to be either completely inept or complicit, could not be trusted to not simply cash us out in such a situation.

As they neared the state line, in a secluded and remote part of Mississippi, Lt. Colonel Jackson pulled off to the side of the road. "This is as far as I can go. I've broken too many rules and burned too much fuel already getting you this far. If I crossed over into Alabama and anything happened, my job with the Guard, which is all I have in this world now, would be gone. We are on Mississippi Highway 70, as soon as you cross the state line into Alabama it becomes Alabama 96. Make sure you locate that on your map to get your bearings," he said as he stepped out of the truck to help them unload their bags and bikes from the back.

"Thank you so much for the help," Rachel said. "You could have simply escorted us off of the airport property when we arrived in Tupelo and been done with us."

"Like I said," replied Lt. Colonel Jackson, "just pay it forward and we are even. If I keep doing the same, maybe someday God will bless my daughters with the same treatment so that they can find their way home to me."

"We will. We promise we will," she said as she gave him a hug.

Nate shook his hand and said, "Thanks again, sir. Your kindness may have made the difference between our success and our failure."

"God bless you, sir," said Luke as he shook his hand.

"Watch out for trouble at all times; it's everywhere these days," Lt. Colonel Jackson said as he climbed back into the truck. With a wave goodbye, he turned the truck around and began his drive back to Tupelo.

"I hope he makes it back okay," said Rachel.

"Being in a truck marked as Mississippi Guard will help, as people will assume he is armed," replied Luke.

"Was he armed?" asked Nate.

"Come to think of it, I'm not sure," replied Luke.

"He must truly be on a mission from God if he is gonna just drive around these days unarmed," added Nate, before changing the subject. "Well, back to the business at hand. According to the map, Alabama 96 will take us to Alabama 90. It's mostly rural green space, which, for us, is a good thing. I learned fast during my solo trip from California to Texas that the fewer people, the better. If not for the bikes, I would just want to hike straight across the country through the woods, but that would take forever. As it stands with the bikes, not accounting for sleeping, eating, resting, and possible hostile threat avoidance, we are looking at a day and a half of solid pedaling to get there. That means best-case scenario, we could do it in two days, but considering the state of things, I think three days—maybe four—are more than likely what we can expect.

“Then we should plan on four days,” said Luke.

“Yeah, you’re probably right,” Nate replied. “So how much food do we have between us?”

“We have six MREs for each of us, so if we eat two meals per day we are good for three days before food becomes a problem.”

“That’s good,” Rachel said. “That gets us most of the way there.”

“I guess first things first,” said Nate as he knelt down and opened his pack. “It’s time to put together our toys.” He opened his pack, unwrapped the two AR-15 uppers and lowers, and reassembled them. He then function-checked them both and handed one to Luke. “I assume you are familiar with an AR?”

“Yeah, I’ve had to use them a time or two over the past year with the TSG,” Luke replied.

“Good,” said Nate. “Now Rachel, are you familiar with handguns at all?”

“No, sorry, I’ve managed to avoid it so far,” she said sheepishly.

“Well, it’s time to learn,” Nate said as he pulled out his Berretta M9 service pistol with its holster and a double magazine pouch. “Help her put that on,” Nate said to Luke.

They spent the next half hour explaining every detail of the M9 pistol to Rachel. Nate had her load it and unload it repeatedly until she felt comfortable with the basic mechanics. He simulated each type of malfunction that she may get in a gunfight and showed her the proper way to clear each of them. He went over basic marksmanship fundamentals as well as basic emergency tactics to help prepare her for potential situations they may face during the trip.

Once they felt that she was as prepared as she was going to be without actual live fire practice, Nate said, “Okay, then, here we go... our first leg of the journey with no outside support. Are you two ready?”

“As ready as ever,” said Luke.

“Yes, let’s get this over with,” added Rachel.

Chapter 32: Guerrilla Warfare

Early the next morning on the Homefront, Evan, Jason, and Griff all decided that, although Jason was a key component in the tactical abilities of the group, his injuries would put him at a disadvantage if he were to attempt to join in on the first raid on the Muncie property. With that in mind, he volunteered to stay behind and handle security at home while Evan and Griff, accompanied by Daryl, who had spent the night, traveled to the Thomas farm to meet up with the other locals for the first wave of attacks. Their goal was to burn the name "The Guardians" deep into the minds of everyone at the Muncie property.

Upon arrival at the Thomas farm, Evan and Griff went to the basement to check on their prisoner. Just as Jason and Griff had said, Evan found the conditions to be deplorable, but he was still alive. "Don't worry; you won't have to put up with this much longer," Evan said to the man as they walked back outside.

In attendance from the Homefront were Evan and Griff. Evan had his single shot .50 BMG, which made him the sledgehammer of the group. There would not be much at the Muncie place that could withstand the *big fifty* for long. Griff brought along Evan's Egyptian-made Maadi AKM that had been fitted with bump fire stock to replicate fully automatic fire. Griff's job would be suppressing fire. The sound of a fully automatic AK-47 type rifle would be enough to keep some of the enemies' heads down while they pounded on them with their more precise weapons. Daryl, who accompanied Evan and Griff, brought his Savage long-range precision rifle in 6.5 Creedmoor, in addition to his flint bombs.

From the other homesteads, Jimmy Lewis brought along his Winchester Model 70 chambered in 7mm Remington Magnum. Charlie Blanchard brought his .308 Winchester chambered Armalite AR-10 and Billy Skidmore brought a bolt-action hunting rifle also chambered in .308 Winchester.

When it became clear that all who were going to show up had arrived, Evan stepped up and got everyone's attention. "Well, gentlemen, that makes six of us. I hoped a few of the others would have shown up today, but for some folks, this is a lot to swallow. What we do here today, we don't do for vengeance, we do for the safety and the futures of our loved ones, as well as those others out there who would fall victim to this group of rapists, thieves, and murderers, should we not act. Griff here is a Marine Corps vet and has a pretty good handle on this sort of thing. He's been putting together a basic strategy for tonight's hit-and-run attack. I'll let him explain it to you, and then we will get down to the business at hand."

Griff stepped forward and had the full attention of everyone there. He started by saying, "As of today, we may be good citizens and militiamen at heart, but we will conduct ourselves as guerrilla fighters. As we have seen all too often in the recent past, you cannot fight an evil force that follows no rules by following the rules of civilized conflict yourself. If we want to win this and secure the safety of our own people without fear of retaliation or reprisal, we have to not only win, but we have to scare the living shit out of any scumbag out there who may have intentions of entering this area for unjust reasons. Now that we have taken on the name of the Guardians, the composition of that group must remain completely anonymous. We want the Guardians to remain a nameless, faceless group of men who will annihilate anyone who dares mess with the families that we protect."

"The definition of guerrilla warfare is a group of armed civilians or irregulars that use military tactics, including ambushes, sabotage, raids, petty warfare, hit-and-run tactics, stealth, and mobility to fight a larger, less mobile force. That's what we must be. If we take on these criminals or the ones who follow them face-to-face, we risk taking losses to our own, either in battle or in retaliation. Those losses would destroy the ability of some of our families to be able to provide for themselves. That, to me, is completely unacceptable. It's easy to avoid; if you don't want these sort of tactics employed against you, stay the hell off our lands with criminal intentions. Is everyone here on board with this? If not, nothing will be held against you. We will still fight to protect your families."

Everyone just stood around and looked at each other for a moment, and then Billy said, "I'm in for the long haul."

"Me too," said Charlie. "We can never let what happened to Isaac and Ollie happen again."

"Hell, yeah—let's do it!" shouted Jimmy.

"Great, here's the plan as I see it," Griff said as he began to go over in detail the plan for the night's hit-and-run attack.

After discussing everything in detail and ensuring no questions went unanswered, Evan said, "Okay guys, let's get a bite to eat and then hit the trail."

There were still some canned goods left in Mildred's pantry, so Evan decided it would be best to fuel up on that rather than tap into what everyone had brought along in their packs. "A man never knows how many days his daypack will have to last him," Evan said. "Don't start burning those precious resources before you have to."

Evan made the group a poor man's stew by mixing several different types of canned beans and vegetables together with some water, and adding what spice he could find in the almost bare cupboards. After they all had their fill, they said a prayer asking for the safety of their families. They didn't pray for their own victory, however, as they felt it was not appropriate to ask for success at the expense of another man's life, no matter how wretched it may be.

After dinner, Evan and Griff removed the prisoner from his basement confinement and brought him before the group.

They decided that the best way to transport him would be on the back of Daryl's horse. They planned on taking an off-road route through the woods to avoid detection, and the horse would carry the prisoner, a folding chair, and Daryl's special supplies.

They lifted the man onto the saddle and tied a noose around his neck. They then attached the noose to the saddle. Evan tied a rope around the man's hands and held that rope like a leash. "If you make one peep or do anything at all to try to get away or signal your friends, I'll yank you off of that saddle and send the horse running," Evan said in a stern and serious tone. "Do you understand me?"

The man nodded.

Once everyone was set and ready to go, Griff took the point position and Evan the rear. That way, there was a handheld radio at each end of the group, which was important, as they would be traveling in a widely spaced-apart manner in order to lessen the impact of an ambush. The trek through the woods was mostly uneventful, with the occasional coaxing of the horse being necessary at times in the tighter spots of the vegetation.

After the long hike through the mountains and woods, they finally neared the Muncie place. Griff brought the group to a halt and rallied everyone together. He quietly said, "Let's hunker down here until nightfall. That's when we will deliver our friend here," he said as he pointed to the prisoner on the horse.

They set up perimeter security and settled in for a much-needed rest after the long hike over rough terrain. They removed the prisoner from the horse and tied him up to a tree with the rope of the noose that was around his neck. They then gagged him and again threatened him with his life if he made even the slightest sound.

By nightfall, a few of the men had fallen asleep. The previous night had been a sleepless one for them, as the worry and anxiety of what was to come had eaten away at their rest. Evan gently nudged them awake and quietly whispered, "Griff and I are going to go scout the place out and make our final plans. Keep an eye on our friend there, and keep your heads and wits about you. I'll use this turkey call to let you know it's us when we return."

"You two be careful," said Charlie Blanchard.

"Daryl, while we are gone, be getting your toys together," Evan said. "It's almost time for your pyrotechnic debut."

Daryl laughed and said, "Will do, sir."

With that, Evan and Griff slipped off into the darkness. They used a very slow and methodical tactical bound to approach the property. Now was not the time to get sloppy. They considered their adversaries to be your average gang/thug type but did not want to underestimate the possibility that one or more of them may have had prior military experience and knew how to set up a proper security perimeter. They could hear music off in the distance and a large bonfire was burning behind the house. It appeared as if a small generator was running in a shed to provide them with the power for the stereo and a few lights.

"Wow," Griff said. "Not only are they careless and reckless, but they are wasteful too. Burning fuel just to play music... what the hell?"

"Why conserve fuel when you can just take what you need by force?" Evan replied. "They probably see the world as having an unlimited supply of everything—for those who are willing to take it, that is."

"True," replied Griff. "Well, the bonfire is a jackpot for us. All of those idiots drinking and hanging out around the fire won't have jack for night vision. That'll help us put our friend into position to get the party started in the morning."

"Not to mention the fact that come morning, they will be worn out and hung-over, and we will be ready and raring to go," added Evan.

"How many can you see?" asked Griff.

"Looks like about twelve around back by the fire," said Evan. "I can't tell what's in the house, of course. Probably at least a few more in there and then there is the guy on the front porch with a rifle who must be their lookout. That's a minimum of thirteen, but one has to assume there are more."

"It must take a lot of food to feed all those people," added Griff.

"Hence the stolen cattle," replied Evan. "One cow goes a long way."

"True...Well, let's get back to the guys and get everything together. We need the cover of darkness to set up," replied Griff.

Evan and Griff returned to the group and they gave a final briefing as to what everyone's job was and what to expect. Evan explained, "Daryl will be the closest to the house to operate his contraption; Griff will be with him with the bump-fire AK to give him a suppressive fire to initiate a retreat if need be. If their fall-back is successful after the blast, Daryl will set up with his Savage model 12 and join in on the long-range harassing fire with the rest. I'll be on the lower west corner of the tree line, and Daryl will move to the lower east corner. Jimmy, you take the upper west. Charlie, you take the upper east end, and, Billy, you be a floater."

"A floater?" Billy inquired.

"Yeah, basically don't be tied down to one position," Evan clarified. "Move around and direct fire where it seems needed the most, then move around some more. The four corners will keep them pinned down from all directions, keeping them confused at size and strength, and the floater will only magnify that. They won't know it's the same guy moving around. Also,

Griff will do the same once Daryl is in his secondary position. A little full auto AK fire will rattle their cages and definitely make them second-guess our force strength. One more thing, being on the move, Griff will be the commander of the operation. He has a flare gun with two different colors. If he pops green, it's time to pull out, rally at the farm for a head count, and debrief. If he pops red, it's an emergency mission abort. If you see a red flare, bug out and split up. In either case, don't go home. You don't want to be followed back to your family. Rally at the farm on green, and every man for himself on red. Just make sure that if things go red, give it a few days before you go home and make sure you aren't being followed if that is the case."

"Any questions?" asked Griff.

"What are our targets exactly?" asked Charlie, nervously. "Are we shooting to kill?"

"Unfortunately, yes," Griff responded. "There is no civil way to play this out. Think of your families and think of Ollie, Isaac, and all of those you are saving by getting rid of this problem."

"I know, I know, I'm sorry. I'm just having a hard time believing this is all real," replied Charlie. "Don't worry, I'll be fine."

"Well, guys," Griff said, wrapping things up, "if there are no more questions, Evan, Daryl, and I will deal with our friend. You all get into position, and when the sun comes up, you will get your signal to open fire."

With that, they all did as instructed. Evan, Daryl, and Griff untied the prisoner from the tree and Griff said, "Okay, time to get you back to your buddies, but one peep or one sketchy move from you on the way there and I'll slit your throat, do you understand?" Griff asked with his hand on his knife.

The man nodded in the affirmative and off they went. While the others proceeded to their assigned positions, Evan, Daryl, and Griff took the prisoner, the chair, and Daryl's flint bomb to the center of the property at the bottom of a long, sloping hill that served as a large front yard. It was approximately one hundred and fifty yards of cleared area to the tree line with a gravel driveway running up the center of the property to the house. As the party seemed to die down and the Muncie gang began to settle in for the night, Evan and Daryl snuck up the driveway with the man, covered by the darkness of the pre-dawn morning. At about halfway, approximately seventy-five yards from the house, they unfolded the chair and sat the man down on it, tying his legs to the chair legs and tying his neck, via the noose, to his hands around the back of the chair. The man was secure and unable to get up and run away. While Griff and Evan were tying him in place, Daryl placed his flint bomb inside a small backpack and hung it over the man's shoulders and over the back of the chair. The man started to squirm, trying to figure out what the pack was all about, but Evan quickly ended his curiosity with a knife to the throat, saying quietly, "One more move and all they will find is a bled-out corpse in the morning."

As the final step, Daryl rigged a piece of fishing line to the flintlock mechanism's main trigger, cocked the hammer, and tied the other end to the man's belt. There were only a few inches of slack from the line to the pack, as was Daryl's design. Griff hung a sign around the man's neck, visible from the front that read, "A peace offering from the Guardians."

As they began to walk away, Evan turned to the man and whispered in his ear, "Move before they come out to get you, and we will shoot you dead where you sit. There will be several sets of crosshairs on you at all times. While you sit here waiting for your friends to rescue you, I recommend you look back over your worthless life, remember all of those you have harmed, and beg God for forgiveness."

Evan then went to his corner, and Daryl and Griff set up in the middle directly behind the chair, just over a hill and behind some bushes. This position was chosen as a back up to the trigger mechanism. Daryl had strung out a fishing line to this location from which he could activate the trigger if the primary triggering mechanism did not present the opportunity.

As the sunrise began to appear over the hills from the east, Evan could not help but think about just how beautiful life was. Just how wonderful everything that God had given the world could be, yet fellow humans keep messing it up, over and over again. He resented that he had to take this action. He resented that bad people force good people into these sort of situations, bringing them somewhat down to their level. *Oh well,* he thought, *what must be done, must be done.*

As the sunlight reached the prisoner in the chair, the man who was on duty to watch the front of the property began to yell for the others. "Frank, get Frank! It's that dumb ass Pete we sent to watch the rancher!"

Several other men appeared with an assortment of weaponry, all pointing their rifles in random directions as if they felt they were being watched by whoever left their cohort tied up in the chair in the dead center of the lawn. When Frank Muncie Jr. appeared, it looked as if he was giving orders to a few of the other men. There was an argument, and then two of them, both armed with shotguns, began to work their way out to the prisoner.

"Well, I guess we know our prisoner's name now," said Daryl. "I would have rather not known that. It makes it a little more personal now."

Griff just patted him on the back and turned his attention back to the two men approaching the chair. As they got a little closer, they read the sign around his neck. One of them chuckled and removed the sign while the other started removing the gag from Pete's mouth. As he worked to untie the gag, the man said, "Pete, you sorry piece of shit. You've always been a liability. You had to go and get yourself caught and led them right to us, didn't you. Frank's gonna have fun teaching you a lesson. You're screwed."

As the gag came off, Pete said, "No, *we* are screwed."

Daryl pulled the line, dropping the flintlock hammer against the frizzen, which ignited the charge, sending Pete and the other two men straight to hell in a devastating explosion that shook the entire home. Nothing but a crater remained in the yard as bits of debris and body parts came falling down to the ground.

Before Frank Jr. even knew what had happened, the Guardians opened fire on the house. Griff laid down suppressing fire with the AK while Daryl fell back to his secondary position. The sound of fully automatic fire from the bump-fire AK sent the men at the house scurrying in all directions. Evan began firing the big fifty at the front door of the house. He wanted to take it off its hinges to make them feel vulnerable, as they would no longer have the simple ability to even shut the door. One shot to the upper hinge, reload, and a second shot to the lower hinge and the door fell violently off its frame. He then turned his attention to the structure of the home itself. He felt if he could get some of the large bullets through the wooden walls, the feeling of safety behind cover would be a thing of the past for them. As his shots hit the walls, the air inside of the home was filled with splinters and shards of wood as the walls seemed to rip themselves apart. The other three, with much less firepower, focused on soft targets. Two of the Muncie gang were cut down before they got inside. One took a gut shot on the front porch and lay in plain view, shivering and convulsing as he died a slow and painful death. Another was shot in the back from Jimmy's position, while Charlie focused on the backdoor, shredding it into jagged pieces with the rapid fire of his AR-10.

Once the remaining Muncie gang members had all retreated into the house, the Guardians focused their fire on non-human soft targets such as windows, rainwater barrels, ATVs, vehicles, and anything else that looked to be of use to them, including the stereo they were using the previous night. After a few moments, return fire began coming from the house. It seemed to be random and sporadic as if they had no idea where the incoming shots were coming from. The Guardians then returned their focus to the windows. They were not sure if they hit anyone inside the home, but they did notice that the rate of return fire was reduced dramatically.

Wanting to end the fight from the position of dominance, Griff popped the green flare and began his withdrawal. Evan and the others saw the flare and began their withdrawal as well.

When Evan arrived back at the Thomas farm, he found Griff and Daryl already there. Charlie Blanchard showed up a few minutes later, with Billy Skidmore close behind. Nervousness set in while they waited for Jimmy, as he was the only remaining member of the raiding party yet to arrive. After another fifteen minutes, he finally appeared out of the woods. After the initial euphoria that they had all survived, an awkwardness filled the air. Several of the men had never been involved in the taking of another life, and although their actions were justified and it had been a complete success, it was a lot to take in.

Charlie Blanchard seemed to be in the worst shape. He was pale and sick looking. Evan asked, “Are you okay, Charlie?”

“Yes, I’ll be fine,” he replied. “I almost went into shock when I saw those men explode right in front of me. I have seen stuff like that on movies and had pictured what we were going to do in my head over and over again, but there is nothing like it actually happening in front of you. Nothing could have prepared me for that. I vomited right there on the spot before I could even start shooting. I’m not sure I hit anyone. As a matter of fact, I know I probably didn't, but I gave the back of the house hell."

"You did great, Charlie," Griff said. "You all did. What we did today was knock those bastards off their high horse. We took away their element of security. We took away some of their strength, and we showed them that their actions have lethal consequences. Best of all, they have no idea who the Guardians are and what their composition and force strength could be. All they know is that a beat-down awaits them and anyone like them."

"Okay, guys," Evan said, "we know we put a dent in them today, but we aren't sure how bad. So when you get home, batten down the hatches and keep a vigilant watch on your families and loved ones. If anyone runs into trouble, call for help on the CB right away. Now get back to your families and keep them safe. We will be in touch."

Chapter 33: Advice from a Stranger

Nate, Luke, and Rachel had been riding nonstop throughout the night since Lt. Colonel Jackson dropped them off. The trip had been mostly uneventful so far, and the clear sky and bright moonlight was a Godsend for this part of the journey. The ideal conditions allowed them to press on long after nightfall. Lt. Colonel Jackson had started them off on a good route. Highway 90 through Alabama was a sparsely populated, rural farming area where most of the inhabitants had the ability to remain self-sufficient after the collapse. Early on, people migrating out of cities such as Tupelo, Decatur, and Huntsville swarmed the area. However, the local population banded together and ensured the looting and squatting were kept to a minimum. Eventually, most of the migrating masses moved on, due to the vigilance of the local militia that formed just after the collapse.

They had not encountered very many people so far during the ride. They did, however, have several armed individuals on some of the farms in the area take on an unfriendly and aggressive posture as they rode by. It was a clear message that migrant travelers were not welcome. This unfriendly behavior was understood and respected by Nate, having worked on a farm during his journey. He understood the plight of a subsistence farm in today's world and just how vulnerable they were to theft and looting. Many people who had grown up in the cities and were indoctrinated with the entitlement mentality had been conditioned to look at farms as public servants, as a place where the public's food is grown, rather than the private property of a hardworking family. This detachment from reality led to many a conflict between farmers and the hungry refugees from the cities. The farmers, who otherwise would have been generous and helpful people, did not take kindly to having people make demands for the fruits of their labor.

Highway 90 eventually merged into Alabama 21, and after following that road for quite some time, the group decided to stay on the rural routes. They connected with Alabama 424 and then on to Alabama 524. This route paralleled Highway 24, which was a major arterial route, keeping them moving in the right direction while avoiding other travelers and those who would make their living in this new world preying on them.

When passing through the town of Russellville, Alabama, earlier that day, they found that a majority of the residential neighborhoods that were not abandoned, were in a state of total neglect and had barricades constructed at their entrances. They assumed people were still living in those neighborhoods and assumed they were being watched, so they just kept on moving. Towns like this had now become eerily quiet. There were no sounds of vehicles, no dogs barking in the background, no children playing. It was just like watching a post-apocalyptic movie, except there was no viral outbreak, nuclear war, or zombie horde; it was simply humanity tearing itself apart. As they entered the center of town, they came across a man standing on a street corner, handing out handwritten flyers. He welcomed them to town and asked them to please take one. Nate cautiously approached the man and accepted a flyer while Luke stood, prepared to act in the event it was a trap.

The man was handing out flyers for a church revival that he was helping to organize for that next Sunday. Nate was polite with the man and struck up a conversation, explaining that they had to keep pressing on. Otherwise, they would have been honored to attend. After a quick but pleasant conversation, the man warned them not to go through Huntsville. He said, "What's not ruled by the man is ruled by the bad man there." Which confused Nate at first. He then went on to explain, "The Federals have a heavy presence there because of the Redstone Arsenal. Redstone was home to many DOD assets before the collapse, and still is. It's home to the Army's Missile Command; NASA has a presence there, and more. That's where they developed a lot of the counter-insurgency technology used in Iraq and Afghanistan and will now use on us if we were to ever start fighting back against their heavy-handedness."

"How do you know so much about the place?" asked Nate, trying to figure out if the man's statements were legitimate.

"I used to work there as a DOD contractor. I worked for an electronics company that had a contract to build components for those systems. So trust me when I tell you, if any Federals see you armed as you are, they will more than likely take you into custody on sight—if they don't engage you, that is. To the government these days, an armed citizen is a potential insurgent. Besides just having that threat to worry about, Huntsville is full people who were simple street thugs, criminals, and drug dealer types before the collapse but are now the kings of that place. You wouldn't last five minutes with a pretty girl like that in your company," he said as he looked at Rachel, tipping his hat to her.

"But if there is such a large government presence, how do the street thugs get away with all of that?" asked Nate.

"The feds only care about what goes on inside the fences of Redstone," the man said. "Outside of that, we are all irrelevant to them. It's not like they have to win our votes anymore. They do patrols outside of the perimeter and through town occasionally, which is how you could bump into them, but it's not to maintain order; they patrol for their own security."

After speaking with the stranger for a while, the group pressed on. Nate had thought about that conversation all night as they pedaled on through the darkness, guided only by the moon. As the sun came up, they were all exhausted and sleep-deprived. Nate decided it was time for a break. His prosthesis was beginning to irritate him and he knew the others must have been nearing that point as well. "Let's find a place to make camp and get some sleep," he said.

"Oh, thank goodness; I need a break so bad," replied Rachel.

They were now just outside of Decatur, which was just across the river from Huntsville. Nate said, "Let's carry our bikes into that thick vegetation over there, behind that fallen tree, to hide them. Then we can hike back into the woods a bit to set up a quick camp."

"Sounds like a plan!" said Luke enthusiastically.

Nate and Luke carefully carried their bikes over their heads and hid them where Nate suggested. Rachel, being of small stature, simply didn't have the energy left to carry both her bike and her pack, so Luke went back, got hers, and hid it behind the bushes as well. They hiked back into the woods and found a bed of pine needles beneath a cluster of pine trees that would make the perfect camp. Being evergreens, they still had their cover, whereas many of the deciduous trees had begun to turn color for the fall and lose their leaves. They each unrolled the bedding they had packed and made a place to lie down for their nap.

"I'll take the first watch," said Nate.

"Watch?" queried Rachel.

"Yes, we need to stand watch 24/7," Nate replied. "We can't afford to have come all of this way only to let our guard down and end up just another group of victims in this mess. Just remember, you are a hot commodity to all of the lawless scumbag men out there."

"Nate!" Luke said with a scowl on his face.

"It's true. You can ignore the reality of things, or you can be prepared for it," Nate replied sharply. "Either way, the reality is there."

"Okay, well, wake me up when you need a relief. I'll get the next watch," replied Luke in a defeated tone.

As Rachel and Luke quickly fell asleep after their exhausting night on the bikes, Nate studied his map and thought back to the advice from the man in Russellville. Sometimes he felt like God was watching over them. Was it just a coincidence that a man spreading the word about a church revival would be on that street corner at that time? Was it just a coincidence that he would have knowledge of what lies up ahead that could mean the difference between success and failure for Nate and his group? *Some things just felt like they were meant to be*, he thought. As he studied the map, he came up with an idea to keep making progress while bypassing the city of Huntsville.

Now I just have to sell the idea to them, he thought to himself.

Chapter 34: A Victorious Return

After the Guardians' first raid on the Muncie gang, all of the men involved cautiously worked their way back to their own homes and families, being careful not to be followed or seen. Upon Evan and Griff's arrival back at the Homefront, both men were greeted by their wives and children with open arms and tears of joy. Although they had been through a lot during the last year, this is the first planned altercation, and Molly and Judith had both been worried sick since the plan's inception. Sarah was relieved when she learned that Jason would not be participating, although she knew that deep down inside, his heart wanted to be side-by-side with Evan. The two had been through so much together, they had grown to become more like brothers than friends.

After the brief celebration of their return, Evan and Griff briefed Jason on every detail of the event. They could see it in Jason's eyes that he was chomping at the bit to be involved. Evan said to him, "That would have been one hell of a hike through the woods with your leg and hip hurting like that."

"I would have gotten through it," Jason replied.

"I know, but you'll be raring and ready to go for the next one."

"When do you see that happening?" Jason asked the two of them.

"We've got to let the next few days play out. The men can't stay away from their families that long, especially considering potential reprisals. After a few days of guarding our own homes, we will regroup and hit them again. The way it stands now, I would imagine we would continue the attacks until the threat is gone. I'd rather not face off with them directly if we can avoid it. These hit-and-run attacks will allow us to chip away at them from the safety of cover, and at the time and place of our choosing. I really don't want to lose any more people from this community. I want short, strategic hits, keeping the momentum of the fight and the initiative on our side. If we get down and dirty with them face-to-face, we give them the chance to turn the tables on us."

"Agreed," Jason replied.

"Now, let's discuss what we need to do in regards to security around here," added Griff.

For the next hour or so, Evan, Jason, and Griff discussed security at the Homefront. They all agreed that, for the time being, any chores not directly related to food production should be halted and those efforts be turned to security watches and patrols instead. Griff volunteered to sit down and work up a watch strategy to be implemented, beginning that night.

"You two go get some rest," Griff said. "We need our A-team on at night when hits are most likely to come.

"Roger that!" said Jason.

Evan and Jason left Griff to his task at hand and headed to their quarters. On the way, Evan got the ladies together and gave them a sanitized brief on what transpired at the Muncie place. They were all happy and relieved that none of the men involved from the confederacy were hurt and that it was a success. However, they worried about what may come in the near future. Momentum and control of the area were on their side for now, but would it remain that way, they wondered?

Molly brought Evan some clean clothes to their room and cuddled up with him for a few moments as he tried to get some much-needed rest. "Maybe you can stay back on the next one?" she said.

"I don't think so," he replied. "We can't keep rotating through our leadership folks. The other guys in the group are new to all of this and need consistency. Besides, Washington didn't lead the Continental Army to victory via carrier pigeon. He led from the front."

She smiled, kissed him, and said, "Okay, General, you get some sleep. I'm gonna go tend to the kids."

He just smiled, realizing the ridiculousness of his own comparison and quickly drifted off to sleep.

As the other men rejoined their families and word of the victory spread amongst the homesteads, several of the men who did not volunteer to go along on the first raid felt as if they had let their fellow homesteaders down. They felt as if they had missed out on a defining moment in their lives. They sat on the sidelines while others risked everything to secure safety and peace of mind for them all.

Chapter 35: Nate's Plan

As Rachel slept, Luke relieved Nate and stood watch while he took his turn sleeping. Around four o'clock that afternoon, Rachel awoke to find Luke leaning against a tree with his rifle in hand.

"Hey there, my sexy guard," she said with a smile.

As Luke returned the smile, they both heard Nate say, "What do you mean? I'm not on watch. Luke is."

"Ha, ha, very funny," Rachel replied. "I thought you were asleep.

"I was trying," Nate said in reply. "I just have too much on my mind."

"Like what?" she asked.

"Like how to get us around Huntsville," he said with a yawn. "We can't just ride right through the middle of there, and with it being on the other side of the river, we are restricted to bridge crossings which are all in the middle of the sprawl. I do have an idea though."

"What's that?" asked Luke.

"We can use the river to our advantage," Nate explained. "If we stay on our current course, we will be just north of Decatur and just northwest of Huntsville when we get to the river. If we can find a boat or a raft..."

"Do you mean steal a raft?" Rachel interrupted.

"No, I mean if we can find something that's abandoned or something that we can use as a raft, we can float right through Huntsville under the cover of darkness. The river turns to the east just past the city, where we could ride it downstream a little farther, getting well clear of the urban sprawl before we go back ashore."

"I'm not sure I want to be on a raft on a river at night," Rachel said in a concerned tone.

"It may be a boat and not a raft," Nate responded. "It depends on what we find. Either way, I think we would be much safer braving the water of the Tennessee River than the thugs in the city."

"I agree with Nate, honey," added Luke. "I say we just go with his plan. Look how far he got on his own."

"Well, let's see what he finds," she said.

"Either way, it's time to get moving," said Nate as he donned his prosthesis and climbed to his feet.

They packed up their bedrolls; each ate an MRE, donned their packs, and hiked back down to find their bikes exactly where they had left them. They continued towards Huntsville refreshed and ready to go.

After riding their bikes another five hours, they found themselves on the outskirts of Decatur, Alabama. They took a much-needed break in the woods just off the road and out of sight while Nate studied his map. After a few moments, he looked up at Rachel and Luke and said, "If we can work our way around the north side of Decatur to the river, we should be able to start scavenging for something to use there. It looks like there are a few marinas located off Joe Wheeler Highway. We can take Highway 24 to Beltline Road and get to the river while avoiding most of the city."

"In the daylight or wait until dark?" asked Luke.

"Well, considering the fact that, without street lights and such, we will have a hard time finding what we need, I think we need to get in there before the sun sets, get in position, and wait until nightfall to slip into the water to get around Huntsville. If we can't find a boat or a raft, we will just have to come up with a new plan then."

"You're the boss," said Luke.

"Okay, then, that's the plan," Nate said enthusiastically. "Let's eat another MRE and then get back on the road. Once we get in there, we may not have another convenient opportunity to rest up and eat for a while."

"Good, I'm starving," said Rachel as she opened her pack and began to sort through her remaining MREs.

They ate their dinner and relaxed for a few more minutes before packing up to hit the road again. This had been the farthest bike ride any of them had ever attempted by a huge margin, and it was beginning to take a toll on them physically. Nate was starting to feel pain in his left hip and thigh from the lack of lower legs muscles on that side to assist with pedaling his bike. He had been compensating with his other muscles and being a recent amputee, it was still all new to him. Still, despite the discomfort, he knew they needed to press on.

Nate donned his prosthetic leg, which he had now gotten into a habit of removing every time they stopped to rest, climbed back up on his feet, and said, "Let's get moving!" in a positive voice.

As they continued on Highway 24, they began to see people off in the distance as they entered Decatur. The people they observed seemed to be equally intent on avoiding them. Nate rode up front with Rachel in the middle and Luke taking up the rear. They had worked out a defensive plan during one of their earlier breaks using this formation. If a threat came from the front, Nate would dismount and cover or engage the threat while Luke covered his and Rachel's retreat to cover. If they encountered a threat from the rear, Luke would do likewise while Nate and Rachel sought cover, following closely behind the other two. This was, of course, if it was a threat they simply could not evade, which was always the first strategy to pursue.

As they came upon Beltline Road, they made their turn to the north. "It won't be too much farther now," said Nate. After traveling approximately a half mile on Beltline Road, Nate noticed a set of railroad tracks and a rail service road going off to the right, in the general direction they eventually wanted to travel. He stopped for a moment and pulled out his map. "Cover us while I look something up," he said to Luke. After a quick scan, he said, "Okay, perfect. Let's take the railroad. It leads to exactly where we want to go. We can cut off some distance while staying out of plain sight as well."

"That looks a little creepy," Rachel said.

"It won't be any worse than being out in the open. Trust me," he said.

Nate took off pedaling up the service road that ran alongside the railroad tracks, followed reluctantly by Rachel and Luke. After another half mile or so, they came upon a rail yard off to their right, full of abandoned boxcars that were now being used as a makeshift shelter. They could see people inside the cars watching them as they rode by.

As the service road came to its closest point to the boxcars, a child of around seven or eight years old, ran out, stood in front of them and began asking for food. This startled Nate and the others, as it was the perfect scenario for a trap or an ambush. Nate and Luke immediately came to a stop and scanned the area with their rifles, looking for anyone who may be making a move while the child distracted them.

A young mother came running out of the boxcar yelling, "Please don't shoot him! Please don't shoot him! He's just hungry and desperate," she said as tears began to roll down her face.

They lowered their rifles, as they could see the sincerity in the woman's eyes. "How many of you are there?" Nate asked.

"It's just me, him, and his little sister," she said. "Well, there are others on the trains, but my two kids are all I have."

They looked towards the car that the young boy and his mother ran out of and saw a young girl staring back at them in fear. Rachel got off her bike and took her pack off. She dug around, pulled out two MREs, and handed them to the woman. "I'm sorry, but this is all I can spare."

"Thank you so much," the young mother said. "We haven't had anything to eat for a few days now. God bless you."

Nate watched as others began to climb down out of train cars. "We need to get going, Rachel," he said.

Luke made the same observation from the rear and agreed. "Let's get moving, Rachel," he said.

The young mother and her son walked back to the train car and climbed back inside. Initially, the people—a mix of men and women, maybe six or seven total—were moving towards Nate, Rachel, and Luke, but when they saw the young woman climb back up into her train car, they changed course and went towards her. She quickly climbed inside and slid the door shut as the crowd reached her car.

"Damn it!" Nate said aloud as he dismounted his bike with Luke following his lead. "Keep your head on a swivel," he said to Rachel as he walked by her towards the cars. He raised his rifle to the low ready and yelled, "Hey! She clearly closed that door for a reason. Back away and leave her be."

One of the rough-looking men turned, looked at him, and said, "Mind your own business."

Nate noticed he had a large kitchen knife in his belt and one of the other men had a three-foot long section of pipe. The man with the pipe started to pry on the door as the woman struggled to keep it closed from the inside.

Nate fired a shot at the man's feet, sending a cloud of dust and flying gravel in all directions. "I said leave her be!" he shouted in an angry voice.

"We've gotta eat too. If that bitch has food, we're all gonna get some," one of the men shouted back.

Luke looked at Nate and they both understood what needed to be done without even saying a word.

"You're a grown man! You should be down in that river fishing and catching your own dinner instead of stealing from a woman and her children. What kind of worthless piece of crap are you?" said Nate, trying to anger the man to get him away from the boxcar.

"Shut your mouth, boy, before I cut your tongue out," the man said as he reached for the knife in his belt. "You can't shoot us all before we get to you. You had better move on and mind your own damn business."

"Maybe not, but I can shoot you," Nate said as he pulled the trigger sending a .5.56mm round directly into the man's center mass, dropping him where he stood.

The women in the group began to scatter and run while the man who was prying on the door ran at Luke, swinging the pipe. Luke fired three quick shots into the man, ripping three gaping holes into his torso while dodging the pipe, barely avoiding being hit. One of the other men who had started to advance on Nate quickly changed course and ran the other way. Nate desperately wanted to shoot the man in the back. He knew this kind of person would always be a threat to that woman and her children as well as any other vulnerable people he encountered in the future. *Do it! Do it!* he thought to himself. His finger flinched on the trigger as he tracked the man with his sights.

Finally, Nate said, "Damn it!" He lowered the weapon; he just could not bring himself to pull the trigger on a man who was running away. He turned and looked at Rachel and Luke, climbed on his bike, and said, "Let's go. No more diversions."

Rachel was shaken by what she had just witnessed but climbed back onto her bike and followed Nate, with Luke closely behind. She could not help but be distracted by the thoughts of what that poor woman must have to go through every day to feed and protect those children.

After they were out of sight of the scene of their altercation, Nate stopped to consult his map. "Let's cut through here," he said, pointing to a rundown RV park and an abandoned industrial facility. "The riverbank should be just beyond the main road on the other side of the park," he said.

He and Nate slung their rifles in front of them for easy access as they all got off their bikes to push them through the park. Nate took the lead again with Luke covering the rear. As they walked through the park, many of the campers and motorhomes looked abandoned and ransacked, but a few clearly had inhabitants. They could see curtains move as they advanced through the park, indicating that they were being watched.

As they reached the road on the other side of the RV park without incident, they all breathed a sigh of relief. As soon as Luke was on the road behind them, Nate proceeded towards the river. An abandoned marina was just in front of them, sheltered in a cove behind a man-made barrier. The barrier would have been used to provide shelter from the river's current while boats pulled in and out of their slips. The only boats that remained were all sunken at their moorage. Nate assumed they were abandoned and eventually filled with rainwater long after the battery that fed the float-activated bilge pump no longer held a charge.

They parked their bikes and carefully entered the marina with their weapons at the ready. There were signs that people had been camping in and around the marina facilities, but none of it looked too recent. Nate entered a metal storage building that had its sliding metal door torn from its tracks by what he assumed were looters and thieves. There were also bullet holes in the walls, allowing light to shine through in an eerie pattern.

As he moved some rubbish about, he found three small canoes. "Jackpot!" he exclaimed. He pulled them from underneath the trash and the unhinged door that was lying across the top of the canoes so that they could get a better look at their find.

"Damn it!" he said.

"What?" asked Luke as he saw the bullet holes riddling the side of the canoe. "I guess those bullet holes in the wall line up with these."

"Yep," said Nate, disappointed. "Help me with this other one." He pulled the next canoe out into the open.

Luke helped him drag it free and said, "This one only has four holes."

"We can work with that," Nate said.

The brothers then proceeded to remove the last canoe from underneath the rubbish to find that it had survived the situation unscathed. Nate looked at Luke and said, "Find some rope. I'll be right back. Rachel, you keep an eye out for trouble while we work this out."

Luke dug around and quickly found some mooring line and brought it back to where Nate was busy working with the canoes. He noticed that Nate had an old milk jug, a few sticks from a tree branch, and a lighter. He used his knife to cut out strips of the plastic milk jug and then broke the sticks into two-inch pieces that were approximately a half inch round.

"What's the milk jug for?" asked Luke.

"Welding rod," replied Nate, busy with his task at hand.

Nate twisted and worked the sections of wooden sticks into each of the bullet holes for a nice, tight fit. Then using the saw on his multitool, he cut off a majority of the excess portion that stuck outside of the sides and bottom of the canoe, leaving the protrusion mostly on the inside of the boat. He then used his lighter to heat up the plastic hull of the canoe around the sticks that he used as plugs. He followed that up by melting milk jug patches over the area. He repeated this procedure on both the inside and outside of the canoe. As the plastic from the milk jug melted, it worked its way into the area around each of the stick plugs, sealing what the stick alone had not. Another layover of a larger piece of plastic was then melted overtop of the hole, making a patch.

"That's brilliant," said Luke. "Do you think it will hold?"

"They are both petroleum-based products, so hopefully they will bond well enough," replied Nate as he continued working.

Upon completion of the patch job, Nate flipped the canoes right side up and placed them side by side on the ground. He lashed them together with the mooring line that Luke found, using the center seat and cross braces as tie down points. He said, "Bring the bikes over."

Uncertain of what he had in mind, but trusting, Rachel and Luke pushed the bikes over to Nate. He then laid the bikes over the center of the two canoes and tied the bikes' frames to the canoes, creating a rigid center structure that secured the two boats tightly together.

"Voilà!" he said triumphantly.

"Bravo brother," Luke said.

"I figured you and I can both sit in the back with oars, one paddling on each side, and Rachel can sit up in front of the bikes in one of the forward seats and act as our lookout," explained Nate. "It's gonna be dark out soon. Let's hang tight in here and get some rest. We can then carry the boat down to the water under the cover of darkness, slip it in, and be on our way.

Chapter 36: Recon

Back on the Homefront, it had been two days since the raid on the Muncie place. All seemed quiet and secure on the neighboring homesteads as well. Evan was getting itchy to get some intel on the current situation. He gathered Jason and Griff to put their heads together to decide what course of action to take next.

"Since no one has reported any hostile activity, I think we are going to have to make a scouting run over to the Muncie place to see what's going on," Evan said to the guys. "Which one of you guys want to go with me?"

"Your call, Griff," replied Jason. "I'm feeling up to it; my leg is doing fine, but since you were involved in the raid, I figured you may want to see the results of your handy work."

"Sure, I'll go," Griff replied. "I'll stay back on the next run and you can get back in the mix then."

"Roger Roger," replied Jason smartly.

"Let's head out tonight to be in position at sunrise to get a good look around," suggested Evan. "I would feel better traveling under the cover of darkness for a while."

Griff agreed and the two men went to ready their gear. Evan and Griff both decided to carry VZ58 rifles as their compact size and side-folding stock would make them easy to carry through the woods in the dark, especially since this was intended to merely be an intel gathering outing.

That night after dinner, Evan and Griff said their goodbyes and set out on foot for the Muncie place. It was a cloudy evening with no moonlight to guide their way, so they opted to leave the bikes behind. It would take longer, but they could move more safely and stealthily on foot, they thought.

That night at the Homefront, Judith, Peggy, and Mildred entertained and cared for the children while Jason, Molly, and

Judy stood watch. Sarah, Jake, and Greg were sent to bed early, as they had the early morning shift. Molly patrolled the immediate area of the house itself while Judy monitored the cameras and the radio in the basement. Jason decided to spend the evening watching over the livestock, especially the cattle, as he knew it would not be hard to track the movement of the herd to the Homefront, giving the Muncie gang a clue as to whom the Guardians were associated with.

Jason perched himself in one of the Homefront's observational tree stands with a thermos full of coffee and settled in for what he hoped would be a boring night. The first few hours were uneventful. He had mostly his sense of hearing to go on, as the dark, dreary, cloudy night all but made his vision useless. There were always plenty of animal sounds in the woods at night to help occupy one's time while on watch. Jason would close his eyes and try to identify each sound he heard, painting a mental image of what that bird or squirrel may be doing.

At about two o'clock in the morning, the sounds of the animals fell unusually quiet. Jason perked up, knowing that the animals in the forest were often the best early warning system one could have. He heard a branch crack off in the darkness. Trying to focus on the direction from where he thought the sound came, he felt frustrated and helpless, as he could not see what it was that he was hearing. He heard weeds and brush move as something or someone slowly passed by what seemed like mere feet from the base of tree in which his stand was perched. Just as the sound passed him, it stopped. There was dead silence, not a single sound other than the gentle breeze blowing through the hills.

Jason desperately wanted to shine the rechargeable flashlight that he had clipped to his chest rig in the direction of the last area of known movement but knew if there were armed men slipping through the woods in the darkness, he would simply be giving them an easy target and would be a sitting duck. He held off against his urges and just waited and listened. The sound of brush being pushed aside continued once again. Jason thought the intruder might be heading in the direction of the cattle. Once it had gotten a safe distance away, he slowly and silently slipped down the tree to the ground. It was still nearly pitch-black outside, but now that he was on the ground, he could see just well enough to feel his way silently through the woods in the direction of the intruder.

As he left the cover of the trees for the temporary pasture they had set up for the cattle, he slipped his rifle off of his shoulder and held it in his right hand while holding his flashlight at the ready in his left hand. At this point, he wished he had a tactical rifle with a rail-mounted light, rather than his big bolt-action Remington and a handheld light.

As he crept his way towards the cattle, he heard a cow let out a terrible pain-filled sound, immediately followed by the sounds of the other cattle beginning to panic and run in all directions. He felt the wind and heard the heavy sound of a cow narrowly missing him in the dark amid what was quickly becoming a chaotic stampede. He immediately switched on his light, only to have another cow change course to avoid the light, only a few feet from trampling him.

As that cow ran past him, his light illuminated the fierce eyes of a large and hungry mountain lion. The cat had just brought down a cow and was now turning its attention to Jason and his light. The big cat charged with a fearsome roar. Instinctively, Jason knew that if he dropped his light to shoulder his rifle, he would lose sight of the ferocious beast. With that in mind, he dropped his rifle and drew his .45 from his holster, emptying all eight rounds of .45ACP+P into the charging cat while he attempted to hold the light on his target. His pistol locked back empty to slide lock, and just as he was engaging the magazine release to reload, the big cat fell to the ground and slid to a stop at his feet.

"Holy shit!" he said aloud with his heart pounding in his chest.

The next day, Evan and Griff returned from their scouting run around noon. Their wives and kids greeted them with a warm reception and after lunch, they met up with Jason for a debriefing. "So what did you guys find?" Jason asked as he lit a cigar from his stash.

Evan took a sip from his coffee and said, "Not much at all, actually. The Muncie place looked completely abandoned. We tore that place to shreds during the hit and it didn't look like they picked up or tried to repair the place at all. The door was still off its hinges from the hits from the fifty and everything. You would think if someone planned to continue to use the place, they would at least have put the door back up. We watched from sunrise until about nine o'clock and didn't see one sign of movement. We then worked our way around to the west side of the property, observed from there for a while, and didn't see a thing there either. It did look like they may have burned a few bodies out back, but that is the only visible sign of activity."

"What about inside the house?" Jason then asked.

"We didn't go inside," said Griff. "We didn't feel we had anything to gain in exchange for the risk. Basically, they just aren't there."

"Did we miss anything here while we were gone? And what's the special occasion for the cigar?" Evan asked.

Jason exhaled a puff of cigar smoke and casually said, "I put some more meat in the freezer."

"How did you do that?" Griff asked.

"You fellas ever eat mountain lion meat?" he asked with a smile.

Evan and Griff just looked at each other with confusion then Jason added, “I was in a stand watching the herd last night and had an altercation with a cow-killing cat. He lost.”

“Well, holy crap,” replied Evan. “If you think about it, the subsistence hunting that a lot of folks have to do is putting a strain on game animal herds without the oversight of wildlife management. Take away the game animal population, and they will have to look elsewhere. That herd of cattle is like a buffet to a mountain lion. Just a bunch of big, dumb, slow, delicious animals, fenced in with no escape.”

“Well, I’m gonna make me a hat or something out of him,” replied Jason.

Griff laughed and said, “There is always a bright side to everything, I guess.”

Chapter 37: The River

As the day gave way to the night in Decatur, the sky began to cloud up and look like they could be in for a rainy night. Nate stood watch while Luke and Rachel tried to nap. He weighed the pros and cons of the change in the weather in regards to his plan. *The starless night will give us more cover in the darkness*, he thought. If there had been a bright moon that night, they would be easy to see from the shore. On the other hand, the near total darkness of a cloudy night would make it harder for them to navigate the river and to find their intended point of landing on the riverbank.

They did not have spare time to waste, however, especially with Rachel being down two MREs due to her generosity earlier that day. They only had one day of food left between them and still had a long way to go. In his opinion, they should press on.

As the night was upon them, Nate woke Luke and Rachel from their nap. “Who’s ready to go sailing?”

“You rigged sails up on it now?” asked Luke jokingly.

“That was just a figure of speech,” replied Nate. “Let me rephrase that; who wants to go drifting?”

“Well, brother, knowing you, I would have believed it,” Luke said as he yawned and stretched.

“It looks kind of nasty out,” Rachel said as she walked out of the shed and looked up at the sky.

“It could be better,” replied Nate. “But on the bright side, it will keep the moon from illuminating us like sitting ducks on the river as we pass by Huntsville.

“Do you think it’s going to rain?” she asked.

“There’s a chance of it, but the sooner we get in the water, the sooner we get out. Besides, after all, that pedaling, we could use a good bath anyway,” Nate said with a smile.

The three of them picked up the canoe-raft-contraption of Nate's and carried it to the water's edge. "We will have to paddle out of this protected area to get to the main channel," Nate said. "Once we get in the channel, we should be able to drift with the current, paddling just to steer and keep us straight."

"Should we put our packs in the boat, or keep them on our backs?" asked Luke.

"I was thinking about that," Nate replied. "I think we should wear them, just in case we have to get out of the boat and run for it in a hurry. We don't want to leave what few provisions we have behind. We should keep our rifles in front of us and ready to go, but maybe run the sling through our belts so that we can't lose it if we tipped over."

"Yeah, that sounds like the way to go," replied Luke.

"Well, Rachel, climb on in the front seat of one of the canoes and Luke and I will shove us off," directed Nate.

"If I could have looked into the future and saw my life, I would never have believed climbing into this thing would be an acceptable mode of transportation," she said jokingly.

"Yeah, it's definitely not the way most of us saw our futures, but I'm just glad you're in mine," Luke said to Rachel in reply.

She just smiled as Nate and Luke shoved them off and climbed into their seats. "Dang it! I got my feet wet. I hope my leg doesn't rust," Nate said jokingly.

"Don't worry," Rachel said. "We sprung for the model with the undercoated chassis."

With a laugh, Nate and Luke began to paddle their way out of the marina. The joking subsided as they began to realize the seriousness of their new phase of the adventure. It was a dark and creepy night and the last of the visible stars faded away as the cloud cover continued to build. Nate hoped that he was not leading them down the wrong path with his bright idea. He just wanted to avoid an altercation, with Rachel in the group, at all costs. Through his previous cross-country travels, he had learned two hard lessons: an attractive woman is never safe in this new world, and the cities are not where you want to be.

The cool fall air, even this far south, was beginning to bite at them as the breeze blew over the water. It felt a good ten degrees cooler on the river than it did ashore. As they rounded the corner of the marina and joined the main river channel, they could feel the canoe enter the current. Nate and Luke used their paddles to turn the canoe downstream, and then they just let the current take them.

"Okay, guys, something to consider here," Nate said. "We need to stick to the right of the channel for a while. There is a strip of terrain that divides the river right down the middle coming up ahead. If we get ourselves stuck to the left of it, we will be landlocked and have to beach it and get out and drag the boat over to the other side. The right side is the dredged side for boats to get through. After it's clear we've passed that divide, we want to move over to the left side of the channel, as it is the smooth and clear side. I can't see the map right now in the dark, but I studied it pretty well before the sun went down."

"That's good to know," said Luke. "I'm sure glad we've got you here to be the one to pay attention."

With that being said, Nate and Luke began to steer the boat over to the right side of the bank. "I really can't see a thing," said Nate.

"Me either," replied Luke. "How about you, Rachel?"

"I'm kind of freaking out to be honest. I can't see a thing," she replied nervously.

Just then, it began to rain, reducing their visibility to near zero. "Is this thing gonna fill up with water?" Rachel said nervously.

“It would take a long time to do that,” Nate replied. “We won’t be going that far in it.”

“Your patches seemed to be holding up well. It will be hard to tell if the patches are holding now, though, with the rainwater in the boat,” added Luke as the rain picked up its intensity.

“I don’t like this, guys; let’s paddle to the shore,” said Rachel nervously.

“We can’t see the shore,” said Nate. “We could paddle ourselves right into a mess of brush and muck. I think we are better off just riding it out here in the channel,” he said, trying to keep control of the situation.

They continued down the river, struggling to see and guide themselves away from the shore when they could. They had passed two major bridges, only being able to see the bridge piers as they passed next to them. They could tell the rain upstream had sped up the current by the speed at which they drifted past each bridge. The river now began to narrow, accelerating the current even more.

“We’ve got three major bends in the river to get around now. Once we pass through the bends, we will come up on one more bridge,” Nate said. “After that bridge, we can beach the boat on the left side of the bank anywhere it looks safe and continue on our bikes from there.”

They rounded the first bend, and then the second, occasionally bumping a log or some other debris in the water, startling them and adding to the stress of the situation. The winds began to pick up, rocking the boat and creating choppy surface water, further disorienting them. Nate held his paddle in the water, straight down to the side with the blade turned in the direction of the canoe in order not to induce drag that may turn the boat. He figured that if he felt the paddle begin to drag the bottom, he would know they were getting too close to the riverbank. He felt a whack on his paddle, and before he could say anything, the boat violently came to a stop and began to swing sideways with the current. Rachel screamed as she became tangled in a partially submerged fallen tree. The current kept rotating the boat, which was now sideways in the river, as Rachel was pulled into the water, entangled in the tree.

Nate and Luke heard the scream and the splash but in the total darkness could not see where Rachel had gone. Nate and Luke both paddled furiously in the direction of the tree, but the current was carrying the boat away. Luke took off his pack and rifle and jumped into the dark waters, swimming as hard as he could towards the sound of Rachel's cries for help, which soon gave way to mere splashes and the sound of a struggle.

Rachel had been dragged underneath the water by the swift current and had become even more entangled in the submerged branches. The straps and buckles of her pack were hopelessly tangled in the web of limbs and branches that were hidden underneath the water. Her pack, now soaked with water, was also weighing her down. She struggled to release the buckles, but in her panic could not get them off. She was more terrified than she had ever been in her entire life. *This is it*, she thought as the last gasp of breath she took before going under was beginning to fail her.

Just then, she felt a hand grab her and tug her towards the surface. Unfortunately, her pack was too entangled in the branches to be able to free her to pull her up to the surface. As Luke struggled to free her, he grabbed his knife and began cutting her straps. Once free of the pack, he pulled her up to the surface where she desperately gasped for air.

Luke and Rachel were now both perched in a tangled mess of dead tree branches in the swift current. There was no way to get to shore as the trunk of the tree leading to the river's edge was submerged and covered with slick algae and mud, and with the current, there was no way they could hang on to the tree while traversing it to the shore.

During Luke's struggle to rescue Rachel, Nate had frantically paddled the boat in the direction of the shore until he was able to beach it in a muddy area about one hundred feet downstream from where they were stranded. He dragged the boat up onto the muddy bank and untied the mooring line that they had used to lash the canoes and bicycles together. He tied the pieces of rope together, creating one long section, and ran up the bank, slipping and falling on the muddy, slippery slope of the bank every few feet as he went. It was the first time he had dealt with mud with his new leg and had not quite gotten the hang of it.

When he got to a point upstream of where Luke and Rachel were stranded, he tied one end of the rope to a branch and threw it in the water. He yelled, "The rope is on a branch drifting to you, try and grab it."

"Okay," Luke yelled in reply. When Luke felt the branch wash into him from behind, he felt around and grabbed the rope. "Okay, I've got it!"

Nate ran the rope around a tree and held on tight. He yelled downstream to them, "The rope is secure. Use it to work your way over to the bank."

Luke held Rachel tight as he tried to work his way down the slippery trunk of the tree while holding on to the rope and branch. He slipped and fell, almost losing the grip he had on Rachel and was now a few feet downstream of the tree. She held on tight while the current and the angle of the rope washed Rachel and Luke over to the bank. As soon as Luke could feel the mud and rocks beneath him, he began to struggle to pull her ashore. Nate ran back downstream to them and helped him pull Rachel, coughing with water in her lungs, out of the cold and muddy river.

For the next few minutes, she lay there crying in Luke's arms as he tried his best to comfort her. After she calmed down and had somewhat regained her composure, Luke and Nate led her up the hill, into a wooded area where they could rest and recover. He then got the two canoes, which were no longer lashed together, and dragged them up the hill, giving one to Luke and Rachel to use for shelter from the rain and one for himself. They flipped the canoes over and took shelter underneath. What have I gotten them into? Nate thought to himself as he settled in for the night beneath the canoe. What have I done?

Early the next morning, the sunrise revealed a whole new day. The rain clouds and high winds had given way to a beautiful sunrise with a thin fog lifting off the river in the perfectly calm air. The birds were chirping again, and the sound of natural life was all around them. They combined their MREs to inventory what was left after the entire loss of Rachel's pack. They had a total of four, which for three people, gave them a good day's worth of food, two max if they traveled hungry.

Nate studied his map and scouted the area to determine their exact location. Once he had it all figured out, he returned to Luke and Rachel and said, "That bridge up ahead is Highway 231. Just on the other side is Hobbs Island Road, which will take us towards New Hope. It's a rural area so it should be our best bet for bike travel. The way I see it, if we go that way and ride for at least twelve hours per day, we will be in Del Rio in two days."

Rachel was still a bit shaken up from the night before and was still wet and cold. Just as Luke began to suggest that perhaps Rachel needed more rest before they continued, she stood up and said, "Well, let's get going then. I want to get the hell away from this God forsaken river, and maybe the wind from the ride will dry us out."

Chapter 38: The Reunion

It had been several days since Jason's mountain lion attack at the Homefront and the increased security efforts had now fallen into the new routine. It was just after breakfast and everyone was lending a hand cleaning up when Sarah, who was standing watch from the upstairs window, reported on the handheld radio that a man was approaching the front gate on horseback. Jason and Griff ran upstairs to see while Evan grabbed his VZ58 and went outside to investigate.

"Looks like Daryl Moses from here," Griff said to Evan over the handheld radio.

"Roger that; I'll go meet him and let him in," replied Evan.

Evan walked down the long driveway to the gate and there stood Daryl Moses in his typical frontiersman attire, holding the reins of his horse in one hand and waving hello with the other.

"Howdy," Evan said with a smile. "I hope you're not bearing bad news."

"No, sir, I just thought I would swing by and chat about a few things," Daryl replied.

"Well, come on in," Evan said as he opened the gate. "We've got fresh coffee on, come on up to the house and we'll sit out back and have a cup and catch up on things. Griff is going out on patrol around the perimeter in a few minutes, but Jason can join us."

"I'd love a cup. Hell, I would ride all the way over here for that reason alone. Coffee is getting dang hard to come by these days," Daryl said.

"Yeah, thankfully, those big wholesale clubs made it easy to stock up before the collapse," Evan replied. "I wish they were still in business today. Our supplies won't last forever with all the mouths around here to feed."

They walked back to the house and Evan, Jason, and Daryl sat around the fire pit in the back yard to enjoy a sip of coffee on the beautiful fall morning. Jason stuck a log on the fire for a gnat smoke and asked, “So, how have things been out your way since the raid?”

“Pretty quiet,” Daryl replied. “I went by the Muncie place this morning and took a peek through my spotting scope. It looked just like the night we left it, except not a soul was there.”

“Well, that’s because those scumbags don’t have souls,” Jason joked as he took a sip of coffee.

“Yeah, very true,” Daryl said with a laugh. “Let’s just say there were no living bodies there then,” he replied. “So what do you guys think? Do you think they moved on? Or did we get them all?”

Evan took a sip of coffee and replied, “Well, I guess it is possible that our barrage on the house killed more on the inside than we know. However, when Griff and I ran out there to check the place out, there was a fresh burn pile in the backyard that we could only assume was to dispose of the dead bodies. That indicates that there were survivors. Has anyone else seen hide or hair of them?” Evan asked.

“Not a thing,” Daryl replied. “I stopped by Lloyd’s yesterday morning, and then Jimmy’s place in the evening and they were asking when we were gonna start the barter runs up again. I guess the talk is a few of the folks are getting low on some of the things we had come to depend on and are anxious to get our trade going again. Everyone is wondering how long we need to stay hunkered down before getting back to business as usual. My guess is that they ran off after that butt whoopin’ we gave ’em.”

“That’s a good question,” Evan replied. “I guess we need to somehow get a consensus from the group.”

"Do we want to get a meeting together in person, or just start using the CBs again?" asked Jason.

"I think the CBs would be a good way to start instead of getting people out on the road," Evan said. "Let's get Judith back on the radio with her daily updates for a few days and get the chatter going again. After everyone is comfortable, we'll get back down to business. We can't and shouldn't hide from those bastards forever."

"Amen to that!" Daryl replied. "Well, gentlemen, I've got to get going. My chores have been slacking and I've got to get some firewood cut before the winter gets here."

With that, the men said their goodbyes as Jason and Evan escorted Daryl back to the front gate and saw him on his way. They went back inside the house and gave the women an update on the status of the other homesteads and asked Judith to return to her daily CB radio updates, sharing what she learns on the HAM. She was excited to do so, as she had missed the sense of community that had been building prior to the attacks. Molly asked Linda to stay with them for just a little while longer until they were sure everything had blown over. Linda agreed under the condition that they would put her to work sewing and mending clothes to earn her keep.

By the next day, everyone was chatting on the radio again and the community was starting to feel as if it had returned to normal. People had begun making deals over the radio for Evan and Jason's next barter run. The list was getting quite long, as people had gone without their routine deliveries for some time now. With that in mind, Evan and Jason agreed to resume their deliveries the following day.

Amidst the chatter on the radio, Charlie Blanchard chimed in and called for Judith. Judith replied, "Yes, Charlie, I'm ready to copy," assuming he was merely placing an order for supplies from one of the other homesteads.

"No, Judith, I'm not in need of anything. I'm just relaying some news for you. Pastor Wallace from the Del Rio Baptist Church just informed me that you have a few visitors waiting for you there."

Judith nearly passed out in disbelief. She was speechless. She didn't even reply to Charlie, she just got up and ran through the house screaming, "They are here! They are here! My boys have found me! Oh, thank you, Lord, my boys are here!"

All of the other women rushed to see what the commotion was about. She was nearly hyperventilating with excitement as she told them the wonderful news. Molly went over to the radio, called Charlie back, and got the details. She told him she would talk to Evan and get right back to him to relay to Pastor Wallace when to expect an escort to arrive to get them.

The joy at the Homefront was overwhelming. Molly found Evan and explained everything to him. "We should have enough daylight to get there and back today," he said.

"I think this is a good occasion to burn some gas," added Jason.

"That's a damn good idea," replied Evan. "We've not used a highway vehicle in so long, I've almost forgotten we even had them as an option. Del Rio is too far for a tractor run, and my guess is our new guests are going to be pretty darn exhausted from their travels."

"Mine or yours?" asked Jason.

"Let's take Molly's Suburban," said Evan. "We will need the third row since Judith will surely want to go with us."

"That'll work," Jason replied.

Evan and Jason went out behind the workshop where the Suburban was parked. It had been connected to a solar battery tender and they were pleased to find it charged adequately to start right up. All of their vehicles had been stored with full fuel tanks to help avoid condensation in the fuel. They had also treated the fuel with a commercially available fuel stabilizer to keep the gasoline from varnishing. They started it up and the truck ran as smooth as when they parked it. They topped off the tires, which had lost some air since it had been parked, but otherwise they were ready to go.

Evan drove the Suburban down to the house where they found Judith anxiously waiting. Peggy was standing along beside her and asked, “Is it okay if I come along? Judith wants me there for emotional support on the way.”

“That’s fine with us. Is Zack squared away?” he asked, knowing that little Zack usually had a hard time whenever Peggy wasn’t around.

“Yes, all of the other women offered to help watch him. He’s playing with Haley now. He’s quite fond of her. She’s like his big sister.”

“Well, that sounds like a plan. Let’s get moving,” he said. “Oh, and Molly, go get Jake, he can be our trunk monkey.”

Peggy and Judith climbed in the middle row, Evan took the driver’s seat, Jason rode shotgun up front, and Jake sat in the cargo area with a VZ58 to cover them from the rear. They had to take their time driving around a few downed trees and washouts, as the roads hadn’t had any maintenance since the beginning of the collapse. The drive to Del Rio only took about twenty-five minutes in the Suburban. They had almost forgotten how easily one could get around in a regular vehicle. They just didn’t have the fuel reserves to do it any time other than a special occasion such as this.

As they pulled into the church, Peggy nearly had to hold Judith inside the vehicle until it came to a complete stop due to her excitement. As Evan put the truck into park, Judith jumped out and began running for the door. The door to the church opened and out walked Pastor Wallace, accompanied by two grizzled men in their mid to late twenties and an attractive young woman.

Judith nearly jumped into the men's open arms. They all began crying tears of joy as the young woman stood and watched the reunion with tears in her eyes.

"Oh thank you, Lord, thank you for bringing my boys back to me!" she said over and over. As they gained their composure, Luke wiped the tears from his eyes and introduced Rachel to his mother.

Nate looked at his mother, wiping the tears from his own eyes and asked, "Mom, what about Dad?"

"Oh, boys... I'm sorry," she said. "Your father died over a year ago when it all began." Nate and Luke both hugged their mother again and shed a few more tears together. "I'll explain everything during the drive home," she said.

Evan and Jason had walked over to Pastor Wallace during the emotional reunion. "God truly does work miracles, doesn't he?" said the pastor.

"He certainly does," replied Evan. "San Diego to east Tennessee in the midst of all the chaos. That's an amazing journey."

"She raised some damn fine men, that's for sure," said Jason. "Oh, sorry for the D-word, Pastor," Jason said sheepishly.

"Oh, that's okay. It was a heck of a journey," the pastor replied.

Evan then walked over to the group and said, "We had better get going; the sun will be going down soon and it will be safer traveling in the daylight."

Peggy had been watching from the back seat of the Suburban. She could not help but notice how handsome both of Judith's sons were, *especially the older one,* she thought, as she could not help but stare at Nate.

Judith and Nate climbed into the third row with Peggy while Luke and Rachel took the middle row. As they settled in, Judith brushed up against Nate's prosthesis and was startled.

Nate said, “Oh, yeah, it wasn’t an uneventful trip, to say the least.” He then went on to detail his journey and how he had found Luke and met Rachel. Judith shared with them how she and their father escaped Norfolk aboard *The Little Angel*, and how that led to meeting their group. Nate looked at Peggy and smiled as Judith explained how important she had been to her over the past year. Peggy blushed and returned the smile. Judith was already thinking of how wonderful a match the two would be.

Back at the Homefront, while Griff and Greg handled the security duties, Molly, and the other ladies prepared a wonderful feast to celebrate their arrival. Molly even broke out some wine that she had squirreled away for such an occasion. Judith would have loved to spend all night sitting up with her boys, catching up, as well as getting to know Rachel; however, she could see they were extremely fatigued.

The women set up some temporary accommodations for them for the night for their much-needed rest, with plans to figure out something more permanent the next day. Everyone was in such a festive and glowing mood, they had nearly forgotten the troubles they had as of late.

As Evan was preparing to relieve Griff as the roving patrol, Mildred approached him. “Evan,” she said.

“Yes, ma’am,” he answered.

“I’ve got an idea,” she said. “You and Molly have been extremely gracious offering shelter to anyone who has needed it, and now there are even more mouths to feed. Now that Judith’s boys and the one’s lady friend have arrived, perhaps we should consider having Judith and her family move into my home with Haley and me over on the farm—after all of this Muncie gang stuff blows over, of course. I can teach her sons to work the place, and we—as in everyone here included—would have double the food production. I include the young lady Rachel in that, of course.”

“Ma’am, that is a wonderful idea and is very gracious of you,” Evan replied with a smile. “As soon as we get past our security concerns, we should definitely discuss that with Judith and her boys. I’m sure you are anxious to get back home too.”

“Yes, I am, actually. Ollie and I spent a majority of our lives there, and I want to be back there with him,” she said. Evan gave her a hug, then went on to relieve Griff and assume his duties.

Chapter 39: The Resolution

It had been a week since Judith's family had been reunited at the Homefront. They quickly acclimated to the homesteading life and immediately became welcome additions to the group. Nate and Luke were trained in the security procedures at the Homefront and thoroughly briefed on the security concerns of the community, as well as the recent events involving the Muncie gang. Evan, Griff, and Jason were pleased to have two more well trained and experienced men onboard, in the event of future hostilities.

In addition, the entire community was overjoyed to have Rachel and Luke around for their medical expertise. In the short time they had been there, several people from the other homesteads had already been asking for medical advice from their new community doctor.

Evan and Jason resumed their barter runs between the other homesteads and life finally appeared to be getting back to normal. It was nine o'clock in the morning, and Evan and Jason were getting ready to head out on their weekly run. As they were hooking the tractor up to the trailer, Judith came running out of the house yelling, "They are shooting up the Smith place! They are shooting up the Smith place!"

Evan and Jason both dropped what they were doing and ran to meet Judith to see what was going on. "What? What is it?" Evan asked.

Judith paused for a moment to catch her breath and said, "We just got a mayday call from Lloyd Smith's wife. Their home is under attack."

"Is it the Muncie gang?" asked Jason.

"They don't know, they are just pleading for help," she said frantically.

Evan looked at Jason and said, "The Suburban is ready to go, let's take it. Go grab our rifles and some ammo. I'll grab Luke in case anyone in the house over there is hit."

"On it!" answered Jason sharply as he ran for the house.

Evan ran out to the shop where Luke was working on a project for his mother and said, "Come with me; one of the other homes is under attack and we may need you."

Evan and Luke then ran from the shop towards the Suburban. Molly came out of the house to see what was going on. Evan told her, "Have Judith try and radio the other homesteads for help. Tell them we are on our way, and tell Griff what's going on and to lock this place down!"

As Evan and Jason reached the Suburban, Jason came running out of the house with an ammo can, two AR-15s, and his Remington. Evan and Luke both grabbed an AR and the three men got into the Suburban. Evan fired it up and tore off down the driveway to get to their fellow homesteaders before it was too late.

Evan drove like a madman. He was desperate to prevent one more innocent life from being taken from their community. He slid sideways around every turn, barely hanging on to the road. After a few miles, Evan said, "The Smith's homestead is just up ahead. We'll find a place to ditch the truck and then jog in on foot to take up a position once we figure out what's going on. As they rounded the next corner, a freshly cut tree was down in the road. Evan slammed on the brakes and brought the big SUV to a screeching halt. He looked up into the rearview mirror and saw several men step out into the road, armed with a mix of weapons. He yelled, "Trap!" ducked down below the dash, threw the truck in reverse, and floored it, backing the large SUV directly into the oncoming fire of the enemy guns at full speed.

Three of the four gunmen dove out of the way and were narrowly missed, but one unlucky attacker was crushed by the large SUV. Not being able to see where he was going, the Suburban slipped off of the edge of the road and down the embankment, rolling over on its top ten feet down below.

"Move! Move! Move!" yelled Evan as he, Jason, and Luke scurried out of the windows and disappeared into the woods.

As they ran, they could hear gunfire ripping into the Suburban behind them. After running about fifty yards, Jason dove behind a log and covered the area behind them. Evan and Luke both peeled off into a position of cover as well. Evan gave Luke hand signals to cover their back while he and Jason remained focused on their pursuers. After a moment, the shooting ended. Jason, Evan, and Luke remained in position, ready to engage their attackers, but they never came. Evan then moved over to Jason's position to put together a plan.

"What the hell?" Evan said.

"If they were after us, they wouldn't have stopped so easily," added Jason.

"Let's give it a few more minutes and then move on if we don't see or hear anything else," Evan replied.

Meanwhile, back on the Homefront, Nate and Peggy were taking a leisurely walk through the woods. They had become nearly inseparable over the past week, as they both felt a connection right away. It only made sense, of course. He was his mother's son and she was quite fond of Peggy as well. They were just making small talk when Peggy reached down and took Nate's hand. He looked up at her and smiled. He couldn't believe the turn of luck his life was taking.

Just then, he heard a cracking branch behind him. He turned to look back just in time to see the butt of a rifle about to connect with his face when everything went dark.

Near the Smith homestead, after another ten minutes of not seeing or hearing anything, Jason said, "Something doesn't make sense. That downed tree was planned to stop anyone who may be coming to help the Smiths. Why wouldn't they pursue us when they realized we got away if they were going through all that trouble?"

"Do you hear that?" Evan said.

"What?" replied Jason.

"Nothing, no gunfire off in the distance. We are close enough to Lloyd's place to hear shots being fired if it was still going on," explained Evan.

"Do you think they've already taken the place?"

"Could be... or this entire thing was a diversion to pull us away from the Homefront," Evan said.

"Son of a bitch," said Jason. "Well, there is only one way to find out. Let's get to the Smith place right now!"

Evan and Jason both got up and began to jog through the woods, giving Luke the signal to follow. They ran the next mile to the Smith's homestead to find the siege of the home to be over. Exhausted, they ran up to the tree line, stopping just short of exposing themselves and yelled to the house, "Lloyd, are you okay?"

"Yeah, we are fine," Lloyd yelled from the inside.

"Where are they?" yelled Evan.

"We don't know; they just quit shooting and left," Lloyd replied.

"We've been had," Evan said to Jason and Luke. He then ran out of the woods towards the house and yelled, "We are taking your ATVs! We've gotta go."

Lloyd just replied, "Oh, okay," as Evan didn't have time to explain.

Lloyd had two ATVs in his shed. "Jason, you take the Honda. Luke, hop on the Polaris with me. We'll cut through the mountains to get there. We can't trust the roads right now," Evan said as they climbed aboard the ATVs and fired them up.

They rode through the woods as fast as they could go, dodging trees and low branches along the way. They connected onto an ATV trail that Evan was familiar with that would get them part of the way there. The rest would be pure cross-country. Evan's mind raced at a million miles per hour as to what may be going on back at home. He could not believe they fell for such a ruse if what he feared may be happening was true.

Back at the Homefront, Sarah, who was standing watch upstairs, saw some armed men milling around the tree line through the spotting scope. She immediately alerted Greg, who ran and grabbed a rifle and joined her. "Where's your dad?" she asked.

"He's looking for Peggy and Nate. They went out for a walk this morning before we heard about the raid at the Smith's and we haven't seen them since."

It was just then that a shot was fired on the house, followed by another, and then another. "Where's Jake?" she asked as she heard him running up the stairs towards the observation post. As he topped the stairs, she looked at Jake and said, "Make sure all of the kids are in the basement with Molly. Make sure they are locked down."

Without saying a word, he nodded and ran back down the stairs to do as she asked.

Griff was still out trying to find Nate and Peggy. They had gone on their walk earlier that morning before the events at the Smith place were known and they did not have a radio with them at the time. He jogged through the woods on the trails that most people frequented to no avail. Then he heard the crack of a gunshot off in the distance towards the house. He immediately came to a stop and listened. He heard another and then another. "Damn it!" he said aloud as he reversed course and began to sprint back to the house.

Griff entered the old barn by the tree line where he could hopefully get a good look at what was going on before he made the run to the house out in the open. He removed his radio from his pocket and said, "Sarah, report."

"Men in the tree line with rifles. Shots fired but not sure from where," she responded.

Why just take a couple random shots at the house? Perhaps to get us to hunker down while they got more men in position? Or perhaps they are ranging and sighting in? Testing our response? These thoughts swirled around in his head as he tried to get his head wrapped around the situation. It was then that the reality sank in with Griff that he had left the house without a rifle in the haste to find Nate and Peggy. He was armed only with a sidearm while facing an enemy at long range.

As Evan, Jason, and Luke neared the house, they slid to a stop on Lloyd's ATVs just out of hearing range. As soon as they dismounted, they started a sprint for the home. When they neared the tree line, they stopped for a moment to listen and observe.

They were within thirty yards of the old barn when they heard Griff shout, "Enemy in the opposite tree line, not sure of intentions. They can reach you from there!"

"Who's in the house?" Evan yelled in response.

"Just the boys and the women. Nate and Peggy are unaccounted for," Griff replied.

"Damn it!" Evan said aloud in frustration.

Just then, a barrage a bullets began to impact all around them and their position. Evan, Jason, and Luke each hunkered down behind a tree for cover.

"How many shooters?" Evan asked.

"At least six or seven that I saw," replied Jason.

“They’ve got a fix on us. If there are others, they will eventually flank us here. We need to make a move and soon,” said Evan.

“Agreed,” replied Jason.

“Griff, can you get to Ollie’s tractor?” Evan shouted.

“Yeah, probably,” he replied.

“Good, crank it up and send it across the field. Once it’s moving and drawing fire, radio the house to open the back door,” said Evan.

Evan then looked at Jason and Luke and said, “Hopefully the movement of the tractor will draw their attention long enough for us to make a sprint for it.

“Will do,” answered Griff.

The gunshots subsided momentarily. They waited for just a few moments and heard the old Massey Ferguson tractor start up. They watched for it to make their move. As the tractor came out of the barn under its own power, they noticed a man in the driver’s seat. They quickly realized what it was and Jason said, “Well, it looks like Griff found a good use for that old scarecrow.”

As the tractor and its straw-filled driver began to draw fire, Evan, Jason, and Luke made a run for the house. As they ran, they saw the back door of the house swing open just in time to sprint inside as the barrage of bullets again focused on them rather than the tractor that had now been disabled by the gunfire.

Molly ran up to Evan and gave him a big hug as Jason said, “Sarah?”

“Upstairs,” replied Molly. Jason ran up the stairs to check on his wife.

“Is anyone hurt?” Evan asked.

“Not in here; the kids are all in the basement with the other women. Rachel too,” Molly added, looking at Luke to reassure him. "Griff couldn't find Nate and Peggy, though. Oh God, I hope they are okay."

"Do we have any idea what these guys want? Evan asked.

"Not a clue," she replied.

Nate awoke to find himself lying flat on his back in the woods. He spit blood out of his mouth and tried to sit up. A terrible headache and dizziness forced him to lie back down as the world began to spin around him. It took him a moment to regain his bearings and realize what had happened. He immediately sat back up and frantically looked around for Peggy, but she was not there. He climbed to his feet, stumbling a bit a first, and then began to look around for clues. He could hear gunshots off in the distance towards the house, and saw signs of a struggle and trampled vegetation going in the other direction.

He made a quick assessment and realized that other than a possible concussion, a busted lip, and a few loose teeth, he was probably okay. All he had on him for a weapon was his knife. He left his pistol in the house. He had been a bit distracted by his feelings for Peggy and had violated one of his own rules of never going out unarmed.

Gathering his composure, he began to follow the trail of disturbed vegetation and footprints, knowing that whoever jumped him and took Peggy had left them behind. After a few moments, he heard a muffled struggle up ahead. In a small clearing, he saw three men, one of them standing with his back turned to him, another looking down at the ground, smiling and laughing, and the third was down on the ground just out of view, due to the surrounding brush.

Nate silently slipped his knife out of its sheath and crept a little closer. To his horror, he saw Peggy on the ground, bound and gagged, with her shirt torn open while the man kneeling down tried to get her pants off as she struggled. The men were so distracted by their act, Nate was able to slip up close behind, and as soon as he was within range, he lunged forward, grabbed the man facing away from him by his long hair, pulled his neck back, and sliced his throat wide open.

As soon as the man began to go limp, the other man standing across from him pulled a shotgun into firing position. Nate shoved the shooter's dying cohort towards him, absorbing a direct blast from the shotgun, spilling the man's guts on the ground. Nate continued to push the man into the shooter, blocking the use of the shotgun while he stabbed him repeatedly in the chest.

Nate then quickly turned to see the man that was on top of Peggy scrambling to reach his gun that he had left leaning against a tree. Nate leapt onto the man, stabbing him in the back, over and over again like a man demon-possessed until there was no sign of life.

Covered with blood spatter all over his hands and face, Nate crawled over to Peggy and hugged her and held her tight. After a moment, he regained his composure and helped her get herself back together. "We've got to help the others now," he said.

"Yes, yes, of course," she said as she found herself lost in his eyes.

Back at the house, Evan and Jason quickly put together a defensive strategy, utilizing Linda and Judy in defensive positions, while Molly and Rachel stayed with the kids in the basement. They put Jake downstairs to guard the outer basement door; Linda was on a window on the upper floor overlooking the rear side of the house facing east, Judy on a window facing north, Greg a window facing west towards the main body of the attackers, and Sarah facing south towards the main driveway. Evan, Jason, and Luke would move between the windows to meet the changing threats that a battle, which seemed inevitable, would surely bring.

Evan borrowed Sarah's handheld radio and transmitted, "Griff?"

"I'm here," he replied.

"Do you need anything?" asked Evan.

"I'm trapped like a rat without a long gun; I've just got my pistol. I doubt you can get anything to me safely, though," Griff replied.

"Okay, well, if you need anything, let us know," Evan said. "You can be our eyes on the ground in the meantime."

"Wilco," replied Griff.

After a few more uneventful moments, Linda yelled out, "I've got movement on this side in the tree line."

"Over here as well," called out Judy.

"Well, hell," said Evan in frustration. "They are blocking off all of our escape routes."

Just then, a voice came over the CB radio that said, "Howdy neighbors. That wasn't very neighborly what you did to our house and our friends. We're here to return the hospitality."

"Frank Jr.?" Evan asked over the radio.

"Why, yes it is," the voice on the radio said. "You see, neighbor, you and yours have put quite the damper on our once prosperous enterprise, and we feel you owe us reparations."

"What do you want?" Evan asked.

"The way I see it," replied Frank Jr., "you shot the shit out of our home, rendering it simply unlivable, so we think it would only be fair if you give us yours. We want your house, your land, and everything on it. Oh, and we'll take any pretty girls you may have in there as well. That young one looks pretty sweet. We've been watching for a while. We know what you have and where you have it."

"That sick son of a bitch!" Evan said in a fit of rage as he paced back and forth. He then stormed out of the room, came back a few minutes later with his .50 BMG, and began to set it up facing the tree line where the main body of the Muncie gang seemed to be located. “If I see that sick bastard, I’m killing him on sight,” Evan said as he chambered one of the massive fifty-caliber rounds.

“Every last one of you will die if you make a move towards this house!” Evan shouted over the radio.

“Yes, neighbor, we realize that,” answered Frank. “We ain’t stupid. We’ve planned for that eventuality. You can either lay down your weapons and surrender willingly or we will burn you out. If we can’t have your house, no one will. We will burn every last woman and child to death while we sit back here, have a beer, and watch. Hell, I might even use your wife’s smoldering ashes to light a celebratory cigar.”

Evan ordered, “Fire at the tree line! Try and flush them out!” as he began firing blindly into the woods with his big fifty. Everyone at the Homefront opened fire, aiming low to the ground and just inside the tree line where they assumed the men might be taking cover.

“Okay, then, I guess that’s your answer,” Frank Jr. answered in a disappointed tone. “That’s a shame, too. I really wanted that young’un.”

They then heard a large diesel engine fire up in the distance. It sounded like it was coming right down the main driveway. To their horror, they saw a large bulldozer come into view. It had steel plates welded on around the cab for armor and the blade had several oil-soaked logs chained to it that had been set on fire. It crashed through the front gate and began to head for the house. Evan and Jason both opened fire on the dozer trying to find a weak spot in the makeshift armor. The operator immediately raised the blade to shield the cab from their shots.

“They might as well have a tank!” said Jason in an exasperated tone.

The dozer came to a stop approximately seventy yards from the house. "One last chance to change your mind," Frank said over the radio.

Evan looked at Jason and said, "Run downstairs and let them know to get the kids ready; we may have to make a run for it, and it's not going to be pretty if we do."

Jason just looked at Evan, realizing the horror that awaited them and their children. They both knew if they were forced to run for it, they would be cut to shreds. "Tell them if we give the signal, to run for their lives and never look back. We will hold them off the best we can while they get away. And tell Molly and my kids I love them."

Jason reluctantly turned and went downstairs to give the terrible, but seemingly necessary instructions without saying a word to Evan in return.

After a moment with no reply from Evan, Frank said, "Alrighty then. Game on." With that, the dozer resumed its advance towards the house. Simultaneously the tree line erupted with gunfire directed at the house from all directions. Everyone near an upper floor window dropped to the floor as the windows all began to shatter as the barrage of bullets found their way into the room through the ballistic shutters.

Almost as soon as the gunfire had begun, the bullets began to be redirected and ceased to hit the house, yet the sounds of the shots continued. Evan slipped over to one of the windows, peeked out through the shooting port in the ballistic shutter, and saw the attackers retreating from the tree line as they were fighting someone off from behind them in the trees. The attackers were being cut to pieces... but by who?

The dozer, however, continued its ominous course unimpeded towards the house with its payload of burning lumber. Evan then saw a man on horseback come barreling out of the trees at full gallop.

"It's Daryl!" Evan yelled aloud.

Darryl's horse ran straight at the dozer from behind. As the menacing steel beast got to within ten yards of the house, Daryl tossed a backpack onto the dozer's engine compartment and then turned away riding as hard as he could. A huge blast rocked the house as the pack exploded, bringing the dozer to a complete stop.

The operator of the dozer opened the reinforced cab and bailed off the burning machine, shaken and disoriented, holding his hands over his ears in pain. Daryl then turned his horse back towards the dozer and charged back towards the man at full gallop. As he came upon the man, Daryl pulled back on the reins to slow his horse, drew his 1875 Remington revolver, and shot the man dead.

The gunshots began to subside, and as the last attacker was killed, the Homefront's defenders emerged from the woods. It was nearly every man from the community: Lloyd, Bill, Jimmy, Charlie, William, and, of course, Daryl. Nate and Peggy were also with them, each carrying a rifle themselves. The community that Evan, Jason, and everyone at the Homefront had worked so hard to bring together had stood side-by-side in a time of desperation and saved them all. They had truly earned the name, the Guardians.

****The End****

(To be continued in *The Blue Ridge Resistance: The New Homefront, Volume 3*)

A Note from the Author

I just wanted to personally thank each and every one of you who have purchased and read *The Last Layover: The New Homefront, Vol. 1*, and *The Guardians: The New Homefront, Vol. 2*. These two books have been a labor of love and a great experience for me both personally and professionally. As I developed the story and the characters, I tried to put in place the feelings and experiences that the average American might have in such a situation. I feel that although this exact scenario is merely one of myriad things that could happen to our great society, we all need to have the mindset that nothing in this world is certain and nothing is guaranteed. Having the proper mindset during the onset of a world-changing situation could mean the difference between our survival and our demise.

I would also like to personally thank everyone who has provided me with support and encouragement along the way, as well as the readers of Volume 1 who provided online reviews and email feedback, which I used to help improve the reader's experience and the quality of Volume 2 and Volume 3. Please follow me on Facebook at www.facebook.com/homefrontbooks and Twitter at @stevencbird.

Respectfully,

Steven C. Bird

CPSIA information can be obtained
at www.ICGtesting.com
Printed in the USA
LVOW10s1804190117
521537LV00004B/796/P